The Witch of the Wilderness

E. R. Griffin

Also by E. R. Griffin

The Queen of Ruin

Bad at Magic

"What She Left Behind"

The Witch of the Wilderness

E. R. Griffin

For Grandma Lolo. I think you would have liked this one. I miss you and love you always.

1. The Girl in the Woods

The forest gives up nothing; it only takes things.

It holds its secrets like a breath. It keeps death better than the grave. I've been told I should fear it. Yet I find excuses to enter it. Its path like a mottled tongue, its trees like wicked teeth, its darkness a maw gaping with hunger. I walk into it, a willing meal.

And each time, I imagine a voice in my ear: *Hello again.*

I wander the broken ground, thin ice breaking beneath my worn boots. Winter waits on the edges of my world. November is fey with its weather, bringing ice and breaking it just as quickly. I rustle my cloak closer around my arms and start my chores, my excuse for coming to this place. I pluck up the first fallen branch I see. It's good for mere kindling, but without this, we'll have little else to warm us tonight.

I go deeper, keeping to the strip of tamped ground I've beaten over the years. I pick up branches as I go. Leaves and twigs crush against my steps and mark my path with sound. Before me, Beast wanders in an aimless path, tired from the evening's work. He sniffs occasionally at a fallen branch, but loses interest quickly and turns his paws homeward.

The branches in my arms weigh down my steps, dig into my ribs. I whistle for Beast to slow. My days are naught but work, and I wish this walk might be a respite despite the burden I carry. I know once my feet cross onto our land, Uncle will be waiting with a new chore. He'll bid me build and stoke the fire that he might read by it while Mem and I darn socks.

I once found solace in the firelit readings. Uncle's voice gentle in the room, reverent of the words in our tattered black Bible. But of late the verses creep along my back like fear, and his voice seems not gentle, but cold, threatening in its softness. Like a quietly spoken curse.

I shake my head and shift the branches more securely in my arms. The sun dangles between the trees, threatening to fall to night. I click my tongue, and Beast abandons a pile of leaves that caught his attention. He trots at my side, tongue lolling.

"Good boy," I say. "Home's not a mile away. Let's make the most of it."

Beast seems to smile, his tongue laid over his toothy jaw. I consider Beast my closest friend, odd as it seems. His simple love and devotion are unique to his kind, I'm sure. The men and women of my village boast no such virtue.

At once his demeanor changes, his relaxed posture stiffening until his tail is level with his nose. He stares off into a thicker part of the forest, tail ticking slowly to the left and back. He lets off a soft whine.

"What is it, boy?" My mind goes to wolves, bears...worse things. I clutch the bundle of branches tighter to my chest. "Come, now. Let's be gone from this place. We don't want to be caught in the—Beast!"

He moves as a bullet from a musket, one moment by my side, the next a dark flash deep in the black of the woods. I make chase, but the bundle in my arms catches against the closely grown trees. With a growl of frustration, I let the bundle drop and weave between the trunks, trying to spot the matted brown fur of my companion.

"Beast! Beast! Here, boy. Come back!"

A whine breaks up the sound of my clomping feet, and I slow, following the muffled cry of sorrow. If he's hurt... I can't let myself think it.

At last, I find him sitting in a small clearing, pawing at a long bundle of cloth. He tips his head to the orange sky and howls.

"What's gotten into you?" I say. "What've you fou—oh."

As I approach, it becomes clear. What seemed a ruined collection of discarded fabrics is the still, white form of a girl, no older than myself. She's dressed warmly in a thick riding cloak and boots, a plain dark wool kirtle that now rides up over her ankles. Her coif lays loose behind her head, the ties tangled with her splayed hair, so red and rich, even crusted with dirt and ice as it is. I hold a hand to my mouth, intent to stifle a scream that never comes. Sorrow fills me, broken up only by hot pumps of fear as my heart leaps against my ribs.

I look at last to her face, white as the ice crawling across her lashes, her mouth blue with death, eyes like curdled milk, colorless and sunken into their sockets. She was beautiful in life, I'm sure. And crowning that beauty, ruining it, sits a pale, branded H above her brow.

Heresy. I wonder what sort of heretic she is. A Catholic, or a Quaker? She looks young, yet she may be grown enough to face such charges. She is certainly no older than my own twenty-two years, though in death it's hard to gauge.

My eyes flutter down, then, and there's another brand on her upturned palm, this one fresher, cut by a blade rather than raised by hot iron.

At first, the jagged curves and slanted cuts mean nothing. But I stare a while, and they bleed into one another, forming a familiar, grinning face. A skull, so like the ones we carve above our headstones. But on her dead flesh, it's no memento mori.

Beast paws at her sadly, and I grab his scruff, lest the Devil leap from her body into his. "No! Don't touch her."

The brand is clear about who—what—this girl was. A witch. Marked by the Devil. Banished from her community for her heresy, the worst possible kind. Somehow, she wandered into our woods. And here the Lord did justice upon her. Here she died in the cold, alone.

But the woods are still the Devil's domain, where he makes his midnight bargains and deals misery to those foolish enough to fall for his allure. The witch is dead in the flesh, but that does not mean her evil perished with her.

It may be a trick of my addled mind, but I hear a sigh between the trees, a woman's sorry breathing.

I tug against Beast's scruff. "Come, Beast. We must get home. Beast!"

He resists my pull, turning mournful eyes toward me. I look again at the witch, though my very skin screams at the danger of casting my eyes upon this evil.

I twist a lock of my own mousy hair, come loose from my coif. Mine is flat and dull, not rich and bright like the witch's. But I suppose to a dog, two girls are simply two girls. Does Beast think her me? Does he see this icy corpse and think of my own passing? Or does he simply mourn a dead girl for the sadness that it is?

Animals do not have such thoughts, I remind myself. They have no souls, as Uncle is quick to remind me when I hesitate at slaughtering a chicken for supper. But still. He seems so sorry to leave her.

"Come, Beast. We'll return for her. But now we must be quick. Uncle will give me a lashing if I return after dark."

At last, I coax Beast away, though he whimpers as we make our way back through the trees to where I dropped the bundle of firewood. I gather it back up, press my feet to the path. That cold, black tongue lolls, and at last spills me out. No more tooth-trees gnawing close. There is open air, a snow-bundled field, and a gray little farm beyond. Home.

Stars have broken out between the clouds by the time my feet cross onto our land. A bruised sky hangs above me. Our little farm is situated close to the woods, but I'm still late arriving at the loose gate. I maneuver it gently, but still it creaks, announcing me.

Behind the house, a hammer stills in its banging. The memory of its metal music clings to the air. My uncle's voice barks an order, probably telling the goats to scatter. I usher Beast toward the front door, trying to get inside before—

"Deliverance."

I go cold at his voice. My uncle carries terror like a fog around him, spreading it to the rest of us when he is near. His large, imposing frame appears around the side of the house and stalks toward me. I shut the door on Beast's concerned face. I prefer to spare my friend exposure to whatever punishment awaits me.

Uncle stares down at me, working his jaw. He spits into the dirt. I flinch, cast my eyes down. "Where have you been?"

I set the sticks slowly beside the door and rise. "I'm sorry, Uncle. We—I—got lost. It won't happen again."

"I should think not, as you've gathered wood in that forest for years now, and you well know your way home." He grabs me by my chin and forces my eyes to meet his. "What really happened?"

I cannot tell him about the girl. Speaking a lie should be my greatest concern—but, God help me, her devilish ways may already be upon me. I don't tell Uncle the truth. "I—I wanted a walk. A little time t-to enjoy—"

His hand tightens, and an ache spreads through my jaw as his fingers bite the joint, stuffing my voice back down my throat. "You wanted to cavort in the woods like a heathen? Is that what you mean to tell me?"

"A—walk," I grind out, eyes tearing up as his grip strengthens. I would prefer an outright blow to this slow boil of anger, which is sure to culminate into something worse.

He tosses my face away, jerking my neck. "Kneel," he says.

"Uncle, please. I meant no harm."

"The Devil gets your soul all the easier if you believe yourself innocent. *Kneel.*"

I obey, letting my knees strike the dirt as one, the pain a mere prelude. He looks about, as though to divine inspiration, and his gaze settles on the bundle of branches I brought in for firewood. He chooses the thickest of them and balances it in his palms.

"Think on your misdeeds, and may the Lord forgive you."

The first strike lands across my back, followed by another which catches my left shoulder. He strikes me seven times, and each bows me closer to the earth. The final blow lands low on my back, and a pain unlike the rest courses through my bones. I bite my tongue to keep the gasp inside my lungs.

"Go inside," he says at last, and throws the branch aside. "Say your prayers. No supper."

"Yes, Uncle," I say to the loamy ground. My fingers curl in the dirt; the mercy of nature is the only thing that keeps me from collapsing. I think I cannot rise, the pain is so intense, but find myself on my feet when Uncle thrusts me up with an impatient hand.

"Inside," he growls.

I nod, mute, and stumble into the house. I think he means to follow, but he instead slams the door on me. His footsteps retreat around the house. Soon, the banging of the hammer takes up again. *The paddock for the goats,* I think through the dulling pain. *He's been fixing that paddock for weeks now.*

Beast whines from his hiding place beneath the supper table. I glance up and find he has company.

"Oh, Mem. How long have you been there?"

My younger sister lies on her stomach beside Beast, her face pink with a brewing storm of tears. "He struck you."

I manage a wry smile. "Only a little."

"You cannot sup with us?"

"No, my love. But it's all right. I'm tired anyway." I kneel before the two of them and scratch Beast's ears, muss Mem's hair. "Shall we say prayers together? I'll wait up for you."

She nods. "Pray Uncle not be so angry."

"Hush." I put two fingers over her lips. "What is the Fifth Commandment, Mem?"

She wilts like a flower in the cold. "Honor thy father and thy mother." A small pinch gathers her brow together. "But he's not our father."

"He cares for us as one." But even I cannot make the dryness of the lie leave my voice. Mem returns my sardonic smile.

"Liv?" Mem shifts onto her elbows, hopeful eyes turned up. "When will Abel come home?"

I have no answer. Our cousin's letters have grown scarcer as the winter creeps in. But I say what I always do, though I fear I am once again bearing false witness. "Very soon, I'm sure of it."

"Maybe Uncle will be happy then," Mem says, her tone suggesting a question rather than a true hope. It was Uncle who sent Abel away to trap fur, thinking to bolster our dwindling coffers. If Uncle misses his son, he shows no outward sign. He only complains of Abel's late return, I wager, because that means the money is late, too.

The noise of uncle's work ceases outside, and I rise, beckoning Beast to my side. "I'll wait up for you," I say once more, and retreat to the narrow ladder leading to our shared loft.

I will wait to say all of my prayers with Mem, but before she joins me, I have one best kept between me and the Lord. I thank Him for my many blessings, confess my sins even as penitence stings the raw flesh of my back. I ask that I might be among the elect and see the glories of Heaven. I ask him to guard me against evil as it lies so close to my door.

"Lord God in Heaven..." I might as well just say it. God knows already what I'm thinking. "Please show mercy to the girl in the woods. Forgive her sins. Amen."

I rise from my sore knees and walk to the small window facing the forest. I peer out at the thick trees. Moonlight brings relief to their dark masses. The forest goes on so long. We are truly in a wilderness here.

I hardly remember London, that dark, smoky place of my childhood. The streets were loud, crowded. I could taste the air. The buildings were tall and pressed close, sometimes leaning into one another or bowing above the bridges. That city was like a forest, thick, peering, hungry. But the teeth of the city never closed around me. The forest...now that it has sampled my flesh, will it ever let me go?

I think of the place between London and this desolate village. After the long sea voyage, we settled in Boston. I loved it, how big and alive it felt after months in a dank cabin, after a childhood of shadowed streets.

We had a modest home nestled among other houses sprouting like spring growth. Mother wanted to stay there, and had she lived, we would have. Father loved it, too. There was a part of him, small and secret, that missed London, even as he complained of the crowds and the smells and the sin. Boston had been a place in between, a growing city made for people with Father's convictions.

But he died the same day Mother did. The bloody sheets were only just thrown above my mother's body when I found Father in the next room with a flintlock pistol in his hand, a blast of powder and blood between his eyes.

That left us in Uncle's hands.

And Uncle wanted a place that could keep his secrets.

3. Prayers

I am not allowed out of my room all night. I sit against the door, listening to Uncle read to Mem from the Bible, his voice carrying snippets of Leviticus through the thin wood. I don't enjoy his readings anymore, but they feel important, required. To banish me from hearing the Word of God tells me how malicious Uncle thinks my trespass to be.

Uncle believes me damned, I'm certain. No man, woman, or child has guarantee of Heaven. The Lord's will is mysterious and just, and should I not find myself among the elect, I know, even before the terrible flames and lashes and unending tears greet me, that I deserve Hell. All sinners do.

But I once hoped that I was elect. That Mem and I would greet Mother and Father at the pearly gates and walk in undying gardens, our family rejoined.

I am not chosen, however. I know it as surely as I know death awaits me, not cold and peaceful as the pagans would have it, but eternal and filled with flame. My stomach seizes beneath the growing ice in my heart. My breaths come short and desperate. I want—how I want just to *know.* To receive a message that might assuage me. But for all I have prayed, I have never heard God's voice, not even as a flicker in my heart.

And now...now, it's much too late. I've sinned in terrible ways. And those trespasses follow me from room to room. They treat my lungs to ice with every breath. One among the elect would not have done such as I have.

I bury my face in my hands and let the dirty nails of my fingers find purchase in the tired flesh.

When at last Uncle finishes reading, Mem joins me in our room. She fishes a small, soft roll of bread from her pocket and places it in my palm.

"Mem," I say. "You shouldn't have."

She smiles. "He didn't see me do it."

"I can't eat it." It's as good as cursed. It was taken dishonestly, and I have been banned from eating tonight. Surely the bread would boil in my stomach, make me ill. I press the bread back into her hand. "I must accept my penance."

A sour look crosses Mem's face. "When does Uncle have to accept his?"

"He..." I shake my head. "He is who the Lord put on this earth to watch over us. Now, please, take that bread back and tell Uncle what you've done. It will be better in the end."

Mem brings the bread to her lips and takes a bite, her eyes on mine, challenging.

"Mem," I hiss. "Why are you acting so?"

"I'm tired of the way Uncle treats you," she says quietly, her eyes drifting to the floorboards. The house is thin, and we've often wondered how soft our voices must be to escape Uncle's ears. How late does he stay up, waiting for one of us to speak out of turn?

"Well, if you've got a nasty bellyache in the morning, you'll know why," I say.

Mem's smile returns, toothy and bright. "We'll see."

I think of the dead witch in the forest. Has her mischief already leaked into my home? Mem has always been willful. But I have to wonder if I've carried part of the Devil back with me.

I ruffle Mem's curling blond hair. "Let's say our prayers now."

Mem nods and gets to her knees by our bed. She begins, skipping over forgiveness and thankfulness straight to a request: "Lord, please heal Deliverance from her wounds, and protect us from Uncle."

She opens one eye, looking at me. I stare back, my tongue locked around "amen." I want that, too. I want to sleep without pain, to wake without fear. But this is too bold.

"Liv?"

I shake my head and say, "Yet we thank you, Lord, for the guidance of our uncle, for the chance at penitence, today and every day. Amen."

"Amen." The word sounds dull in my sister's mouth.

We climb into our cramped bed and I shut my eyes, feigning sleep. But Mem knows me too well. The traitorous rhythm of my breaths, too quick for sleep, spur her to speak softly.

"We could run away."

I turn my face on the pillow to see her better. "Where did you get such a wicked idea?" I say, my voice muffled by the squashy fabric.

"We could go to London. The king can't be as bad as everyone says. We could hear plays."

"Mem. Speak no more of this."

She shifts beside me. "What shall I do when you marry, and Abel is still away? I shall be alone with Uncle."

The brokenness in her voice shatters something in me as well. I rise to my elbow, looking into her large eyes. She's in that place between the smallness of youth and the blossom of her first blood. Innocence and womanhood meet at this age. Her worries will only grow. The world will only seem crueler.

"Is that what you're so worried about? Mem, no one has asked for me." I smile. "I'm afraid you cannot rid yourself of me so easily."

She punches my arm, unamused. The blow glances away, tickling more than hurting. "Thomas will. You know he plans to, once he's returned."

The ice that always holds my heart shoots through my chest, down into the ache of hunger in my gut, making me happy I didn't eat. Even so, bile burns in my throat. "Thomas has years yet at Harvard. Besides, he'll have better prospects than me. Especially as a reverend."

"You'd be happier away from this place," Mem says after a moment.

"Mem. You are the brightest star in my sky. I wouldn't leave you here alone, even if Thomas did come back."

She smiles, believing me, though I know even this truth saddens her. She feels but a fraction of Uncle's cruelty, has never fallen beneath his fists. She wants better for me. But I can never leave her. I imagine, with me married and gone, that Uncle's hatred would transfer, that his anger would need a new target.

"Tell me something about Mother," Mem says.

I close my eyes. I hate talking about Mother, especially with Mem. Her name—Remembrance—is no mere, pretty thing. Mother died moments after Mem bleated her first cry. And they look so alike. It is Mother's face blooming each day stronger on my sister's face. They share the gentle hint of rose in their cheeks, the yellow hair touched by the same sunlit hue.

Uncle didn't care to name Mem. So, I did. I gave her the only name that made sense.

Mem waits, eyes sad but hopeful.

I should extol Mother's virtues—her goodness, her patience, her obedience. But tonight, in the secret dark, I find myself remembering other things.

"She hummed when she cooked. She made the most wonderful meat pies, back in Boston. Covered in flour to her elbows, she'd spend hours humming her songs and kneading dough."

"Did she let you help?"

"Every time. She...called me her little brownie."

Mem's brow crinkles. "What does that mean?"

"Brownies are...fabled creatures. Not real, of course. They're fey and kind and they're said to live in households and help with chores, always with delight."

"But they're not real?"

"No, no. They're a thing from stories."

"I should like a brownie myself," Mem huffs.

I laugh. "You've got me, which is twice as good."

She nods. "Aye." Then, "What songs did she sing?"

"I...can't remember." I frown at the low ceiling of our loft. There's a cadence in my head, but it's all murmurs, no words. There is music, but the notes have gone flat. "You know, they might have been all her own. Now that I think on it...I'm not sure her songs existed before she began to sing them."

Mem smiles. "Then I'll make a song, too. One that only we'll know."

"I should like that. Sleep now, Mem. And no more talk of running off. We'll always be together. And we can get through this. All right?"

She sighs and presses her face deeper into her pillow. "Right. Goodnight, Liv."

I kiss her forehead, and hold her little hand in mine until she falls asleep.

Mem's heavy sleep has always seemed a burden—waking the child at first light is impossible some days—but tonight, I thank God for her weighted limbs and gentle snores. She won't notice my absence.

I carry my boots, treading in stockinged feet across the dusty wood planks of our home. The fire still glows in faint orange clumps, even at this late hour. Uncle must have stayed up late, reading his Bible. Or pondering what to do with me.

Beast rouses at the sound of my approach, but I stay him with my hand. I cannot risk him in the forest when there is only faint moonlight, and creatures larger and fiercer who might do him harm. He whimpers but obeys, resting his jaw on the floor with a look of annoyance.

"Next time," I mouth, smiling, as I slip out the door with my cloak.

The icy ground sends lines of cold like searching fingers through my stockings and up my legs. My very blood seems to cool at the contact with the ground. I quickly shove my feet into the boots and lace them, then throw the cloak over myself. A little slice of moon wraps itself in cloud cover, darkening the already dim path from my home to the forest.

I stumble toward the shack where Uncle keeps his tools and feel around for the rusted, bent shovel. The tools in the dark seem somehow more violent, sharper, as though their purposes might extend beyond labor. A vision of wolves and bears stalking between the trees flashes through my mind; the sharp-edged shovel promises safety.

Shuddering off the cold and the darkness of my thoughts, I hold the shovel tight and make my way toward the woods.

4. A Specter

It feels strange, to remember the way. I only ever take one path through the woods, choosing felled branches from the same few trees when we need kindling. It worries me to recognize the break in the trees Beast led me through earlier. As though the forest is whispering me back, its wind-breath in my ear.

As though the witch beckons with invisible fingers.

Fissures of terror split my heart when I come upon the body; it is badly changed from the few hours since last I saw it. The rotted clothes are torn, and bloodless tears are ripped through skin to bone in the arms, chest, and face of this miserable girl. Her mouth gapes impossibly wide, the lips torn into a new, grotesque smile. Claws and jaws have done their work upon her.

I expect a sense of vindication—this is what happens to a witch; this is what such a fiend deserves. But regret alone boils in my chest and warms my face. Shame coats me. I ought to have come sooner, properly buried her before the carrion creatures had got to her.

I should never have left her.

A new thought, as cold and unwelcome as the sight of the ruined body: She had died recently when I first came upon her. I had only seen her death from the view of justice: of God striking down the wicked.

But something killed this girl, and it had been in the woods with me, only minutes or moments before I found her.

I clamp the new worry down, keeping it between my teeth. There's work ahead. I move several feet away and strike the shovel down. The metal meets hard earth; the ice of our long winter lingers in the ground. But I cannot despair. Somehow, I will make this witch a grave, and perhaps my respect will spare me any lingering misery she sought to do upon the living.

Perhaps I will have fled this place before whatever did her in returns.

I tear at the ground in painful strokes, lifting only bits of dirt at a time. By the end of an hour's work, I have a trench that will barely fit her body. The sparse dirt covering would not prevent animals from feasting upon the rest of her.

So, I continue. I let my body suffer the agony of this labor until the sky takes on the lighter blue tones of encroaching morning. Satisfied I will get no further, I drop the shovel and go to the witch.

I thank God for the cold, which has lessened the smell of her blood and viscera. Even so, dragging her torn body, limbs bent strangely and pooling foul liquids, makes me grateful for my missed supper. I gag when her head bends back and reveals the work of a wolf's jaws upon her throat.

I stop, kneeling beside her to rest and quiet my stomach. I breathe through my mouth, my exhalations white on the air like specters bearing witness to this atrocity. I spread my fingers across the ground, truly feeling it, focusing only on the painful cold and the rigid dirt. When my eyes open again, I keep them away from her face, her mangled limbs.

A small book dangles halfway from her cloak pocket. I pluck it out, curiosity stronger for a moment than fear. It's thin, worn, its red leather cover cracked and tied shut with a dirty string. I know whatever it is, it must be evil. Some artifact of her craft, perhaps a spell book from the Devil himself. It ought to be buried with her. Better still, burned and removed from the earth altogether.

I place it in my own pocket. I'll burn it in the fireplace at home.

Restored, I manage her rigid body into the pit and quickly replace the cold dirt. The sky transforms from blue to white-orange, the dawn here before I'm ready. I take up the shovel and run back home.

The Lord is merciful. Uncle has not yet risen, even though the day has begun. I whisk through the house, Beast at my heels, tail wagging. Safely in my room, I shed my sodden, dirty cloak and kirtle and let them pile at my feet. I scrub my face and hands, coated in cold dirt, until our wash basin is black with my secret task. I murmur prayers all the while, asking forgiveness and mercy, and thanking God for that which he has already shown me.

Clean at last, I pull on a fresh shift, then turn to stuff my dirtied clothes beneath the bed. I startle to find Mem upright in bed, blue eyes upon me, lips parted as though ready to speak.

"Good morning, Mem," I say cheerfully, though my heart plummets. How long has she lain awake watching me?

"You were gone."

"I was not," I say, forcing a laugh into my words.

"You were murmuring. Just now. What words did you say?"

"They were prayers, Mem. What's gotten into you?"

Her head lists to one side, a sloppy movement better suited to a ragged doll than a girl with bones and muscle. "She came while you were gone."

My blood cools. Has Mem seen the witch? Has the vile spirit of the girl whisked into our home, tormented my sister?

"Who, Mem? Who did you see?"

Mem gasps, almost laughing, as though she hardly believes her own words. "*Me*. Myself, grown, but ruined. White as snow and rings around my throat."

My befouled clothes slip from my fingers. "What?"

"Rotted eyes and gasping mouth. I stood there." She nods to the foot of the bed. "And I spoke. 'Where is she? Where has she gone?'"

I clench my jaw, hoping the rigidness of my jaw will spread to my spine, make me solid and strong in this moment. "You saw...yourself? Grown old?"

"Not *old*. But grown."

Her voice is music, the rhythm like a prayerful hymn. All this time, she's shown no fear, only a strange serenity.

"Rings around my neck, blue, purple. Is that how I'll die, Liv? Has God sent me a vision of the future?"

My mouth opens, but only a breath of prayer comes out. *God, help her.*

"But I was looking for you. And I told myself, 'I know not whence she's gone.'"

"Mem, this is—speak no more of it. It's evil. It's dangerous."

"I'm not scared," my sister says. "Not now, and not then." She lifts her arm and points toward the door, though her eyes stay on the place beyond our bed, to the place where she saw a specter. "'Him.' That's all she—all *I* said."

I fall to my knees, prayers and memories crowding my mind. Which to speak, which to tell?

Beast nestles by my side, whimpering.

"Liv? It's all right. She wasn't wicked. She was almost kind, but sad, too. What will make me so in the future?"

I shake my head. Numb lips form the only truth I know. "You didn't see yourself, Remembrance."

"But I *did*."

"No. That wasn't you."

I shut my eyes, prepared to start a prayer. It dies in my throat. Frost fingers curl against the slope of my neck. An entombed chill seeps from their press and seizes my body. Her rot-breath fills my ear.

"List, and speak what thou know."

5. The River

My memories of London are a smear: fog and dark, smell and cacophony. My first true, bright memory is of water, the sky bleeding dawn in a glimmer across the waves. I was too young to understand why we left England; kings and churches held no place in my mind. I only knew the gleam of water, Mother's hand on mine. The New World, they called it, lay beyond the bands of sunlight striking off the ocean. We were nearly home.

We made land in Boston and lived there. Father had money, and so we had comfort. Mother cooked and kept house; I helped. The years were quiet and spent too quickly. Shortly after my first blood, Mother shared her happy news. A baby was on the way. A sibling for me, when I had never had hope of one.

Mother was huge with child when Uncle Ezra came to our door, a lanky boy at his side. He had gone separately to the New World, and had arrived in Plymouth years before my family had designs of leaving England. He'd married and been widowed upon the birth of his only child, Abel. Father called him a lout whenever his name came up. But he was kind to his brother then. Too kind.

Uncle stayed with us. What money he came with had been squandered, my father said. Uncle said it had been *spent*, given over to investments that had seemed sound enough. It was clear Uncle needed support. But my attention was not intended for these matters. I stayed away from Father and Uncle's arguments, their late nights of whispered fury. I helped Mother. I waited for my baby sister.

I only paid attention to their men's talk once.

"Boston—it's a sinful place, a waste of this godly land," Uncle said, deep into a cup of cider. "It's a little London, that's all. Holier places wait, brother. Waste not our fortune on this barren city, and let's settle together where a man may worship God as he demands."

Father made a sound too mean to be a laugh. "And where is this Holy Land, Ezra?"

"The holiest places are those untouched by man's design. There are settlements, small villages flung into the woods beyond here. Maine is good. Empty, peaceful—"

"I'll not give into the vanity of the Church, Ezra, but I will have some earthly comforts. You can keep Maine. Perhaps you'll find your fortune there."

I think, now, that it was this quip on my uncle's fortune that settled things in his mind.

What happened after that last argument and our being loaded into a cart on our way to Maine exists only in my mind, and his. I've never told anyone. It didn't matter how we got into that cart, anyway. All that mattered was that I held my newborn sister in my arms, that we were going to live with my cousin and my uncle far away, and that I needed to be quiet. Safety came from silence. And so, I would not speak.

I didn't tell anybody what followed me from Boston.

But now, Mem had seen it, too.

"Say nothing to Uncle."

I rise from the floor, unable to look at my sister.

"I won't." She toys with a lock of sunlight-blond hair. "Is it a blessing? Or a curse? To see one's own death?"

"That wasn't you." I flinch at the edge in my voice. Mem doesn't know, doesn't deserve this. "It was a dream."

"It *wasn't*—"

"Speak no more of it. Now come. We've work enough to last a week, and the sun's already high."

"Liv! What about prayers?"

I halt my exit, but don't turn back. "Start without me."

I leave my sister's crestfallen face and go to the kitchen, Beast close at my heels, his low ears sensing the anxiety filling the house. I scratch his head to calm myself as much as him. We clomp slowly down the stairs, my stomach clenching the closer I get to the kitchen.

I expect to find my uncle about the house, but all is quiet. I slip from the kitchen to the cramped room where he sleeps, and there he sits, in his highbacked chair, holding his head in both hands.

I begin to creep away, but my feet scrape a traitorous melody on the scarred floor. His head snaps up.

"Think it's funny, eh?"

I drop my eyes, shake my head. "No, sir. I'm sorry. I—I wanted to know what you'd like for breakfast."

"Rotted vegetables and stale bread, I suppose. It's all we have. If I didn't have two little sluts to care for..."

I clench my jaw lest purest vitriol spew forth. "I'll go into the village today, if you like. Buy some—"

"*Buy?* Didn't you hear me? I've nothing for myself, money, bread, or else, because you and your useless sister drain everything from my pockets!"

He rises, and as he stomps closer, the sickening waft of old cider follows him. He's been up all the night, I realize, drinking between bouts of unconsciousness. He hasn't sobered.

So, it is no shock when he stumbles and falls facedown to the floor.

He groans, propping himself on arms as unsteady as driftwood. "Think you're clever... up all night..."

I startle back. He knows of my midnight journey, my flight into the woods—

"—scratching at the walls, thumping around." He tilts his face to mind. Scraps of graying beard cling to his face. His teeth are yellowed, a few gone entirely. His eyes, bloodshot and jaundiced, stare into mine. "I know she's not real. You think you'll fool me. But I know it's just you, being clever."

My body goes limp, and I cannot say whether it's with shock or relief. "You see her, too."

He laughs, shaking his head. He's still on his hands and knees, and he looks so...pathetic. A beggar man in the streets. A supplicant before a reverend confessing at last. "Clever, clever witch. Think on your sins."

Think on yours, I wish to say. But I press my lips together and nod. "I'll see what can be done about breakfast."

The day is filled with work enough to bury the memory of this morning. At least for a while.

Due to my confinement last night, there are chores waiting. I spend my first hours after breakfast at my mother's old spinning wheel. Mem, meanwhile, sits at the loom, her eyes drifting from her work to a book propped in her lap.

"Don't let Uncle catch you idle," I whisper.

"It's hardly idle to study and work at once," she says.

Outside, hammer falls sing out. Uncle is back to working on the paddock. How his head, soggy with drink and no doubt aching, can stand those constant hammer falls, I don't know.

"Think you he'll hunt today?" Mem asks after a few moments of silent work.

"I have doubt if it," I say before I can school the bitterness in my tone. Uncle forbids me to hunt—it's a man's work, his work. And yet he's been idle of it. He'd rather Mem and I sell our goods in the village, to purchase food from families with hauls to spare.

But the other families can well make their own candles and soap and thread. We make coin only from those with pity in their eyes.

"The harvest was poor," Mem says.

"Aye."

"The garden is dying."

"I know, Mem."

She looks up from the loom. "What will we eat tonight? Or the next?"

"Mem—"

"We can't go on like this," she whispers. "We'd be better off on our own."

Before I can answer, the sound of hammering stills. I fear Uncle has heard our whispered dishonor, yet his footsteps back into the house are too slow for anger. He slams through the front door, grabs his musket from where it stands against the wall.

I would like to think this means he's going hunting, but he always brings his musket into the village. And when he goes into the village, no matter his business, he ends up at the tavern.

He grabs his walking stick last, still unsteady from his night awake at the bottle. He says nothing to us and departs with a slam of the door.

I wait a long moment to ensure he's truly gone, then rise from the spinning wheel. "I'm going to do the washing. Finish that, then start on the soap, hm?"

Mem groans. "Not the soap, Liv. Anything else."

"We've need of it." I ruffle her hair. "Finish that and you can read until Uncle returns."

"Have it your way." She gives me a sunbeam smile. "If you happen upon a very sick deer while you're out..."

She jests, and yet the very thought had crossed my mind. I could hardly explain to Uncle why we suddenly had food for our supper, but perhaps he'll be so mad with hunger he for once wouldn't protest.

I haul the wash baskets out the door and trek a worn path through our fields. The river snakes through the open plains beyond our farm, but there is a shaded place where they meet the woods before trickling into that forbidden darkness. It's my favorite place, silent and alone. Most of the other women out washing choose the field. But I have need of my solace.

I hear the river before me, its quick babble like secrets told between schoolgirls. I nestle into the very edge of the forest and kneel before the water. It moves eternally. The water that is here now was a moment before in the woods. The water that flowed in a spring long past has probably met the ocean and scattered around the world.

But for the river's ever-changing nature, it's a place frozen for me. There is a single moment held between these trees, sung over by the whisper of the water.

Are you so afraid of me, Liv?

I plunge the first filthy piece of clothing into the water. The chill shocks my skin and crawls up my arms. I scrub soap into the seams of shirts and pick dirt from the threads of shifts.

I work my body, and it quiets my mind. This roar of memory becomes a chant, then a breath. It may never leave me, but it's a quiet haunting when I have something to do.

I hang our clothes along tree branches. It would be idle to sit here waiting for them to dry. But…Uncle is away drinking before the noonday meal. Mem has likely abandoned the loom and forgotten the soap in favor of her book.

Dammit if I can't have one moment.

I turn to the water. Despite my scrubbing this morning, my skin still feels filthy from my work in the woods. My hair, too, is lank with want of a washing. I glance down the river, toward the open field. Nobody is within miles of me.

I shed my kirtle, then carefully, with another long glance toward the open field, slip out of my shift. I touch one toe to the water. The shock of cold rips a breath from me. But a moment later, the icy pain is replaced by a feeling of rightness. I step further into the river and wade closer to the forest, until I find a deep portion where I can sink my whole head under.

Liv.

His voice. Not surprised or embarrassed. He had been looking for me.

I had wanted to be found.

Will you come out of there?

And I'd smiled. *Why don't you come in?*

I release the tangles in my hair. I scrub the lot of it with soap, then run the bar along my body. A decent person would haul water to her home, heat it, and bathe in the secret of her own walls. But I've been coming here to wash since I was young.

It had always been my secret and my thrill. Even my shame cannot keep me away.

Joy had turned quickly to fear. Once Thomas had disrobed and slipped into the water with me, I felt damnation knocking at my heart. But by then, I knew myself already lost to Heaven. Because a girl with God in her heart would not have desired this at all.

He saw the war in my eyes, the tremble in my shoulders. He asked the thing that broke my heart. *Are you so afraid of me, Liv?*

I pressed myself to him, then. He held me against the bank, a hand cupped behind my head. He—

Barks rip through the memory and I turn toward the bank. Beast stands by the emptied wash baskets, barking and twitching his tail. I rise from the water and quickly pull on my dry shift. It soaks through, and my kirtle bunches the damp fabric as I pull it on next.

Beast twists in the circle and barks again, louder. Something is wrong.

I leave our things to dry and run for home, Beast close beside. The front door is open, and shouts thicken the air inside. I stumble to a halt to find Uncle returned, standing over Mem. He wags a book in her face.

"Idleness! Heathen waste!" He throws the book into a newly stoked fire. Mem screams as the flames catch it up.

"Poetry! Written by a godless whore, no doubt!"

"Uncle!" I say. "What are you doing?"

"Question me not," he snarls, whipping around. His mouth it open to deride me further, but he fixes on my sodden clothes, my water-wild hair. His yellowed teeth clench.

"Whore," he says.

I startle back. "Uncle! I was only at the river to—"

"To fornicate? To show your sluttish self to the Devil himself? Shrink not from me," he says, storming forward as I take small steps back. "Hold fast and receive thy punishment."

He shoves me aside and goes for the door, and his walking stick.

All at once, everything goes to hell.

Uncle lifts the walking stick, starts toward me.

Beast barks, hair rising, and plants himself before me.

Mem scrambles to her feet.

Uncle roars and rips Beast away, flings him, whimpering, into the wall. I scream, and not for the walking stick that strikes my ribs. I collapse under blows yet still crawl to my friend. He scrabbles to his feet, and his barks resume.

"No, Beast, shh." I stifle a cry as the walking stick lands across my spine. I feel the pulse of Uncle's rage, the sucking of air as the walking stick rises sharply, poised to strike again.

But the blow never comes.

There is a small, soft cry behind me.

The stick clatters to the ground.

Beast quiets, watching.

I roll to my back and find Uncle staggering back, gasping, Mem's thin arms coiled around his throat. She dangles from his neck, eyes tight, determination quaking her.

"No more!" She tightens her grip against him. "*No more!*"

Uncle backpedals until he strikes my sister into a wall. Her grip breaks and she crumples like hunted fowl blown from the sky.

"Whores!" Uncle spits on her. "Demons!" He grabs her by the hair and flings her into me, and there we sit cowering. Beast nestles into my side, faithful even in fear.

Uncle's anger dissolves into a worse, crueler thing: A smile, bladed and cold.

"What now, little witches, eh? What would you have me do? Show mercy? Let you scamper away, say your prayers of repentance?"

He steps closer. I clutch Beast to my side and scramble for Mem's hand. But she is not beside me. She crawls closer to the wall, backwards like a scuttling crab. Uncle laughs at her fear.

"Using your head at last, child? Pity it's far too late for your fear."

Mem stops at the fireplace, still warm with embers. Her round face, beautiful with Heaven's own light, darkens against the glowing logs.

"The Devil take you," she says, and reaches her hand into the pit. She lifts a mound of fire-pocked wood and charges forward, flinging the contained flame to Uncle's shocked face. He bellows, embers catching in his beard and scarring his lips.

"Run!" Mem screams.

The three of us launch out the door, no cloaks, no boots. Beast darts ahead, signaling the way. I know, with a mixture of elation and dread, exactly where he will lead us. It seems such the wrong place, and yet, where else might we go?

We fly into the woods like witches.

Twigs snap as we rush into the forest. Branches reaching into the path slap at my face, cutting with their thin fingers. We've run only a little ways when Mem tears her hand from mine. She stops dead in the path, her eyes fixed on a narrow gap in the trees.

"Mem?" I touch her shoulder. She turns to me, eyes wide.

"Did you see?"

My mouth opens, but it takes a moment for my voice to follow. "See what?"

"Someone…" She shakes her head. "It was nothing. Come on. We have to hide. He'll find us if we stay to the path."

I shut my eyes. She's right, of course. Already Uncle must be preparing to hunt us down. I imagine him stuffing his bent feet into his boots, lifting his musket from its place by the door.

"All right," I say.

Beast leads the way, following a path I have twice walked now. When we reach the small clearing where the witch is buried, Mem pauses, looking around.

"This place feels…"

Evil, I think.

"Sad."

I meet her gaze. "Don't touch anything, all right? The Devil plays many tricks in the forest."

Her eyes find the disturbed ground. In the full light of day, I can see what a poor job I did filling the earth back in. The crumble of dirt sits over the grave like so much silt, ready to blow away at the first stiff wind. I try not to imagine what the witch's face will look like, bloodied and torn and pocked with rot.

Mem sits at the far end of the clearing, away from the grave, and Beast settles in by her feet. I look from the grave to my sister. Is she truly safe here? Some part of me fears the witch, but at the moment, I fear my uncle more.

"Where shall we go?" Mem asks after a moment.

"What?" I tear myself away from the grave and face my sister. Her face is bright, hopeful.

"Where shall we live now that we've left Uncle? Can we get our own house? Shall we go back to Boston?"

"Mem, we—we aren't *leaving*."

"But...Uncle..." She shakes her head. "He hurt us, Liv. He burned my favorite book. He called you a *whore*."

"He only needs time to calm down," I say. "He's still our elder, our caretaker, and we'll do God's will and obey him."

"No," Mem says.

I frown. "Remembrance Daily Ashe—"

"God would not ask this of us!" she cries, rising to her feet. "God wouldn't do this to us, not if he loves us as you say!"

"Mem!"

"Tell me why God wants you beaten! Tell me why he ignores my prayers for our safety."

"His will is...mysterious." My eyes drift back to the disturbed earth, to the witch's grave. Evil indeed has crept into my life. Oh, what have I done? What have I invited into my home?

Mem says nothing, and soon, the silence of the forest takes on weight. It hangs around us like a damp kirtle, drags against my skin. I know the witch is buried. I know that. Yet I feel eyes—her eyes, I'm sure of it—staring at me. The gaze trips along my spine, and at last I spin, hoping to catch the spy—be it specter or something fouler. But nobody is behind me. Nobody peers through the trees or the loose ground.

And yet...I think I hear a laugh. A sharp note of wind, perhaps.

"Liv?" Mem tugs on my sleeve. "What are we going to do? Truly? Because you cannot ask me to endure this anymore. You can't ask it of yourself."

"I'll think on it," I say, and place my hand atop her head. She's so young still, and at an age when justice seems such a simple thing. She cannot know the will of the Lord, the pain he asks his servants to endure.

But I'm afraid she'll soon understand.

I stoke a small fire, but it's weak. The wild cold of November has killed so much of the forest, and already I've scoured it for wood and kindling. What little I manage to gather from the clearing barely makes a palmful of fire.

"I'm fine," Mem says, though she shivers. She wears naught but her shift and kirtle, and winter is more than a suggestion this afternoon. Her blue toes curl against her foot. Even with Beast nestled against her, I know she won't last long out here.

We'll have to return home soon. But the more we can stall, the better. Give Uncle time to sober.

"I'm going to find more wood," I say. "I won't go far. Beast, stay."

Beast's tongue lolls and his head tips curiously to the side. I can't help but smile, so fierce is the rush of affection I have for him.

I pass the grave, not looking at it, and step into the trees. They're grown close, and I maneuver carefully between sharp branches, looking for dead wood along the forest floor. I pick up a few small but solid pieces and freeze, still bent over.

There are footprints in the dirt. I kneel, holding the branches close, and use one hand to brush aside the leaves and pine needles fallen upon the forest floor.

I gasp and startle back, dropping the wood I've gathered. Two sets of footprints lead toward the clearing. One, a set of shoes similar in size to my own. I think they must be the witch's.

But beside them, as though walking with her, guiding her...a pair of cloven hoofprints.

I look all around the prints, trying to make sense of them. An animal with a cloven hoof ought to leave four prints. Yet the markings in the soft dirt make it seem as though...as though some creature, neither man nor beast, walked with the girl.

I quickly gather the slim branches back up, and then, with my bare foot, I smear the prints, destroying their trace in the dirt, as though that will destroy the creature itself.

We cannot stay here. Something walks in these woods. Something that led the young witch to her death.

I return to the clearing. Both Mem and Beast perk up at my approach. I kneel before our pitiful fire and carefully set the new branches to the flames.

"Thank you, Liv," Mem says.

I sigh, then look into her smiling face. "We cannot stay. It's not safe."

"It's not safe *there*, either."

"Uncle is a man, given to sin just as any other," I say. "Yet we must respect and obey him, and allow the Lord to work—"

"No," Mem says. "No, you're always going on about forgiveness and patience. But he never gets any better."

I shut my eyes. "You're right. I *know* you're right. But please, just trust me. I—I have an idea." I clutch her hands in mine. "But first we must go home. We'll freeze out here."

"We'll *die* there."

"Mem! There is something out here that—"

"List!"

The voice which spoke came from above, a cracked sound that no human voice would make. I glance up to see a crow perched in a tree above us, watching with a marbled eye trained on me. It cocks its head, flashing the other black eye.

"List! List!"

I balk at the creature. Without removing my eyes from it, I say, "We're going home. *Now.*"

To my relief, Mem nods. "Fine." She seems as rattled by the wicked bird as I.

We hurry from the clearing. The damned talking bird doesn't follow, thank our merciful God. Beast walks ahead, wary but aimed toward home.

"You promise you'll think of something?" Mem asks as our little farm appears between the trees.

"Yes, Mem. I know what we can do."

She won't like my plan. I don't like my plan.

But there's nothing else I can do.

7. The Parsonage

Uncle is gone when we arrive home. Empty cider bottles sit broken by his favorite chair. Upon the kitchen table, the big black Bible sits open to Proverbs. My eyes fly straight to the verse I know my uncle loves most.

He that spareth his rod hateth his son.

I wince, the pain on my back flaring like a reminder. If I believed better, if my heart could hold onto the words I recite to justify Uncle's behavior, then I, too, would sit with this verse. I would seek scripture of repentance.

The verse knocks dully against my ribs. I shut the Bible and turn away.

I change my clothes upstairs, minding I choose one of my nicer waistcoats, then go back down to find my boots by the door. I can only hope Uncle has gone out to the tavern, that he doesn't mean to return any time soon. I return to the kitchen and find some bread and cheese for Mem and a strip of dried meat for Beast.

"Stay here," I say. "I'll return as soon as I can."

Mem frowns around a mouthful of bread. "Where are you going?"

"I'm going to find help. Just..." I take a breath, stalling the tears gathering in my throat. "Do your work as you always would."

Mem pulls a face, but nods. "Hurry back. I don't want Uncle to find me here without you."

I nod, and turn before she can see the glimmer or the guilt in my eyes.

I drape the hood of my cloak low over my forehead as I near the first small homes of the village. My eyes stay low, only occasionally flitting up to assess the rustle of leaves, the seeming clod of a footfall. But I encounter no one until the homes give way to a spread of crude buildings—Winnow's, the tavern Uncle frequents, rises on my left; the meeting house, its two stories intimidating the smaller structures below, looms ahead.

A few people mill outside Winnow's, and their eyes prick my skin as I walk. Their murmurs follow me as I pass by, alighting a little footpath between thin trees.

The parsonage is a lovely, warm home, at least compared to the rude cabin Uncle built for us. Its stately black façade suggests solemnity, but I know happiness kindles within its walls, too. Memories try to weave through the barriers I put up long ago, but they find no purchase. I have one thing to do, one thing to agonize over, and sentiment has no room in my mind.

I steel myself and knock.

Goodwife Wilson herself answers, a good sign.

"Is that Deliverance Ashe? Well, now." Her smile is too small for the healthy roundness of her face. "I barely see you at all, child. Why has your uncle not attended meeting of late?"

I smile, think better of it, and press my lips together, abruptly grim. "I'm afraid...he's not well."

If she takes my meaning, she doesn't show it. But Uncle's near demonic devotion to drink is known in the village, and Goody Wilson nods. "I see. Come in, my dear, it's terribly cold. Not," she adds, closing the door behind me, "that it's much warmer inside. The parishioners have been quite stingy with our firewood allowance. Poor Waitstill is too patient with them."

She chatters as we walk through the parlor, at last gesturing me to a chair near the fire. "When you marry a good man and become a full member of the congregation, pray dear, remember that we cannot serve you for free."

"Of course, Goody Wilson."

"Pray remind that uncle of yours, then," she adds. "He's a one that never offers firewood."

I could explain that well enough, as it's only my stick-gathering that heats our home these days, but I hold my tongue.

She fusses a moment with the fire poker, breaking concealed flame from the logs, then settles in a chair across from me. She takes up an embroidery wheel. "What brought you here today, my dear? I have plenty of work left yet this day."

I take a long breath of the slowly warming air. "Then you might be more receptive to what I've come to ask of you."

She looks up, a reluctant interest blooming on her cheeks. "Yes?"

"My sister, Remembrance... I—my uncle—would like her to start serving in another home."

Goody Wilson blinks. "Would he really? Oh my. But isn't she needed?"

"Of course." *Of course.* But I can't let sentiment or practicality stop me now. I need my sister safe. "But food is scarce. Uncle hasn't much money left."

"After what he got from your father's estate?" Goody Wilson leans forward, her embroidery forgotten. "Has he squandered it?"

"I'm afraid so." Perhaps I should feel ashamed, sinful, even, for confessing it. But gossip is worth more than money to the people of my village. And in rumors, I can pay her handsomely.

"In fact," I say, false shame dimming my voice, "I fear he'll send me off as well. Nobody's shown interest in me for a wife."

"Oh?" She nearly topples from her chair, so eager is she to catch my words all the sooner. "But that's dreadful! You'll be destitute!"

"As long as my sister is secure in a good home, I'm pleased to await the Lord's fate for me."

"And you thought to ask me? Well, child, of course I'd delight to help a poor, starving child. But I've got help aplenty. God has blessed me with hardworking girls who always tend to their chores."

"Oh, but Mem can do so much. And she'd fit in wonderfully, I think. Your Prudence is the same age, is she not? They'd be fast friends."

Goody Wilson surprises me with a genuine smile. "As were you and my Thomas, once."

I look down to hide the color pulsing in my cheeks. "Yes. How...how is Thomas?"

"He's excelling at Harvard, as we always knew he would. Listen to me. I shouldn't be boastful. But a mother is always proudest of her only son. And your cousin? I haven't seen Abel in—has it been a year?"

I nod, warm embarrassment replaced by chill dread. "He writes when he can."

"Trapping fur, yes?"

Another nod. My throat is too clogged with tears I'll never shed to speak any more.

"Well, Deliverance, why not wait on his money, rather than send your sister off? Not that it's my business to tell old Ezra what to do."

She knows, I expect, that this business has nothing to do with my uncle. Rather, it has everything to do with keeping Uncle away from Mem. Goody Wilson is a good woman, devout, obedient. But she is intelligent, too. Smart enough to know everything and say nothing.

"Abel hasn't written in months," I say at last. "For all I know he's dead or held captive."

"I will include him in my prayers," she says, meaning it.

"I thank you. But, Goody Wilson, in the meantime..." I swallow. "Help my sister. Please."

Mem won't soon forgive me. But I'd rather she hate me forever than live another day under Uncle's wrath.

The reverend and his wife are wealthy, despite the seldom-paid salary for his ministering. They can give Mem comfort. She'll be with girls her own age. Uncle is too much a coward to fight for her back. He owes nearly every man in the village a debt. It's a miracle nobody has claimed us as servants for repayment yet.

The air seems colder as I walk toward our ramshackle dwelling, that rotted thing of straw and timber I can hardly call a house. Beast meets me at the gate, a mournful, accusing look on his face.

"I'm sorry, friend. Goody Wilson doesn't care for dogs."

He whines, thumps his tail against my leg.

I step into our home. The stink of lye and boiling fat drifts from the kitchen.

The soap. I forgot I bade her make it today.

I find her standing by the fire, stirring our small, scarred pot. She blinks, coming out of the haze of her work, when I clear my throat.

"Liv! Where have you been? I'll have you know, I put this off as long as possible." She turns fully toward me, the bubbling pot forgotten. "Did you find help? Where were you, anyway?"

"The parsonage," I say slowly, not meeting her eyes. I take the boiled soap from the fire.

"You spoke to Reverend Wilson? Did you tell him what Uncle has done?" Mem lowers her voice and peers over her shoulder, as though Uncle might appear any moment. "Are they going to arrest him? Put him in the stocks? Oh, that would be delicious, wouldn't it?"

"Mem," I chide. She rolls her eyes.

"Well, what are they going to do?"

"Mem..." I set the pot on the table and finally meet my sister's gaze. "I need to talk to you."

Mem's belongings fit in a single satchel, the bag loose and light over my shoulder. Mem trails behind me on the path, wordless. She hasn't spoken since our conversation in the kitchen, where her begging dissolved into shouting, and then crying when I would not change my mind.

I say nothing, either. There aren't words for this, only action. She doesn't understand, and I'd just as soon leave it that way. Why Uncle has spared her so long is both mercy and mystery. But after her actions today, I know it cannot last. His wrath will fall on her.

The parsonage seems somehow less homey upon my second visit. Mem halts a few feet behind me, watching the trees about the house as though monsters twine through their branches. Beast leaves my side to go to her, sniffing at her still hands.

"Mem? Come."

She shakes her head. "I don't want to go. I want to stay with you." She scratches Beast's ear. "And him."

"You'll never know how much I don't want to do this. But we—"

"Who will make the soap if I'm gone?" She looks back toward the path to our pathetic farm. "Your soaps are terrible. And the candles? You need me."

"Of course I do, Mem." My voice is more impatience than sentiment. "But needing you is nothing when I consider what's best for you."

"What's best," she says, tears warbling her voice, "is if we stay together. No matter what. Even with Uncle."

She's heard his screams, seen his mottled red face in the mornings after too much drink. She's now felt his fury when it finds a target. But she doesn't *know*. She has no inkling of what he's truly capable of. I feel a wild temptation to speak the truth. I feel my tongue curl around the traitorous words I've longed to tell another.

Our mother did not die because of you.

But I cannot. God has placed me in his house, in his protection. I must obey him. The Lord's will is mysterious. So mysterious, I find myself doubting it entirely.

"Uncle is not well," I say at last. "And much as I wish things were different, Mem, they're not. I've nowhere else to go. No prospects. But you can be safe here. You can read books without fear, study all you like. You can become a proper woman in this place. And someday…" I swallow. "If I'm married, I'll send for you. You'll come stay with me then. But for now, please, know I do this out of devotion to you."

Mem's tears are fully falling now, no longer choked only in her words. "He'll hurt you."

"Nay, Mem. He weakens every day. He relies too much on his cider for comfort. It makes him wild, but it also makes him sick. And if he goes on disrespecting God's commandments and neglecting meeting…I doubt the Lord will see fit to treat him with mercy."

"Do you think he'll die?" She says it with too much hope, light in her eyes.

"We shouldn't wish for such things. The Lord will deal justly with our uncle."

Mem chews her lip for a moment. "What if she can't find me here?"

I swing Mem's bag to my other shoulder, sighing. "Who?"

"The Blue Lady."

My fingers loosen in surprise; Mem's bag makes a sad, light sound upon the earth. Beast hurries to the bag and sniffs at it, hoping for a treat inside.

"The what?"

"The vision I saw. The one who looked like me? She promised she'd speak with me again."

"That was only a nightmare, Mem," I say.

"She sang to me a bit," Mem says distantly. "It was nice. I think I should be lonely if she couldn't find me."

I choose to ignore her strange speech and retrieve her pack from the ground. "I'll visit you as often as Goody Wilson allows it. Now come."

Mem spares a last look toward the path, Lot's wife longing after Sodom. I take her hand—warm flesh, not salt—and pull her forward, toward her new life.

Uncle is still not home when I return. The soap has congealed in its pot, still sitting on our kitchen table. Mem's fabric dangles from the loom, unfinished. The empty laundry baskets still sit by the door where I dropped them. I'll have to go back to the river and retrieve our clothes.

As I set to tidying the house, I realize Mem was right. I *do* need her. The chores will be entirely mine now.

But our work is wasted, isn't it, on Uncle and our sad lives here? If we hadn't wool and soap and food, we would merely follow the natural progression of our lives, down, down to ruin, and eventually the house might fall upon our bones and entomb us.

I saved my sister from that.

I can't be still, and I can't face the weight of this pointless work. I whistle for Beast to follow, and without knowing why, knowing its unwise even as my feet take me forward, I go into the woods.

The witch's burial place hums at me over the air, a rumble of potential reaching for me. I know I could find her without markers, that I could stumble blind and still find her body below a few feet of hard dirt.

Beast, still smelling her, perks his ears toward the place and wags his tail.

"No, boy. We're done with her."

He growls, disappointed, but follows me along the safe path. I stop to pick up newly fallen branches, needing action, purpose.

I go farther than I usually do. The woods lay deep before me, laced with fog, dark with shadows. The evening sun casts hard lines of light through the trees. The contrast is at once compelling and frightening. It's as though sky exists above but grants only small hints of itself to the eternal dark of the forest.

I don't go back. Even when the sunlight falls lower and dimmer on the forest floor, I stay on the narrowing path. I've filled my arms with branches. Beast trots beside me, pleased with the extended exercise. Shadows drape themselves over me, cooling the air further. The clouds of my breath mingle with the fog and I feel it, my becoming an extension of this place. How I could simply lie down and meld into the forest floor, skin falling off, bone crumbling to sand. With my sister safe I could finally sleep here.

Hellfire seems false in the cool dark. This place does not mean life, but it stunts eternity into something simpler. Death, pure death, where that is it, the end, no waking, no dreaming. Just sleep...

I fall, the branches scattering away from me, save one, which pushes into my ribcage. Wincing, I rise to my knees. Beast sniffs at me, whimpers.

Why did I fall? Nothing lies in my path to trip me. The ground is smooth, trodden. I glance around, suddenly sure something watches me from the woods. Sure I am not the only soul in this forest.

"Hello?"

My voice is buried in thick bark and clustered leaves. It doesn't travel beyond this space.

And then...a rustle. A footstep.

My eyes snap toward the sound.

A black cloak. A face.

She shines between the trees, pale as settled snow, her eyes like thin ice as they watch me. Her lips, bloodred and broken by the cold, part as though she means to speak.

Beast's hackles rise. He snarls.

The girl runs. Her cloak whips into shadow and melds into the leaves.

"Wait!"

I make to run but stumble again, crashing back to my knees. Beast presses his nose to my hand, snuffling, and I find blood coating my palm. A sharp rock broke my fall and my skin.

Was she a girl? She stopped me following her, kept me in this shadowy place. And now my sense of direction wanes. I don't know which way to turn. Without the sun, the way home is anywhere, nowhere.

I rise and wipe the blood on my cloak. My hand bumps something hard.

The book. I never took it out of my cloak. And yet, I swear it wasn't in my pocket a moment ago...

I take it out and turn to the first page. Two names are written there.

Katherine & Elizabeth.

The book tumbles from my shaking hands. The branded girl, buried. And another, still walking, breathing the thin air of the forest. This book was theirs and they signed their names to it.

The book lays open before me, the breeze lifting its pages. The words inside are insensible from a distance, but I see they are hand-scrawled, clumsy. I lean closer. Latin. I don't read it. Perhaps the reverend does. Thomas, certainly. He was always going on about his language studies.

But I could never show this book to Thomas. He's away at Harvard, for one. And he would certainly feel compelled to turn me over to the constable, should a strange red book with two witches' names in it be found in my possession.

No. Damn what it says. Damn my curiosity.

It must be burned. Tonight.

Uncle is still not home.

It's the middle of the night, I'm bruised and cut, covered in brambles, my hair leaking from its coif. And it's as though God approves of my misdeeds, because nobody is here to witness my shame.

I wonder where Uncle is, if he's gone searching for Mem. But I made Goody Wilson promise. I made her understand.

I build a fire to warm my flesh, cold as the dead, and consider the flames, growing in licks and leaps. I should put the book in. I should. I should...

I check the door. I can't let Uncle catch me, and if he should return home right as I toss the book into the flames, if he should find its remains, ashen in the dead pit in the morning...

I take a candle, one of Mem's better-made ones, and light the wick. Beast follows me upstairs, to my loft. It's cold and empty without Mem, the untidy bed too big suddenly. We slept cramped against each other and somehow the promise of room to kick my legs is grim and lonely. I set the candle on a small table, leave the book beside it.

The flame bleeds lovely colors across the bloodred cover. It dances to music unknown to human ears. We watch it awhile, Beast and I, companionable and silent.

Finally, I lift the book, let it fall open to crisp pages. The cramped words within are in a language unfamiliar to me, but I dare not linger on them, lest their magic catch me.

I move the book toward the small flame. It catches an edge, but won't burn far. The flame licks and crowds closer to the insidious words but dies as it nears them, as though they will to stay. The flame collapses, spent.

The hearth, then. I pray Uncle stays away a while longer. I'll scrape every remnant of the book from the burnt sticks and ash and toss it in the river.

But when I arrive downstairs, I find the hearth cold. Dead embers flicker and wane.

It's impossible. I only just lit it. It can't have...

"Damned thing," I hiss at the book.

I storm from the house, Beast close behind, and walk around our property to the crumbled little well beyond the fence. I submerge the pages, sinking them with my hands. The water will take longer but will surely rot them where the fire failed. Maybe the words will wash away, coiled ink slowly ripping the magic from the pages. When I let go, the book floats. But it'll have to be enough.

I return to my room, and it smells of burning. I remember the ladies of Boston, cloistered in their fresh scents, alluring and false. Had I one bottle of perfume I might mask the stench. Uncle will know. My secret stinks of ash and flame, fills my little loft.

I stay up the rest of the night, awaiting my uncle's footsteps over the threshold.

He never comes.

When the sun is at last too high to ignore, I begin my day as though it were any other. I make a small plate of eggs and set the largest portion aside for Uncle, as I always do. I leave it cooling on the table as I wash and clean. The food congeals as I begin darning socks. I have one sad pair completed when a knock lands on the door. Its aggressive pounding makes me pull a stitch, and the end of the sock comes undone.

"Who the devil…"

I open the door and feel my face lose its blood. The constable, Goodman Walsh, leans against the doorframe, looking much calmer than his insistent knocking suggests. He smiles, eyes on my parted lips.

"Hello, Deliverance."

"C-Constable Walsh. God give you good morrow."

The smile twitches into something meaner. "You're wondering where your uncle is, I'm sure."

"Oh." My heart wilts in my chest. "Yes. He hasn't been home all night."

"He's—well. I don't want to frighten you, my sweet girl, but your uncle spent the night in jail."

I hope I don't look as satisfied—*vindicated*—as I feel. "Is that so? What, um…" It seems impolite to ask what he's done. I ought to show concern, sorrow. I feel neither of those things and find my body too light with release to generate them. "What was his crime?"

"You're not surprised to hear this," he says instead of answering.

"He has a temper." Everyone in the village knows it. Gossip ceases to be such when the fact is so well known.

"I suppose he does. He made a spectacle of himself at Winnow's last night. Drunk." He watches me, finds I'm not shocked. His smile edges wider. "He was screaming at someone."

"Who?"

"No one."

"But…you just said…"

"He was screaming as though someone were there, but I tell you, girl, there wasn't a body before him. Sitting in a corner, talking to himself in a hush, and then he explodes. Shouting, tossing his chair, making a fuss over something being said only he can hear. I witnessed it myself."

It's ridiculous, stupid behavior. But... "He was sent to prison for that?"

The constable's teeth join his lips in a wide, pleased grin. "Well, you see, towards the end, a few people suggested he was holding discourse with a spirit. Maybe the Devil himself."

This—I never could have expected this. My uncle is cruel, horrible, but he's devout. He would never make congress with spirits and devils. "Are you suggesting that my uncle is—what, a wizard?"

"You don't agree?"

"Of course not! It's absurd. My uncle is a Christian man."

Walsh nods. His smile glints like a knife blade teetered over flesh. "Then what make you of this?"

He tugs his hand from his pocket. Clutched between gloved fingers is the small red book.

I school my features, burying recognition, guilt. "What is that?"

"I found it floating in your well. I had a look around, of course. Witchcraft is a serious accusation. I needed to be sure. But it appears to be a book of spells. Perhaps the Devil's own book, and his witches' signatures within."

I doubt the constable knows the language in the book better than I. He's guessing at what the words are. Trying to make a case without evidence.

"Who's to say it's his? Anybody could have tossed it in our well."

"You needn't defend him any longer." The constable's big hand closes over my shoulder. I have to remind myself not to back away. "Everyone knows how he's treated you, Deliverance."

His hand slips up my neck. His thumb slides against my jawline. "We know how cruel he is. The bruises you have..."

He's too close. Something trickles along my skin, a concoction of fear and disgust. But his gloved hand doesn't leave my neck. His thumb presses into my lower lip. I'm still. I cannot move, because there's wrath in this seeming affection.

"You've suffered too much," he says, and I taste his breath in my mouth. "But he's put away now. He'll be tried and likely hang."

My mouth drops open. "On such flimsy evidence?"

I hate my uncle. But I cannot be the reason he dies. Nobody deserves this.

I gently back away. The constable lets his hand slip slowly from me, his eyes lingering on my face.

"Please, sir, don't be hasty. Let me—let me speak with him."

"I wouldn't associate with him if I were you. It'll only make you look guilty, too. In fact," he sighs. "Your protestations, I must say, give me pause. As does the look in your eyes when I showed you this." He hefts the book in his hand as though it weighed a ton. "A Christian girl ought to recoil from such an object. But I swear you looked as though you...longed for it."

"No! I don't— Please, sir. I just can't believe my uncle would do such a thing."

He closes in again, his face nearly touching mine. I smell the rot of his teeth, the sour sting of his breath. "Is this your book, Deliverance?"

I make myself hold still, despite every inch of my flesh wanting to curl away from this man. "It's not. Now please, I'd—I'd like a moment alone to think on this. And pray," I add, knowing he will want to hear it.

"Of course." The constable's smile is too close to my mouth. I back away, pretending I don't see the flash of anger in his eyes. "After I collect payment."

"Payment? For what?"

"Your uncle's expenses. We fed him a meal last night, and this morning. We gave him a blanket and pillow. These things cost money, Deliverance."

"But I have no money," I say, calmly as I can. "Nor does my uncle."

"I'd be willing to take compensation of another kind."

My stomach lurches. Surely...he can't mean... He steps closer, and I stumble back into the house, my spine hitting the edge of our kitchen table. But—thank God—he passes me by, throwing me an amused look as he opens our cupboard and begins to rummage.

"Your thoughts so easily stray to such wickedness."

"S-sir?" My breath feels like a rock in my throat.

"You're flushed. Panting." His smile slips wider. "I can't tell if you're frightened or excited."

"I'm upset," I say. "And scared for my family."

"Hm." He turns back to the cupboard and lifts a cracked plate with a scowl. "God, you live like this?" He lets it drop to the floor, shattering it.

"Constable Walsh, what are you...no!"

He finds a teapot at the back of the cupboard, its design of poppies faded, but still beautiful.

"This is a fine piece. Might fetch a penny."

"It was my mother's," I say, my stinging eyes locked on the precious porcelain pot.

"She had exquisite taste." He tucks the teapot under one arm. "Most of this is useless. Oh—hand me that soap there. And those candles, too."

I shake my head, more in disbelief than refusal. After all, I can't really refuse, can I?

"Bring it out to my cart," he says. He pauses, considers the kitchen chairs, then drags one off behind him.

I gather the box of soap, the candles Mem made with such care, and follow him out the door. His horse and cart wait down the lane. I hear a lonely bleating from it.

My head whips toward the paddock Uncle had labored over. Three nannies cluster anxiously at the edge, bleating at the constable's cart. Walsh has our only male goat by the horns, and he hauls him agonizingly closer to the cart.

"You—you're taking our goat?"

"He's a fine specimen."

"You can't—"

"I'll take the nannies, too, if you think they'll be lonely without him."

I shut my mouth, shake my head. I take the boxes to his cart. I'm not surprised to find all our firewood stacked in the far corner opposite the chair. I try not to look into our billy's eyes as the constable loads him onto the cart. He bleats once. I shake my head.

I can't help you.

"Didn't you have a hound, too? Mangey thing. But I might find a use for—"

"He ran away," I lie, keeping eye contact, challenging him to disbelieve me. If he does, he gives in. He places my mother's teapot atop the soaps and hops to the head of the cart.

"Oh. Those are nice."

At first, I don't know what he's talking about. Then I see his eyes on my apron pocket. The ruined socks stick out.

He pushes his big hand under my nose. "Come now. Don't be stingy."

He's just being cruel, pointlessly hateful. I drop the badly made socks in his palm and he crushes his fingers over them.

"I'm sure I'll see you again very soon, sweet girl." He tugs at a strand of hair come loose from my coif. "You're a woman alone now. I feel it's my duty to check in on you."

"I'll be fine," I say, letting a little of the hate I feel drip into the words.

"Even so." He gives me one last, lingering look, then snaps his horse's reigns. The cart's wheels clatter away, along with our supplies for winter.

10. A Prelude to Ghosts

I shove our kitchen table against the door and sit by the fire, watching the entrance, waiting for the constable to return. His threat rattles in my mind. He sees my impurity somehow. He'll think nothing of taking me when the mood strikes him.

Beast whines. I look up, see the dim light of the kitchen. I've sat for hours, and Beast is hungry.

I rise and scour the icebox. We have a small hank of venison left. Tooths of frost cross the meat like veins. It's been buried at the bottom of the icebox, forgotten for so long. It'll do, though. I cook it, leaving the whole portion for Beast. I'm not hungry, and not sure I ever will be again.

There is too much feeling in me. The twist of my stomach and the weight of my heart feel diseased, a plague that rages only the innards. I understand suddenly why Uncle loved his demons so. Drink and violence would at least banish this sickness for a while.

I go to the corner of the kitchen, to the loose floorboard Uncle thought we never noticed. I lift the board and see his stash of beer and cider within. There's even a bottle of rum tucked away. I pluck that out and uncork it. A strong, spiced scent like burning sugar fills my nose.

I tip the bottle to my lips and take three large swallows. It tastes like the stories I've heard of Barbados. It feels like a candle leaking wax down my chest.

Beast finishes his meal and lays on his stomach by my side, ready to keep vigil with me through the night. I take another swallow of rum, staring at the door. Let the constable come and find me drunk and mad. Perhaps I won't be such easy prey if I let my mind loosen, bend with the sweet swimming in my blood. I'll drink the whole damn bottle. I'll smash it against his head when he comes. I'll take the glass to his eyes and fill his mouth with blood. I'll...

My eyes flicker against the waning day. I haven't slept in... When did I sleep last? Surely...

My eyes fly open. My head rests against Beast's side, his slow breaths pressing into my cheek. The bottle of rum stands near, much diminished. I push myself up, shaking my head against the ringing in my ears.

No. Not ringing. The sound building in my skull is too watery, too low and soft. It has a rhythm only occasionally disturbed by a flat note.

"...lay me beneath the stars..."

I scramble to my feet. Beast shoots up, ready to defend me. Against what, though?

"Your smile cannot bind me..."

The voice is coming from the other side of the house, accompanied, like strange music, by the clatter of knitting needles.

"M-Mem?" I call.

The woman's voice answers: "...your wiles do not charm me."

I step into the doorway.

"My wicked heart can't love."

A figure sits in Uncle's chair, slumped, her blond hair falling around her body in loose, tangled strands, thick with dirt. The click of knitting continues, though her hands don't move. They hang limp over the arms of the chair, save for the twitch of one long, blue finger.

I think of the girl in the forest. I think of the old beggar woman who wanders the village demanding food and coin. I think of anybody else this could be, because I know her, and she cannot be here.

"Said...nothing..."

The music of the figure's voice is gone, replaced with a cold rasp, tree branches against an icy window.

"Saw him...do it. Said. Nothing."

Her head twitches to the side, and though her eyes are curtained behind hair, I know she watches me. Hair falls away from her mouth, exposing cracked white lips.

"Deliver...me."

At last, the hair blows away from her face as though by a great wind, and I see her. Those features I'd memorized in life, ruined in death. Her neck is ringed purple. Her nose is rotted away into her blue face. And her eyes, white and sunken into the lids, gone like water in a drought.

If I scream, I don't hear it.

Beast's barking wakes me. My heart hovers somewhere high in my throat, the terror of my nightmare still fresh. I push myself up and look around.

I'm in the doorway to the sitting room.

Was it not a dream? It had to be. I walked here in my sleep, some compulsion driving me to playact the terrible scene conjured in my mind. That's all.

I decided the day Mother died that I could not believe in ghosts. If I did, my nightmares would be real. And if my nightmares are real...

But Mem saw her, too. My fingers drift toward my throat, unconsciously marking the same lines I saw on my mother's neck.

It's a nightmare. That's all. I'm only thinking of her because Uncle is in jail, and Uncle... I shake my head. I can't even think it. It's no memory. Only a suspicion. A dream I had. A prelude to my ghost.

Beast's barking continues, and I find him by the solitary window in the kitchen. He growls, his nose pointed up, encouraging me to see for myself.

Our land is thick with dark, indistinguishable from the sky above. But there is something pale and bright in the paddock. Movement. A slim hand. The edge of a white face.

A girl in a dark cloak.

I move away from the window lest she see me. Why has she come? To find her book, that must be why. She's lost without its spells and charms and knows somehow it was here last. I wish her malevolence upon the constable. Let her reclaim her property from that man. Pray they kill each other in the struggle.

The sorry bleating of one of the nannies brings me back to the window. There's the girl, fastening a rope around the goat's neck, tugging her away from her sisters.

The injustice is what moves me. I have been robbed of everything. I will not lose another blasted goat.

I grab my cloak from the peg, stuff my feet into my boots, and walk out into a misting rain that feels close to snow. I stop by Uncle's shed and choose a pitchfork before rounding the house, where the girl is still struggling with the nanny.

"Who are you?" I say, my voice surprisingly low. The girl stops pulling at the goat and stares at me. Her eyes flit from the pitchfork to my face.

"I— I'll curse you," she says, without conviction.

"Am I not already?" My voice rises. I take a step closer. "Let her go. Now."

She freezes. Laughs. I want to drive the pitchfork into her stomach. "I wouldn't expect such spirit from a Puritan."

"And I expect no mercy from a witch." I fix my grip on the pitchfork and aim it toward her. "But I'm tired of people taking what's mine. So, let the goat go, or we'll match your powers against the end of a pitchfork."

She drops the rope. Raises her hands. "I didn't realize I was stealing from one of my own. I thought an old drunk lived here and assumed she wouldn't be missed."

"You've been watching the house?"

"I keep an eye out. But I've never seen you be—oh." She steps closer, bringing her face into the moonlight. "You were in the woods."

"You caused me to fall."

She rolls her eyes. "I did not. You walked like a drunk. Or a dreamer." She smiles. "I liked the look of you then. I'm more impressed now."

"I will not sign your book, if you mean to suggest it."

Her laugh matches the iced rain, cold and falling away. "You seem too intelligent for that sort of talk."

We stand there, at a sort of impasse. She doesn't mean to rob me, yet she hasn't left. I blink at her, waiting. She bites her lip.

"Are you...often in the woods?" she says.

"Lately," I say.

"Have you seen... She'd be about your age. Red hair, dark eyes."

This girl doesn't know, then. "I saw her."

She perks up. "Where has she gone? Into the village? I was too scared to look, but if you tell me where she's gone—"

"I buried her," I say, enjoying the cruelty of the words, savoring the shock on her face. "I found her dead on the ground with a brand between her eyes. I ought to have left her for the animals—" I wince. Tears have sprung into the girl's eyes, and I soften my tone. "I couldn't leave her like that, though. So I buried her where I found her."

"You're lying," she says, hatred between her teeth, in her eyes. "You're...you're a hateful hag like the rest of them."

I scoff. "You think I'm—"

"I know you're lying!" she screams. "Just tell me where she is."

"She'd dead."

"Stop it. Just stop—stop saying that!"

"I'll take you to her body now."

"No!" She drops to her knees in the muck of the paddock. She's silent a moment, shaking. And then she screams, fingers burying deep into the ground. The goats scatter. Beast shrinks against my side. I absently put a hand to his head, trapped in the girl's grief, unable to leave her as the sound of her agony shatters on the air and fades in pitched notes into the forest.

"Lizzy," she whispers, touching her lips. "Oh God, Lizzy."

I remember the names in the book. Elizabeth. Katherine.

"Your name is Katherine, isn't it?"

"Kit." She takes a shuddering breath, as though the normalcy of this question is causing a rift. She wants to carry on in her grief, but she's forcing herself back together in front of me. "Everyone...calls me Kit."

I lower the pitchfork at last and set it on the ground beside me. "I—I can show you where she's—"

"Don't say it again." A sob breaks the last word. "She cannot be...she's all I..."

"Kit?" It feels wrong to say the girl's name, even worse to lay a hand on her shoulder. She startles at my touch, flinging herself back to her feet.

"No. No, no. Not Lizzy. You're lying. I'll find her, you..." She freezes. "You knew my name."

"F-from the book. Your friend—Lizzy?—she had a book."

"And you *took it*?"

"I didn't—"

"Where is it?" She steps fast toward me. "What have you done with it?"

"It's gone! I thought it was the Devil's book. I-it wouldn't burn, so I threw it into the well, and—"

Before I can finish, explain about the constable, she flies away from me, toward the well. She paws at the water's surface like a desperate animal, crying all the while. When she realizes it's futile, she smacks the water.

She turns back to me, braced against the well. "It's all I had left of her."

Stunned, shaking, all I can manage is, "I'm sorry."

She screams through her teeth, but the fight seems to have left her. She turns, her dark cloak spraying mud at me, and retreats into the woods, mixing with the darkness until I can see her no more.

11. Alone

It snows the next day. Fat white flakes like wet sugar, gathering on windows and heaping before my door. If it were only me, I'd let the snow grow into impenetrable piles, lock me into my home for the winter.

But I have Beast, and he's pawing at his bowl with a baleful look. The house is dropping in temperature and the constable took all our firewood, leaving only my pathetic collection of branches and kindling. The darkness comes early and thick and there are no candles to burn.

I have to work.

I start with feeding Beast. I beat snow out of my path with Uncle's walking stick and make my way to the sagging shelter where the goats and chickens and one lonely pig live in strange harmony. I gather eggs, then a chicken, the hen who lays the least. I stroke her feathers and whisper apologies as I take her to the tree stump, where Uncle used to kill our dinner.

Plucking and preparing the chicken takes too much of the morning. While the meat boils above the last of the branches I have to burn, I spin flax for a candle wick. By the time I'm finished, the meat is cooked, and Beast is too happy to eat his half. I force myself to finish my portion, though my stomach is still weak and wants to reject it. I melt tallow over the remaining embers of fire before it dies and leaves the house cold.

At least tonight I'll have light, though my candle, when it's finished, is lumpy and cannot stand on its own. I prop it between Uncle's Bible and some captivity narrative I meant to read but never did.

The last thing I need is wood to burn. Which means going into the woods. Her woods.

Kit seemed so much more a girl than a monster. I cannot reconcile what I believe of her with the broken girl I met last night. Whatever she dabbled in was evil, but perhaps the Devil used her weakness to elicit her name in his book. Desperate people make foolish decisions.

Beast insists on following me into the woods. I try to stay close, but I find so few branches that my path diverges from safety. I find myself walking, only somewhat conscious of my path, to the place I buried the witch. Elizabeth.

Lizzy.

It's unchanged, save for the layer of snow upon the raised mound. As though in blessing, I find plenty of downed branches around the dead girl's grave. I gather them, shaking the snow off the bark, while Beast sniffs around, recognizing this place. He whimpers, mournful.

"I know, boy. It's a sorry place." Among the branches I find a sizable rock, smooth and gray. I set my bundle of branches aside and lift the stone onto the head of the burial place.

"Ashes to ashes, dust to dust," I say. I place my hand over the earth, where I imagine her still heart would be. My fingers sink into the cool snow, leaving their mark. "May God have mercy on your soul."

The trees rustle, and something dark and quick fills my vision. I scramble back, a weak scream breaking from my throat and scattering white on the air. A crow stands upon the makeshift headstone, head cocked toward me, one beady eye watching my movements.

"Shoo," I try, weakly.

The crow squawks back, and...it can't have, but I swear...it sounded like...

"*What* did you say?"

The bird tips its beak toward the grave. "Thank you," it shrieks in its strange bird-voice. I think I might faint dead away, but the bird takes flight, fluttering back into the trees without another word.

I'm beginning to doubt the Devil has anything to do with this. Perhaps my mind is fragile. My nightmares first, and now talking birds. Nobody would believe me.

I look up through the falling flakes of snow, waiting, but nothing emerges. No specter or witch or chattering fowl. Gathering the fallen branches, I whistle for Beast. I hope never to come back to these cursed woods.

I find someone waiting by my gate. A small figure in a familiar black cloak.

"I didn't expect such sympathy from a prude," Kit says to the ground.

I pause a few feet from her, wary to get any closer. "You saw me?"

"We did." She nods to the gate post. The crow from the forest sits there, watching me.

"Hullo," it creaks.

I shriek, stumbling back into Beast. "How do you make it speak?" What I really want to ask is if she'll please make it *stop*.

"I don't." She reaches out a single pale finger and strokes the bird's wing. "He learned it by himself. Very clever, my little Beaky."

I scowl. "*Beaky*? What sort of name is that?"

"It's a fine name, thanks very much." She looks up at last and pulls back her hood. A beautiful, freckled face stares down at me. Her black hair falls in thick, smooth curls across her shoulders. But despite her beauty, my eyes are drawn to the ugliest part of her—a brand upon her forehead. An H for *heretic*.

I shift the wood in my arms; it's suddenly too heavy. "What did you do to earn that?"

She touches the brand above her eyes, grinning. "Nothing. But what I did, they chose to call heresy. It's simpler, I suppose."

"Are you a witch?"

"Nay." She crosses her arms. A smile ticks on her cheek. "And you? I've never seen a Puritan girl go so often into the forest."

I don't rise to the bait. "What of the book?"

"Do you read French?" She steps closer, challenging me.

I coil into myself. "I thought it Latin."

"So, you read Latin?"

"Nay."

"Your Devil must do, then. Is Latin what they speak in Hell?"

"No. Maybe. What?"

"The book was in French," Kit says. "Lizzy spoke it. Her mother was from Calais. She taught me. That book..." She sighs. "It's none of your concern, really. But we'd write each other stories. Poems. It was a distraction. And a little hope. I suppose a good story is better than a cruel reality."

I nod, because of course she's right.

"Anyway. I thought you might feel better knowing I'm not a witch. I won't be leaving any cursed poppets at your door." Her thin smile vanishes, all joviality washing out of her paling face. "And I wanted to thank you. For burying her. And...and marking it. Now I can visit." She pats the crow on the head. "I hope he didn't frighten you. He only wanted to say thanks himself."

I choose to ignore that last bit. "You...must have been close. With Elizabeth."

Her laugh is watery, strangled. "More than you realize, prudish girl."

I'll ignore *that*, too. "I'm Deliverance. Liv."

"Liv, then." She pulls her hood over her head, shadowing her already dark hair. "Well. I doubt I'll be welcomed in your village, so I'll take my leave."

I find no words, but my face says it all. She nods.

"Listen, Liv. The old drunk is gone, isn't he?"

"For now," I say. "He's been arrested. There'll be a trial. I—I don't know what to expect."

"It won't go well," she says. "In a place like Boston, perhaps he'd stand a chance. But out here... People come to these remote places when they've already decided the world is evil. They can't burn the world, but they can walk away from it. They can make a paradise out of loneliness and remove anyone who threatens it."

I stare down at the path, the little beaten road that has transported me daily back to this place. I've never been home, not since I lost my parents. Uncle wanted what Kit speaks of, a lonely place to build a rotten kingdom. But it was not out of holy devotion.

"My uncle is no witch," I say. "But he doesn't deserve mercy."

"I see." She looks around at the pathetic house, our scraggly land waiting for winter's cover to hide its dying garden and unplucked weeds. "Liv, I don't want to offend...but you seem the type of person more likely to die of cold or starvation than make it through a single winter alone."

I scowl. "I'm quite able to... Oh, never mind. You're probably right." I realize my sad collection of branches is still in my arms. I dump it by the gate.

Kit raises her eyebrows. "I only mention it because Lizzy and I lived out there, in those woods, for months. Things only got dire when the cold came on. I can hunt, skin game, build a good fire. If you want my help...perhaps I'll consider it, given how you showed Lizzy a small kindness."

"That..." I sigh. I cannot accept help from this strange girl. She claims not to be a witch, which is no proof. A witch would deny her sins to death, but an innocent is ready to confess. That, anyway, is what Uncle has always taught me. Yet knowing this, knowing what this girl might be, still my lips part and words fill my throat and trickle from my mouth, desperate: "That would be wonderful."

Kit brightens. "Then I'll come back sometime. Tonight, perhaps. I've been tracking a herd of deer through the woods."

"I thank you."

"Just tell me one last thing."

I nod.

"When you found Lizzy...if you had to guess...what killed her?"

I think back to the body, the seeming perfection of her skin save for the dirt and ice. She looked as though she had merely laid down and died.

"I would say the cold," I tell her.

Kit shakes her head. "No. It wasn't that cold. Our camp wasn't far. She would have made it back. There were no bite marks, claw marks?"

"Only after I returned. When I first saw her...there was ice in her hair and dirt on her skin." I remember, then, the prints in the dirt, the ones I stamped out. "But there...there were footprints. Hers, I think, and another's."

"A person's?" Kit says.

I shake my head. "They were cloven. Like a goat's, only...only if a goat walked on two feet, and was huge besides."

A small, dry laugh trickles from her lips. "Like the Devil."

I shrug. But yes, I think. Like the Devil.

"Thanks." Kit nods. "I'll come back. Hold tight, Liv."

I watch her go, wondering if I'll truly see her again. If I've made a friend through all this strangeness.

12. In Hope or Dread

I cook the morning's eggs, give most to Beast. He gobbles them happily. I manage one, but my stomach has been knotted since the constable came. Even with the promise of Kit's return, I find I can't relax. The day drifts by in a frenzy of half-done chores and barely eaten meals.

Only when the sun is fully sunk below the horizon do I go up to my room. I bring a burning tallow candle and the captivity narrative I've so far neglected to read. Maybe another woman's harrowing story will put my own misery into perspective. Beast nestles beside me in bed, his warmth soaking into my back. It's almost as good as having Mem here again.

Eventually, I drop the book on my stomach to drift and dream. But I wake fitfully throughout the night. A flicker of nightmare starts my heart, and then my eyes snap open. I fall back asleep only to have it happen again.

Something tugs at the blankets by my foot.

"Come on up, boy," I think I say, but my mouth doesn't move with the words. I try my hand, but it, too, is frozen by my side.

The tugging continues.

Why Beast is pawing at my blankets, I have no idea. He knows he's allowed on the bed. He's lying right beside me after all...

My heartbeat picks up. Beast is beside me. Even now. So who...?

Kit? I try to say. Again, my mouth is frozen and mute. I struggle to turn, to kick the yanking hand away. But my body doesn't obey. The tugging moves up. Someone trails their hand along my leg, over my stomach. Pressure settles on my chest as though someone leans with all their weight upon me.

My eyes snap open.

Above me floats a familiar face. Sunken, watery eyes and a blue, cracked mouth. Bruises around the eyes and bloodied whites stare down at me. The shattered mouth opens above mine in a scream that tears through my skull. I think I match her pitch until I realize I *can't* scream; I'm rendered silent by some horrible power, and I can only endure this specter above me.

"Deliver me," it hisses. The pressure of its hands is enough to stop my breath, but I cannot struggle.

Stop. Please. I don't know you. I won't remember you.

"Deliver..."

"Deliverance?"

"Me..."

"Liv? Liv!"

All at once, I'm freed. The specter vanishes as I sit up, arms swinging, tears free to fall. I gasp and hold a hand to my pounding heart. Beast wakes with a start and noses me, curious.

"Liv? Are you all right?" Kit kneels by my bed. She stinks of labor and the forest; blood lines her fingernails. Her wild hair and fevered eyes should alarm me, but instead, a certain warmth fills my chest. Her chapped lips are bright from the cold, bloody where she bites them. Her brow glimmers with sweat. A scrape traces the sharp edge of her jaw, and dirt streaks her cheeks.

"What happened to you?" I manage.

"Oh. Nothing. A lady is never very pretty after a night of hunting." She smiles.

I force my breaths to leave my lungs more slowly. I shut my eyes, but the face is still there, in memory, a thing of rot and cold and wrath. I decide it's safer to face the dark than my dreams. I open my eyes.

"Are *you* all right? You were..." Kit shakes her head. "If I didn't know any better, I'd say you were possessed just now." Her nervous laugh grates on my already thin nerves. "Your eyes were wide open, but you didn't move. It seemed you wanted to scream."

"I did."

She considers me a moment. "What did you see, Liv?"

"Nobody."

"No*body*?"

"I meant...nothing." I scrub my eyes, my arms still shaking. "I didn't expect you back so soon."

"I brought a buck. A big one. He'll feed us for a week if we're careful." She leans across me to scratch Beast's ears. "And you, boy."

Beast pants happily and licks her hand.

I try to bring myself into the peace of this small moment, but my heart won't leave my throat. My hands won't stop shaking.

"Kit? You said you're not truly a witch."

"Of course not."

"But do you...believe? In that sort of thing."

"No." She rises, brushing the dirt of the forest off her cloak. "I don't believe in much anymore."

I wish I had such a luxury. To forget what I saw these last two nights. To never again feel the phantom lap of hellfire across my skin. But what I've experienced is too much to dismiss. That was no mere nightmare.

And that face looming above me...it has the look of retribution.

"You can...do this?" I ask.

Kit finishes tying the buck's ankles together. With a smile over her shoulder, she hoists him high. The carcass dangles from the rafters of our ruined barn, its eyes bulging, neck exposed. She grabs a knife from the floor and twists it in her grip.

"You might not have the stomach for this," she tells me.

She thinks so little of me. I stand firm, locking eyes with her so she'll know I have no intention of going. I slaughtered that poor hen, after all. I'm familiar with gore and—

Kit sinks the knife carefully into the buck's belly and pulls.

And it's not the sight that does me in.

It's the smell.

The enormous, clouding stench of dead meat and blood. The hen had smelled badly, but this...

Outside the barn, between heaves of thin, yellow vomit into the snow, I hear Kit laughing.

"All right out there?"

I grip a handful of snow and take a bite of it, letting the cold, clear taste of ice wash the bile from my mouth. Despite her teasing, I give myself a moment.

"I figured you were more accustomed to housework," Kit says when I return, clammy and breathing slowly through my mouth. I pinch my nose against the growing stink.

"I have to say," I tell her, seeing her covered in blood up to her elbows, "you do seem a witch like this."

"Useful, you mean? Hardworking?" She doesn't flinch as she piles the guts of the beast on the barn floor. "I was a servant in Lizzy's house. They didn't bother to make me a good woman."

She tosses what I think is a heart onto the ground. "So, they gave me work like this. It comes in handy."

The buck's body seems mostly empty of guts. "What's next?" I ask.

"I flay its skin and take the meat from the bones."

"Well. Um. Do you, er, need me for...?"

"No, Deliverance. Tend to the chores that won't make you vomit. You've had precious little food in the past few days as it is. Best not waste it on the snow."

Despite her condescension, I agree. I'm little use here. But there are no chores left to be done. No lye and fat for candles, no flax to spin. Not even socks to darn.

"I need to buy supplies," I say.

"Go ahead," she tells me, working a length of entrails free. "I'll be a while."

"I haven't any money," I say. "My uncle drank it all."

"Ah." She holds up a gory hand, signaling for me to wait, before wiping her palms on her dress. I gape at the act—filthy though her dress is, she's only making it worse. Much worse. Satisfied that her hands are clean—prematurely so, to my judgment—she reaches down into her boot and tugs out a little coin purse. She tosses it to me.

The coins rattle in my palms, their music dulled by the cloth bag. I blink. "Where did this come from?"

"Lizzy and I left prepared. We never did find a village where we felt safe, but...we were ready if we ever did."

"Did you earn this money?" I say. "Or is it stolen?"

She cocks her head. "Everything is stolen, Liv. The land we're on, the air we breathe, the stories we tell at night."

I blink. "What are you on about?"

She gives me that thin, half-bladed smile. "I served Lizzy's family nearly my whole life. I wasn't paid, barely fed, and made to sleep in the stable with the goats. I figure that's my payment, twelve years too late."

"I can't use stolen money," I say, and toss the purse back. "It'll burn my hands. Or what I buy with it will be cursed, or go to rot, or—"

"God, you Puritans think the funniest things."

I scowl. "What are you, then?"

"Hm?"

"You mock me for being a Puritan. Pray, what are you?"

She drops the smile and chucks another bright, bloody organ to the barn floor. It's a shade of purple richer than a king's clothes. "My family were Friends."

Friends—she means Quakers. Of course. So she *is* a heretic, then. Maybe not a witch, but hardly any better.

She laughs. "What's that face? Don't like my religion?"

"It's fine," I say, though I hardly mean it. "You said they *were* Friends? Did they convert?"

"My parents are dead," she says. "Arrested in Ipswich and hanged for heresy. The jailers didn't know what else to do with me, as I was so young, so they sold me to the highest paying family. Lizzy's."

"I'm...sorry." I don't approve of the Quaker religion—I can't. But I don't see why her parents needed to die for their strange beliefs. Quakers are false, but they're not exactly harmful.

"It's long past," she says. "My parents always told me everybody had an inner light, a goodness inside them. They died for that belief." She steps aside as a glut of blood and viscera slops from the deer carcass. "Sort of makes it hard to believe."

"I suppose it does."

"Still," she goes on. "I'd rather live hopefully than in dread, wouldn't you?"

"Dread is what life is about," I say. "We hold to the hope of Heaven, knowing life upon earth is bleak."

"Aren't you just a joy." She lobs the coin purse back to me. "Buy whatever you need. If your fingers rot off and your purchases spoil, you can tell the Lord it was all my idea."

"Fine," I say. "And...thanks, I suppose. Unless this kills me, of course."

Kit grins. She's so different from me, so free with her expressions and her words. Her grief was a raw, hopeless thing tearing out of her last night. Her easiness, a river babbling under her smile today. She has given me stories and heresies and jokes as though they all live within her, ready to be passed around like coin. A currency of knowing, of sharing things that I've so long learned to strangle out of myself.

I turn quickly from the barn, whistling for Beast to follow.

I buy wheat, corn, and tallow from Goodman Jacoby's shop. I'm tempted to empty Kit's coin purse and buy an already made blanket, too, but it seems prudent to save something. So, I buy only what I need most.

I pass Winnow's, and think of Uncle, chained in the jail beyond the edge of town. He'd been drunk, surely, the night of his arrest, and chattering only to himself.

But I think, then, of the specter I've seen. Her ringed neck and blue-hued mouth. *Deliver me,* she says. What sort of things would she whisper to my uncle?

"Shopping, are we?"

I startle, nearly dropping my sack of purchases. Constable Walsh stands before me, tipping slightly, his eyes hazed with drink. I've stood too long, lost in my mind, outside of Winnow's. I hadn't noticed him walk out.

"I'm preparing the house for my uncle's return," I say. "What with the turn in the weather, I thought it best to stock up. I find myself unexpectedly short of resources," I add, my boldness at once warming me and icing my lungs with dread.

"I see that." He nods to the sack in my arms. "I thought you hadn't any money."

I stare straight into his eyes. "I found it necessary to take a loan."

"A pity. Your uncle has left you destitute, and here you are, ready to repeat his mistakes."

"I must have food and drink, sir."

"Indeed. Well. There are ways for young women to make money in this world. Though not with her purity intact." The constable smiles. "I'm sure I'll be seeing you again soon, Deliverance."

I walk around him back down the road from the village. I should have thought of this—of course God is punishing me for using Kit's stolen money. He sent the constable here to catch me in sin, and now, he'll take everything I've illicitly bought. That, and whatever he can rip from what's left of my dignity.

It's no more than I deserve. And yet my blood heats, my face warms. My heart pounds. And I realize I'm angry. Angry at the constable, at Uncle, at this village. Maybe even at God.

I quickly mutter a prayer of repentance, but it feels false on my tongue. I hurry my steps toward the path back home, and I'm nearly there when a sharp voice stops me.

"Well, look at you, then."

I turn, wilting with relief. "Goody Baxter. Good day."

The old beggar woman examines me with a sharp hunger in her squinting eyes. She's gone blind in one eye, and its milky texture reminds me, unwantedly, of the witch.

Lizzy. Call her Lizzy.

"You've made off, haven't you?" Goody Baxter cackles. "Turning tricks for coin, are we?"

"Goody Baxter!" I blush furiously. "That's quite inappropriate."

"Care to share?" The old crone hobbles toward me. She's stooped, wrinkled. A harsh, curdled smell wafts from her unwashed clothes, her filthy skin. I take a step back, but she only shuffles nearer.

"I don't have your looks," Goody Baxter says. "Can't get coin for what's beneath *my* petticoats."

I toss the coin purse to her. It's nearly depleted anyway. "There. Now good day, Goody Baxter."

The old woman grins and greedily shakes the few clattering shillings into her palm. "Thank you, thank you, girl. God bless, of course."

"Indeed." I huff off, furious at myself for being so easily riled. Perhaps everyone in the village knows of my sin, or suspects. Wickedness must live in my eyes and carry on my voice. I suppose, if they truly knew, I'd have spent my time in the stocks already. I'd have a letter of my own branded upon my forehead.

Thomas told no one. He didn't need to. His escape was quick and met with praise. A minister's son, off to Harvard. How perfect, how aligned with God's will. Never mind a secret night spent on the riverbank with a drunkard's niece. The pain, the guilt, it was always mine alone to carry. He could become someone new. I could either face the stocks or rot with my secret inside me.

Beast meets me halfway up the path, wagging his tail. He gets onto his hind legs to sniff at the food I've bought.

"Down, boy," I laugh. "I should think you'd be more interested in that buck our friend is preparing."

Beast does a little twirl and bounds toward home. I follow quickly. A snarl comes from my stomach. Hunger. Maybe it's the idea of fresh meat, or days only nibbling at eggs, but my appetite roars back into my body.

I drop the food in the kitchen, then check behind the house for Kit. I find her kneeling by the wash basin, dressed only in a shift. She has the sleeves rolled up, and she's carefully scrubbing gore from her arms and hands.

"Well, well," she says without looking up. "I see you weren't struck down by lightning."

I sigh.

"Nor did you burst into flames." She looks up, grinning. "Are you ready to convert to Quakerism?"

"Surely you jest." But I'm smiling back. "I even did a good deed. I hope you don't mind, but I gave the change to the old beggar woman from the village."

"How *friendly* of you."

"You're intolerable." I lean against the side of the house and watch her. Kit's filthy, beyond the blood still staining her skin. Her shift is nearly gray with dirt, hanging loose at the chest.

"I can loan you some clothes," I say.

"Sadd colors only? Oh, what the hell." She rises. "I've been wearing the same dress for seven months. I'll take what you've got."

"Seven months?" I repeat. "How did you survive so long in the wilderness?"

"I told you," she says. "I'm very good at surviving."

I eye the brand above her brow. "I—forgive me, but—I thought they hanged witches in Massachusetts?"

She presses her lips together. "They do. If one persists in denying it. We confessed."

"You *confessed?*" I blink. "Yet you tell me you're no witch."

"I *am* no witch," she says. "But try telling a Massachusetts judge as much. I've seen what happens to those who claim their own innocence. We settled for guilt that wasn't ours, and we were branded as heretics and banished."

I take a deep breath. "And...what made them think you were a witch to begin with?"

She shakes her head. "The men of that town have a very small idea of innocence and goodness. Stray even a bit from it, and you might as well be a witch, especially when a neighbor's cow stops producing milk, the minister's wife can't conceive, and a half-blind fisherman swears he's seen a figure in the woods with horns and a lovely walking stick."

I nod. "They thought there was witchcraft about—"

"And we made very convenient witches."

"You had to lie to live," I say, hating how this makes me feel. To bear false witness is a sin, a breach of the Ten Commandments. And yet what choice did she have?

She'd seen her parents hanged. She knew what awaited her.

I clear my throat. "Do you...like corn?"

Kit grins. "Yes, Deliverance. I like corn."

"Good. Then...I'll start dinner."

She nods toward the barn. "I'll bring the main course."

"Oh! Save the fat. I need to make more soap. The constable took all mine."

"What a bastard," she says mildly. My mouth drops open.

But rather than scold her, I find myself laughing.

14. Heaven

I haven't had venison in over a year, since Abel left to trap fur. I had forgotten the rich taste, the tough grain of the meat. Kit smirks over her plate.

"What?" I say, mouth full. I find it's easy to abandon decorum in Kit's presence. She allows it, nay, *encourages* it.

"Your face," she says. "You look like you've reached Heaven at last."

I swallow, smile. "This may well be the closest I get."

"You don't really think that." Kit grins. "You're the haughtiest girl I've ever met. Heaven will be relieved to have you. They might clear out space to make room."

"I'm beginning to think you *are* a heretic."

"Quite," she says.

I take another bite of venison, letting the juices leak down my throat. "In answer to your heresy, however, I can only tell you that none is guaranteed salvation."

"Even if you ask for it?"

"Aye. God has chosen the elect. It's not for us to assume we're among them." In fact, such haughty assurance would almost certainly mean one was *not* elect. To think of such arrogance.

"Mum told me God was in everyone," Kit says quietly.

I nod. "The inner light, you said."

"Aye. But then...well, I never felt much light in me as the years went on. Can I tell you something without you banishing me back to the woods?"

I blink. "I—yes. Go ahead."

"There are days...I wondered if God were real at all. I thought of the people across the world, across time, who thought different things. Who never had any idea of God—mine or yours. And..." She shrugs. "Well. What if they're right? What if no one's right? What if we all are?"

"You talk in riddles."

"This is the plainest I've ever spoken. It's only a curiosity, but...I think there are too many beliefs, sometimes, for any one of them to be right or wrong all the way." She meets my stare and smiles faintly. "You've gone pale. Have I horrified you?"

I look back to my plate, find it empty. I set it on the floor so Beast might lick the grease from it, which he does gladly. "I wonder, too. But Uncle said doubt was Satan's whisper."

"Maybe." Kit rests her elbow on the table, cups her cheek in her palm. Her dark curls tumble into her eyes. Blue eyes. I hadn't noticed before, but they're the color of a twilit sky before the passage of a storm. "Or maybe that whisper is you."

"Right. Well. I thank you again for the venison."

She snorts. "Finished discussing religion already?"

"It's not an appropriate conversation."

"They speak so in coffeehouses in London all the time."

"Well, I'm not some...some damned *Anglican*."

"Yes, that'd be just *too* wicked."

"I—I'm much too tired for such talk."

She drops the last bite of venison into her mouth before handing her plate over to Beast, too. "Then sleep, Deliverance. I can clean up."

"I, no, I feel I should—"

"Liv. You look as though you'll collapse any moment. Go to sleep."

I nod. "Aye. Thank you." I start to walk away, but stop. Plates and cutlery rattle behind me as Kit gathers them together for washing. She hums something, a song I don't know.

I clear my throat and turn around. "You're rather kind and decent. For a Quaker."

She chuckles. "And you're not so unbearable, for a Puritan."

My mouth twitches, and...I'm smiling? Nearly, anyway. "Goodnight, Kit."

Sleep comes the moment my eyes shut, but it seems to vanish just as quickly.

I wake with a start. Something moves at my feet, something clawing and—

I sit up, laugh. It's only Beast, scrabbling at nothing in his sleep as he does when he dreams. I check out the window. Snow drops from the sky. Already our property is coated in a white sheen. There will only be more in the morning. There's almost beauty in it. Peace.

The closest I'll get to Heaven.

Snowfall. Beast. Mem. A good meal and a warm fire. These things are more Heaven than the stories I've been told.

But that's horrible. To think God's promises of pearly gates and streets of gold insufficient. To recoil at the thought of an eternity of worship. What sort of sinner am I? Surely this is proof enough I'm damned. Surely—

My thoughts scatter as I turn back to the window. There, in the fresh fallen snow, are tracks. Two feet moving from the forest. The prints go over the gate, as though whatever left them merely hopped over the fence. They vanish from my view.

Whatever left those tracks is on the property. And it moved fast, from the forest to the house in the mere seconds I'd looked away from the window.

I slip from bed and throw my cloak around my shift. Beast scrambles up at my movements and hops from bed, close at my heels as I descend the creaking staircase.

At the front door, I shove my feet into my boots and slowly open the door.

The footprints are there, sunk into the snow, right before the door, as though whatever came from the forest had waited here like a guest hoping for entrance.

My heart claws against my chest. The prints are not human. They're cloven. Bipedal. Like the prints leading to Lizzy's grave.

I slam the door and throw the latch, breathing hard. The prints showed the creature moving away, but that means nothing. It may still be on the property. It may seek another way in. I rush to the back door and check that it's latched. Unsatisfied, I shove a chair against it, then go to brace the table against the front door.

Kit emerges from Uncle's room, drowsy and rubbing one eye. "What's that infernal sound?" she groans.

"There's—there's a—" I shake my head. "The Devil is here."

"Oh, God." She throws her head back. "Liv. The Devil's not coming for us."

"I saw his prints! What sort of creature walks on two feet and has cloven hooves?"

"A very clever goat?"

"This is serious!"

"What makes you think the Devil's got cloven hooves? Where does it say as much in the Bible?"

"I—that's not the point!" I toss my hands. "Some monster from the forest is here, and it's singled me out. It's—"

I stop myself from saying it, but it's there between us anyway. *It's your fault.* I let this heretic into my home, and now the Lord is punishing me. I buried a witch, housed a Quaker, defied my Uncle, harbored ill thoughts to the constable.

"I'm damned," I say. I already knew it. But it hurts. The knowledge of the fire that waits for me—the pain—the suffering—all because I just can't be good, can't stop sinning, can't stop making the wrong choices.

"Liv. Liv, here." Kit's arm is suddenly around my shoulders, and I realize my breaths have become sharp, shallow. And yet her presence seems to free me. She holds me against her, and my lungs give up air more freely. She rubs her hand against my arm, and my throat opens back up.

"You're not damned," she says softly. "I don't think somebody who worries so much over her eternal soul could ever be damned."

"It doesn't work that way," I say, but the fight has gone out of me. I'm slumped against a heretic and I'm happy there, happy in a way that twists my heart and warms my gut. Beast licks at my dangling hand and whines.

"I'm sorry, boy," I say. I scratch his ears and his tail thumps.

"Can you sleep?" Kit says after a moment.

"Nay. Not with that...thing out there."

"I'll wait up with you, then."

"Kit—no, you should sleep."

"I'd rather keep watch. I still say one of your goats has learned a neat trick, and I intend to catch it in the act."

I stoke a fire, and Kit fetches the blankets from Uncle's bed. We settle in around the hearth, all three of us, a damned girl, a heretic, and a dog. Kit tugs me against her side.

"Sleep if you can," she says.

I look up, a protest in my throat, but her smile stops me speaking.

"I'll keep watch," she says. "Promise."

I drop my head against her shoulder.

The closest I'll ever get to Heaven.

Somehow, I slept.

I blink awake to find myself curled under a blanket. Kit lays only a few inches away, her chin tucked against her chest. We're turned toward each other, not touching, yet sharing the same warmth, like we're enclosed together.

Her lips are softer this morning, healing in the warmth of the house. They're still so bright, and I suppose they're always like that, the deepest shade of sunset. Her eyelashes rest against her cheeks, long as shadows.

Yet she looks anything but peaceful. A divot lances between her brows, which are bent toward each other in tension.

She's prepared for something terrible, even lost in a forest of dreams. The waking world must whisper at her respite.

My own nightmares have peeled themselves from sleep and now walk the house. I wonder, do Kit's dreams have legs, too? Does she snatch glimpses of them in shadow and rain?

Beast noses my back, and I turn. He does a little spin and then whines for the door. My stomach drops.

The footprints. Is it safe to go outside? I rise carefully, trying not to disturb Kit, but it seems life outdoors has made her a sensitive sleeper. Her eyes fly open the moment I shift away from her.

"Is the Devil afoot?" she mumbles.

"I don't think so. Sorry," I tell her. "Beast needs to go outside."

"I should check on Beaky," she says around a yawn. I'd nearly forgotten her crow.

"That bird stays with you always?"

"He's my pet," she says. "I told him to wait in your barn. I'm sure he spent the night gallivanting regardless."

We throw on cloaks and stand together at the door, neither moving to open it.

"Do you...think it's safe?" I ask.

"Yes," she says, still not moving.

"Well, then."

"Right."

Kit throws the door wide.

The snow that has since fallen has blotted out the prints from last night, but I feel them there still, a presence, a specter. Beast rushes out, bounding joyously in the snow, only pausing to pee upon the gate.

We walk the property, checking the paddock, then the barn. Sure enough, Kit's crow sits obediently in the rafters. It holds what I sickeningly recognize as a length of the deer's innards in its beak, chewing clumsily. Upon seeing Kit, it drops the guts and flutters down to land on her shoulder.

"Good morrow," it croaks. I shudder.

"*How* does it do that?"

"He's intelligent," she says. "Most birds are."

I think of the chickens in their coop, the hens I've slaughtered for dinner. I pull a face. "I certainly hope not. But I meant, how does it speak?"

"The same way it caws?" She shrugs. Beaky nips at her earlobe, annoyed by the movement. "I don't know. But every crow I've met has been able to pick up a few words."

"So he's not...you don't suppose he's..."

"The Devil?" she says, drawing the word long and dry.

We leave the barn. I let the goats into their paddock while Kit collects eggs from the hens. Beast plays in the snow, pawing at buried smells, while Beaky flutters off to the roof of the house, eyeing the path into town.

"That way," he squawks.

I still, turning my head slowly toward the crow. "*What* is that way?"

"That way," he repeats.

Kit emerges from the coop holding a handful of eggs, smiling. "Seems Beaky has found our mystery prints."

"That's not possible," I say, but then, Beast stiffens, apparently catching scent of something in the snow. He wags his tail once and darts toward the road. Beaky lifts from his perch and follows.

Kit grins. "I think they want us to follow." She presses the eggs into my hands and takes off after the animals with a whirl of her cloak.

"I—oh, hell." I carefully tuck the eggs into the pockets of my cloak and hurry after them.

Beaky flies ahead. Beast, a few paces behind, covers the ground, dragging his nose through the snow, close on the trail of...something. I hope it's not the hoofed phantom. I don't know what will become of us if we find the monster. It's daylight, but the grim sky is slate and heavy with snow. I don't think this weak light will banish the night's monsters.

Kit tromps ahead, fearless, her boots breaking a path through the snow. I step in her wake, my shoes a near perfect match for hers.

Beaky swoops toward the forest and begins to circle, cawing—wordlessly, thank the Lord. I can't abide that unnerving trick of his.

Beast bounds toward the woods, Kit close behind. I struggle through the snowfall after them.

"Slow down," I say.

Kit turns, laughing. "Keep up, Deliverance."

I push my muscles harder and bound after her. She shrieks and tries to plow forward, but a huge snowdrift rising up along the side of the road trips her. She tumbles forward into the snow, and me after her.

We're tangled, laughing, cold—and yet, warm. Close. I blink, looking down at her face. And she stares back, a red tinge beneath her freckles. Before I can identify the look in her eyes, she's tugging herself out from under me, brushing snow from her cloak.

"Sorry," she says. "I didn't, um. I didn't mean to trip you."

"You didn't," I remind her. She tripped, and I—I sort of just followed. Caught up in the laughter. Happy, for once. The footprints had left my mind. In the whirl of her cloak and the sharp note of her laughter, I'd forgotten to be afraid.

I rise and scrape snow from my cloak, only to pass over something gunky, cold. I wince. The eggs in my pockets. I smashed them, and now they're coating the fabric, little bits of shell dripping in rivulets.

I look up at Kit. She's holding her hand over her mouth, shaking. But not from the cold.

"Are you laughing at me?"

She snorts. "I'm sorry, it's just...you make the funniest faces when you're angry."

"I do *not*."

Our argument is cut short by Beast's howl. Kit whips around. I break into a run. Beaky swoops down and lands on Kit's shoulder.

"Found it," he caws. "Found it."

I see Beast ahead, sat on his haunches, howling toward the blustery sky. The woods are right before him, and, halfway out, a bundle of dirty, wrinkled fabric.

Oh, no.

I skid in the snow, stopping at Beast's side, and find myself staring into the cold, waxy face of Goody Baxter. Her eyes still have their color, though they're blank, seeing naught. Her mouth is hinged wide, as though in a scream. Little crusts of dried blood line her nostrils and the corners of her mouth.

Kit stumbles to her knees beside me, eyes tight, mouth set. "What happened to her?"

"I don't know." I'm tempted to believe she wandered out here in the cold. She holds a nearly empty bottle of whiskey, and I shut my eyes. The coin I gave her—did she use it to buy this drink? Did she get drunk and fall asleep out here because of me? She might only have frozen because of my thoughtless charity.

But— I sniff, then gag. There's the distinct stench of iron on the air, masking the sharp sugar scent of the drink. I reach forward carefully and tug the scarf away from her neck. It comes away gummy with congealed blood. Her throat is torn and gaping wide like a second mouth.

I turn away from Goody Baxter and vomit into the snow. Kit sighs.

"We've got to work on your stomach, Liv." She tugs the scarf farther away. "Animal attack, perhaps?"

I nod, eating a mouthful of snow to calm my stomach and cool the acid taste in my mouth. Beast whimpers and nuzzles against my side.

"I know, boy, I know."

Beaky lands in the snow beside Kit. "Murder-murder," he says.

I frown. "Are you sure that thing's not bewitched?"

"I'm telling you," Kit says, "they all talk. Crows are very clever, and if you spend time with them, they learn to speak."

"Fine. But why's it saying *murder*?"

"Maybe he thinks she was killed," Kit says. "Ever think of that?"

"It's a bloody crow! What does it know?"

"God save the king," Beaky squawks.

"That's it." I rise, suppressing a shudder. "I'm going to get the constable. We've got to report this."

Kit raises her eyebrows, and I read the question there. She's afraid I'll report her, too.

"Go back to the house," I say, smiling. "Take your familiar with you. I won't breathe a word of your presence."

She holds her hand out, and Beaky hops onto her wrist. "Bloody royalist," she tells him. "You're going to get me in trouble with the Puritan."

"God save the king," Beaky repeats.

"And who's the king?" she coos at him.

"If it answers that..." I say, but Beaky only snaps his beak and blinks.

"Oh, well," Kit says. "He'll get there. *William the Third.* Can you say William the Third? How about Governor Andros?"

"Get out of here," I say, shooing her and her demonic pet.

I wait until Kit is safely back on the path to the house, then I take one last look at Goody Baxter. I shut my eyes and murmur a quick prayer for her soul. She was a beggar, a crone, but she deserved a better death than this.

I finish my prayer, and as I open my eyes, they snag on something I missed before. Goody Baxter's hand, twisted in the snow, blue-white from the cold. Yet a harsh line of red interrupts the mottled, dead flesh.

I lean down, and...no.

A crude skull, square teeth and circle eyes. The same symbol I found on Lizzy.

I backpedal away from the old crone. Was she a witch this whole time? It's easy enough to image her stooped over a spell book, clambering onto a broom to make her midnight congress with the Devil.

But the thought drains away. Easy to imagine, hard to believe. She was an old woman, bent of bone and weak of flesh. She could hardly spend a night cavorting through the forest, flying the skies, slipping through doorways to make her mischief. She spent her days posted along the roadways asking for coin. She was thin and wearing away like a piece of discarded fabric.

She had no magic to her.

But then, what of the scars? If she didn't receive it from the Devil, and Lizzy didn't, either, it means someone marked both women after they died.

I turn toward the village and run, Beast by my side.

16. She Comes at Night

I hurry into the village, my tired legs burning from the exertion of plowing through the snow. Still more falls, cooling me through my cloak. My skirt is soaked through to my knees, and my stockings squelch in my damp boots. I take a moment to breathe and compose myself before turning toward the meeting house.

Sure enough, the constable is there, and Reverend Wilson with him. They speak in hushed tones at the far end of the meeting house beside the pulpit.

"Come, Waitstill," the constable says. "You can't really think an older codger like him is the only one. The Devil's got his pick of all these pretty ladies, and he chooses an old drunk?"

"Speak no more of this," Reverend Wilson says. "I won't have accusations flying about the village. They may do thusly in Massachusetts, but I won't have it here."

"You'll let witches run free for the sake of *peace*?"

Reverend Wilson rounds on the constable. "Bring me a shred of proof, and you'll have your trial. Until then, speak no more of this."

I clear my throat at last, aware I've been eavesdropping. Both men turn toward me. Reverend Wilson smiles. Constable Walsh does, too, only his mouth is bent at a cruel angle.

"Why, Deliverance. We were just speaking of you."

I blanch. "You were?"

"Your uncle," Reverend Wilson cuts in, eyeing the constable. "But never you worry. What brings you here, girl? Do you wish to see your sister?"

"I would very much like to," I say in a rush, "but I'm afraid there's a terrible problem."

"Well," the constable says. "Out with it, girl."

"Goody Baxter, the old beggar," I say. "She's—she's out by the forest. Dead. Her—her throat is—an animal must have—"

"Oh, dear child." Reverend Wilson steps forward, bowing his head somberly. "You've done well to tell us. Please, come with me. We'll get some cider in you, and you'll rest by the fire. Constable? I trust you'll see to Goody Baxter?"

"Aye, Reverend, aye." Walsh winks at me, then stomps toward the door. My body only unclenches when the door has slammed behind him.

"I apologize for the constable," the reverend says. "He's been following a witchcraft case in Boston rather jealously. The Goodwin children—have you heard? No, no you wouldn't. Never mind about it. Cotton Mather is making much of it, of course, and now I'm afraid our good constable is seeing the supernatural everywhere."

"Why would he want such a thing?" The words tumble out before I can school them. I wince, prepared for an admonishment, but Reverend Wilson only sighs.

"There's greatness to be had in catching out a witch. To find a whole coven? A conspiracy which takes the entire village with it? He'd certainly make a name for himself in Boston."

"Does he—does he truly think my uncle a witch?"

Reverend Wilson doesn't answer right away. My stomach twists. "Your uncle will receive a fair trial," he says at last. "I'll see to that." He smiles and claps a hand on my shoulder. "Now come. I promised you cider and a warm fire. Remembrance will be delighted to see you."

"How is she?" I ask as the reverend leads me from the meeting house.

"Quite well. Very able. I thank you for sending her to us. Her skills at soap-making are masterful; I've never seen such handiwork."

I smile. "She's excellent, yes. Far better than I ever was, indeed."

"Come now. My Thomas seemed to think you quite apt at homemaking." He smiles down at me. "I do hope you'll consider him, when the time comes."

Heat creeps along my cheeks. A wild corner of my mind wants to laugh and tell the reverend I've done more than consider his darling son. Thank God—mine, Kit's, or anybody's—my sobriety returns, and I manage a demure, "Of course."

A jolly laugh erupts from his belly. "You were always meant for him. I knew it the moment your uncle brought you here. Thomas was smitten the day he met you."

"I haven't heard from him," I say. "I wasn't sure, well...that his affections remained."

"Everything in God's time, dear girl." His smile is sure. I try to return the look, but there's a weight to my skin. My eyes drop to the snow and we walk on.

We arrive at the parsonage, the beautiful home so different from anything I could have given Mem. An ache opens in my stomach, the knowledge that I'll never be able to give her a proper life tearing at me as though the notion has claws. In this village—in this country, this world, maybe—there is no place for a woman alone. I cannot provide for Mem.

I need Thomas. Always before I considered him in terms of wanting. Wanting his kisses, his hands on my bare waist. Wanting him so badly I compromised my soul just for the chance to know his love. But standing outside his beautiful home, the place holding my sister back from the dangers of the world, practicality sets it. It's as obvious as pain. I cannot have a decent life without him. I'll become like Goody Baxter. I, too, might die outside of the woods, a bottle in my hand, a scream in my throat. I'll be buried as a pauper and remembered only for the coin I begged off better people.

My life seems suddenly like a knife blade, point down on a table, able to fall either way so easily. He might still want me. And if he doesn't?

I follow Reverend Wilson into the parsonage, and soon I'm engulfed in the happy chatter and giggles of his many children. The Wilsons have nine in all, a miraculous number. Thomas, the eldest, is of course away, which leaves the eight girls, ranging in age from seventeen to one. Children are spread across the room, sitting with chores—knitting, darning, sewing—all passing the time with idle talk.

"Liv?" Tace, the oldest girl at seventeen, holds baby Hope. She weaves between her sisters scattered on the floor. "What brings you here?"

"I—" I look up at Reverend Wilson, but he's already passing us, giving Tace a mere pat on the shoulder as he hurries from the busy room. "I hoped I might see Mem?"

"Oh." Tace smiles, relieved. "I thought you wanted to see Thomas."

"I, no. He's not back...?"

"No. No, that's why... Well, here." She deposits Hope into my arms. "I'll go find her. Probably in the garden with Pru again."

The girls in the room are all focused on me now, staring, blinking. Like me and Mem, they've all been given grace names, but for as long as I've known the family, I still mix them up sometimes. I know Prudence is Mem's young friend from meeting. But Humility and Obedience are too close in age and looks for me to tell apart sometimes. Silence is the four-year-old currently plucking at an abandoned embroidery wheel. Temperance is fifteen and serious, eyeing me over her loom. And the little toddler currently tugging Tace's knitting apart is Repentance.

"Hello," I say after a long moment.

"Hi," one of the girls, possibly Humility, says. "Have you come to take her back?"

"No..." I frown. "Why?"

"She speaks to shadows," Obedience says. "All night, chattering to nothing. It's dreadful."

"Di!" Tace steps back into the room, a look of murder on her face. "Hold thy tongue. I'm sorry, Liv. They're only jealous a new girl has got Mother's attention."

"Is that true?" I ask quietly. "Does Mem...speak to shadows?"

"Well..." Tace shrugs. "Children babble in their sleep. It's not so strange. Like I said, Di's only jealous. Repentance! No! Naughty girl! Sorry. Mem's in the garden, you can go on back." She takes Hope from my arms and storms toward the toddler. "*Repentance!*"

I leave the girls to squabble over the ruined knitting and pass through the house to the garden out back. Prudence is there, brushing dirty snow away from the wilted stalks of carrots. She glances up, then nods her head to the side. I follow the gesture to find Mem standing by the Wilson's well, her lips moving, a soft whisper like the sound of snow carrying across the garden.

"Mem?" I hurry toward her, a sinking in my gut as I approach. She doesn't look up, only stares down at the surface of the thinly frozen water. Her reflection glances back, warped. Slowly, Mem reaches out a finger, taps the ice. It breaks under the barest pressure, shattering her reflection.

Mem sighs. "You'll come back, won't you?"

"I'm right here, Mem," I say.

"Not...you..." She shakes her head, looks up. "Liv? Liv!" She winds her arms around my waist, buries her face into my stomach. "Please say you're taking me home! These girls are horrible!"

"Mem," I hiss. "Shush. You've always been dear friends with Prudence."

She pulls away, shrugging. "Yes. But Obedience is horrible, and Humility tells me I'm odd, and that little Repentance is always shrieking and ruining the socks I make." She turns wide, shining eyes on me. "I heard about Uncle. I know he's gone. Why can't I come home?"

"Because, Mem, I—I have nothing. What food there is will be gone soon, and..." I sigh. "If Uncle is convicted—they'll take the house."

"No, it'll go to Abel," she says slowly.

"Nay, Mem. The constable will want it for payment." I cannot hide the bitterness in my voice. "Besides, we have no way of knowing when Abel will come back." If Abel will come back.

"So all is lost?" She says it like a challenge, hands on hips, staring dead into my eyes.

"No," I say. "For now, though, all is very, very dire. Here, you're fed, you're warm." I kneel, getting to her eye level. "Tell me, is everything all right? Tace said you were—having nightmares."

"They say I talk in my sleep," Mem says, smiling. "But I'm not sleeping." She nods to the well. "She's talking to me. Telling me things."

My blood falls like sleet through my veins. "You've seen that woman again?"

Mem nods. "She followed me. She comes at night, usually. I thought she was me, grown. But she's not. Is she?" My sister, my small, innocent, beautiful sister, frowns, and for a moment she looks so old, weary. "Liv, what did Uncle do?"

"What..." I try to laugh, but it comes out dry, broken. "What do you mean?"

"What did he do to Mum and Dad?"

I rise too quickly, draining blood from my head and ruining my balance. "What a silly question," I say. "Don't—you don't say such things to the Wilsons, do you?"

"Nay. They don't believe me about the Blue Lady."

"Blue Lady...?"

"Because her neck, it's blue. She says someone took her air." Mem lowers her voice. "She says Uncle took her air." She tilts her head, and a faint smile creeps along her cheek. "I look just like her, don't I? 'Remember me.' That's what she says when she goes."

Deliver me.

I back away. "I have to go. You behave for Goody Wilson, all right? And play nice with the other girls."

"Liv?"

I pause in my retreat. "Yes?"

"That's why he brought us here, isn't it? Because he took Mum's air?" She scowls. "I hope they hang him. I really do."

"Cease this talk," I whisper. "You cannot say such things. It's—"

"Wicked, yes." She rolls her eyes and mutters, "As wicked as standing by while he did it, no doubt."

My feet give out beneath me. Snow scatters around me. The Wilsons might see me, they'll wonder, and yet...

How am I meant to care about such a thing? Mem knows.

"I didn't...there was nothing I could do," I say, but my voice sounds like snowfall, quiet and cold.

Mem steps forward and places a finger under my chin. She tips my face to hers. Her blue eyes are older somehow, and familiar.

"Then deliver me."

I scramble up and flee.

What is this drivel?"

The moment I step through the door, Kit is up, the neglected captivity narrative in hand.

"The book?" I say. "It's Mary Rowlandson's memoir. It's quite harrowing. I'm told."

"Oh, spare me. She's so maudlin." She tosses the book onto the table.

"Well, she *was* kidnapped."

Kit readies the smile I've come to know means she's prepared to say something that will scandalize me. But at the same moment, she must catch sight of my own expression. And how haggard must I look? She steps closer, that now familiar divot of worry between her brow.

"What happened? Did the constable—?"

"Oh. Goody Baxter." I'd nearly forgotten. My encounter with Mem drew all else from my mind. "He went to investigate."

"You were gone awhile," she says, and I hear the fear in her voice. She wonders still if I would turn her in.

"Aye, the reverend was there, too. He took me to see my sister. I—I didn't tell you, did I? I've a sister, eleven years old. I bound her out to the reverend's family."

Kit frowns. "Why did you do that?"

"I wanted her away from my uncle," I say, defensive. "It was before I knew he'd been arrested. Anyway, she's better off there, still. Who knows what will become of me?"

"I'm sorry," Kit says. "I wasn't trying to imply—just, well. I've been a servant, you know. But it sounds like you've found her a good family."

"Was Lizzy's family terrible?"

"Oh, aye." She laughs, but there's no truth to the miserable sound. It's more a breath, a dying one. "Quite horrible."

I nod, and for a moment, we're both quiet—I, remembering Uncle's fists and lashes. Kit no doubt remembering something similar, or worse. I know better than to ask.

"Were you always close to Lizzy?"

Kit's color deepens. "Yes. She was always good to me. We...had things in common. You said you saw your sister? How was she?"

I note the quick change in topic, but choose to follow it. Truely, I want to talk about it with someone. "Well, seems my dead mother's haunting her."

She blinks once, slowly. "Pardon?"

I blow out a breath and drop into the chair across from Kit. "I'm going to tell you a secret. But it's got to stay that way. This is something no one can know."

"All right." Kit nods for me to go on.

"My family came to Boston when we left England. It was only me and my parents then. We got a small house. Everything...everything was lovely, then. Mum was soon with child. But then my uncle came."

Beast comes to my side and sets his head in my lap, sensing how much pain has filled my body, knowing I need him.

"He wanted my father to loan him money. My uncle came to the colonies ahead of my father, but he wasn't prepared. He had very little to his name, and no skills. His wife died of illness shortly after they arrived, leaving him with my cousin Abel.

"But my father refused him the money. He said he'd let my uncle stay with us, get settled in Boston and find work, but he wouldn't give him coin. My uncle agreed. But it was a ruse."

I take a deep breath. "The official story of my parents' deaths is that my mother died in childbirth, and my father, distraught, shot himself between the eyes."

Kit reaches across the table, takes my hand. "Liv—"

"But that's not what happened," I plow on, heedless now. "I was in the birthing room. And I heard it. The gunfire from the next room. My mother and I listened as my uncle shot my father." I use my free hand to flick tears away from my eyelashes. "Mum was crying in her terror, even as the birthing pains must have been at their worst. Because suddenly, there were new cries. Mem. She was born seconds after my father was dead.

"My mother cried to hold her. I scrambled up and...and found my sister there beneath the sheets, bloody and screaming. There was no midwife, I was twelve, old enough to help, and Mem had come so suddenly. But I—the cord, you know. There was the cord, and... So I thought, I'll fetch something for this. The gunshot seemed a dream. My sister was screaming for her mother.

"But right then, Uncle came into the birthing room. He told me my mother was struggling and needed prayers. And I think I said 'No, the baby is born'. But if I spoke, he ignored me. He got close to her and—I didn't realize then, only after I saw her, and the marks on her neck. He strangled her."

I draw in a breath rattling with tears. "And I stood by. I stood by while Mem screamed and my mother died. He drew a filthy knife from his coat then. I—I think, sometimes, he meant to kill Mem, too. He paused above her, and his eyes...they were a demon's, I tell you. He was a monster, then, smelling of musket shot.

"At last, he sliced the cord binding Mem to my mother. He handed her to me, naked and slimy and screaming. He told me my mother had died of a difficult birth. But I was *there*. I know what happened. I saw her mangled neck and—" I stop as a sob tries to rise in my throat. "He was telling me what he wanted me to tell others. And I was so scared. I went along with it. I've lied for all these years, because how do I choose between two sins? How do I decide if I'll bear false witness or be disobedient? Uncle was the only family I had left."

"There's nothing else you could have done." Kit squeezes my hand. "You were only a child."

I ignore her comfort. It's undeserved. "He took my father's money. Sold my family's property, our possessions. He brought me and Mem and Abel here, where he could live out his days away from suspicion and disdain." I press my lips together. This next part is where I begin to sound mad. "But the thing is, she followed me. My mother. Her spirit, or her memory— something has terrorized me ever since we left. I'll go days without seeing her, weeks, sometimes months. But she always comes back. Her ghost, hovering above me. And she always says the same thing. *Deliver me*."

"Liv." Kit brings her other hand to mine. "You witnessed something horrible. Of course the image has stayed with you. But I think it's only nightmares."

"I thought so, too," I say. "Or, I wanted to. But…now Mem sees her. And that's not possible, not if it's only a memory. Mem was alive a minute when my uncle killed my mother. She can't know anything about her, and yet the way she describes her—her looks, her hair, even the rings around her neck from his hands." I take a breath. "I'm afraid it's a reckoning, or a punishment. That my mother has come to avenge herself, because I should have told someone."

"You did the only thing you could to save yourself and your sister. Your uncle is a madman. He'd have killed you, too, if he thought he needed to."

I look down, away from her blue gaze. "I feel so guilty."

"Of course you do. That doesn't mean you *are* guilty."

My laugh sounds closer to a sob. "But I am. Everyone is, but me more so. I've done...so many things wrong. I'm wrong. And no matter what I do—"

Two things happen at once. Kit's hand moves to cup my cheek, her thumb brushing against my lip.

And the front door slams open.

Beast rises, barking furiously. I scramble back, eager both to dive beneath the kitchen table and fling the chair at the intruder. Kit whirls toward the counter and grabs the long knife she used to flay cuts of venison yesterday.

"Woah!" The voice is familiar, but I cannot make out who it is. The room has gone dark since the start of our conversation, the dimming daylight creeping away from the windows. I scramble toward the hearth and strike the flint to bring a fire out.

In the orange light, a familiar figure melts from the shadows. My heart lifts, even as my stomach plummets.

"Abel!" I rush to my cousin and toss my arms around his neck. He lifts me once, twirling me a few times before setting me back on my feet.

"I'm sorry to have surprised you so," he says. He looks at Kit, who still holds the knife like she's ready to lunge. "Um."

"Kit," I hiss, and she sets the knife on the table, however slowly.

"Can't be too careful," she says.

"Who's your friend, Livy?"

"Katherine," I say. "Kit. I—oh, God. There's so much to tell you."

18. Poems

I tell Abel what is mine to tell—that Uncle has been arrested, and Mem bound out to the Wilsons, that the constable collected "repayment" in the form of our supplies and goat—but nothing of Kit, save she is a friend who has been helping me since Uncle's arrest.

Abel shakes his head, furious in a cold way he shares with Uncle. "My father is a godly man. How could they even think him guilty of witchcraft?"

"Constable Walsh claims he held discourse with spirits," I say. "Though I think it more likely he was only muttering to himself."

Abel sets his jaw. "I'll speak to the constable in the morning. I'll see my father released."

I wish you wouldn't, I nearly say, but clamp my lips together with my teeth.

"And you?" Abel turns to Kit. "I'm sorry, but I don't remember you about the village."

"I'm...new."

Abel is waiting for more, but Kit doesn't offer it. I take the opportunity to distract him.

"You must be hungry. There's venison!"

"I'll cook," Kit says quickly.

"Right." Abel cuts his eyes to me. "Liv, a word?" He nods to the back door, and I follow him, throwing Kit a brief smile. She nods, but I can see the tension in her body. Abel was not part of the plan. She's scared.

I'm a little scared for her.

Abel stops beside the goat's paddock and turns. "Who is that girl?"

"She's...a friend. Like I said."

"But where has she come from? And what sort of woman is she? Hair loose, head uncovered—if *anyone* in this village is a witch—"

"Nay, she—she only lets herself look thus when it's just us. We weren't expecting you." I frown. "You haven't sent a letter in months. I thought you might be dead."

He sighs. "I nearly was."

It's only now that I note the biggest change about him—the warped scars along his face and neck, covering even his hands. Pox.

I put a hand to my mouth. "Abel—I'm—are you all right?"

"I managed well enough. The pox spread through our camp, killed nearly half the traders before it burned out. I've been recovering a while, but I..." He scowls. "I didn't feel well enough to continue trapping. I'm back for the winter. I'm afraid I haven't brought back the money I hoped, but with Mem bound out and my father... I suppose we don't need so much now."

"Your father will be free," I say for him, secretly hoping it's not true. "Reverend Wilson promised a fair trial."

"Aye. Well." He nods back to the house. "Does Kit earn her keep?"

"More than I do," I say, smiling. "She hunted and prepared the venison you're about to enjoy."

He snorts. "The woman hunts?"

"Abel." I sharpen my gaze at him. "Is now really the time to worry about the...the bloody *propriety* of anything? I was desperate, and Kit is brilliant and skilled and—"

"Aye, all right. Calm yourself, cousin." Abel grips my shoulder. "In that case, she's welcome, as long as she's no trouble."

"Thank you."

"You seem quite taken with her, besides."

My face floods with heat. "*Taken* with her?"

"Well, aye. You've never been one to keep close friends. Aside from Thomas, but..." He smiles.

"I—I— Go inside and wait on dinner, will you?"

He chuckles. "Are you quite all right?"

"Of course! I just need to—the chickens." I nod to the coop, whence the hens glare at me. I grab their sack of feed and scatter their dinner. Abel gives a bemused laugh and turns back to the house.

"You've somehow gotten odder, Livy."

I surely seems I have.

We're quiet through dinner. Ordinarily, I'd ask Abel about his time away, his adventures. But the scars on his face remind me that there are no happy tales to share. Kit is tense, chewing her food too long, gazing at the door as though she might break for it at any moment.

The missing presences are too obvious—Mem's chatter, Uncle's aura. While I could do without the later, I feel Abel's worry over his father. It's heavy, like ice on water.

Kit abruptly lifts her remaining hank of venison and drops it on my plate, then rises and heads to the sink. She scrubs her plate with enough force to erode the stoneware.

"Are you all right?" I ask.

"Um. My stomach is troubling me." She tosses me a rueful smile. "Think I'll take a walk."

"Shouldn't you lie down?" I rise, too. "If you're feeling sick, I mean."

"I—no. The cold air will help."

"That makes absolutely no sense."

She nods, rubbing the back of her neck. I think she's about to agree, to sit back down and finish her cider. But then she's walking to the door, outside, gone.

Abel sighs. "Are you sure we can trust her?"

"Of course. She's only a bit eccentric."

I force myself to sit back down and finish dinner. Abel— perhaps taking after his father already—takes a second bottle of cider and settles in by the fire. The big black Bible rests on a small table by his elbow. A small, tired part of me wishes he'd reach for it, offer to read the Scriptures aloud.

A larger part of me knows that if I wanted spiritual guidance, I would have opened the Bible myself days ago. That same part of me screams that I'm only worried about Kit and demands I go after her, now.

"I'm going to bed down the goats," I say, throwing on my cloak.

Abel only grunts into his bottle.

Beast follows me outside. We quickly round the goats back into the barn. I do a quick sweep of the property, the inside of the barn, hoping Kit hasn't gone far. But I know where she is, even before I encounter her horrible crow waiting for me at the gate.

"That way," Beaky caws, his beady eye flicking toward the forest.

"Tell me truly," I say. "Are you an agent of Satan? A familiar spirit? Speak any word if you be a witch."

The bird says nothing, only eyes me.

"Clever bird," I say, with grudging admiration. Beaky flies off ahead of me, no doubt guiding me to Kit. Beast hurries along at my side, tongue lolling, grateful for the adventure.

I find Kit where I knew she'd be—in the clearing, knelt over Lizzy's grave. She's carving something in the snow with her finger, and I freeze, sucking in a breath. She cuts me a look.

"It's not a spell," she says. "It's French. Is French all right, Deliverance, or does that go against your Puritan sensibilities?"

"I know it's not a spell," I say. "I...just got the sense that I was interrupting."

"You were. But I can't fault you for it." She looks up at the heavy blue sky. "It'll be full dark soon. And darkness here is so absolute. I remember in London, there was always a light somewhere. Always noise. My Gran took me to Southwark once. Told me how, when she was a girl, there were plays and bear-baitings. Noise all around. Of course, it's still noisy there. But your lot at least managed to do away with the plays."

"Did she hear any plays?"

Kit grins. "The King's Men themselves, performing *Hamlet*. Do you know it?"

"I'm afraid not."

"'One may smile, and smile, and be a villain.'"

"What?"

She looks down, to the words carved into the snow. "It's from the play. My Gran never forgot it, and she told it to me whenever some petty cruelty befell me. I think she wanted me to know...that just because someone says they're good, and believes they're good, they can still be evil." She starts writing in the snow again. "Lizzy's father always smiled. Said he loved all his daughters. But that didn't stop him dragging her to the constable, demanding she hang."

"He *wanted* her to hang?" I shake my head. "I thought—the brands—"

"They were a mercy, but not his. The judge ruled for branding and banishment."

"Why did he think you both witches?" I say at last. "Was it that book?"

"Aye. But not because he thought it full of spells." She stops writing, closes her eyes, and recites:

> "Come, my Celia, let us prove
> While we may, the sports of love;
> Time will not be ours forever;
> He at length our good will sever.
> Spend not then his gifts in vain.
> Suns that set may rise again;
> But if once we lose this light,
> 'Tis with us perpetual night.
> Why should we defer our joys?"

"That's beautiful," I say.

"Ben Johnson," she says. "It was one of our favorites. We knew there were things we couldn't say to each other. Not in that house. So, we wrote them. Lizzy taught me the French. But her father knew the language, too. And one day, he found the book."

I think I know the answer, for it's been stirring in me, too. But still, stupidly, I say, "What...um, what had you written?"

"Love notes, Deliverance. Poems. Scandalous daydreams." She clenches her fists in the snow. "If I'd been a boy...it still would have been horrible, of course, but...but they might have spared her. Given her jail time and banished me alone, maybe.

But it was *unnatural.* And anything unnatural these days makes you a bloody witch."

She throws a scattering of snow toward the trees. Beaky caws and flutters down from a branch, landing on her shoulder.

"Sorry," he creaks.

I smile. "The talking bird probably didn't help."

She snorts. "Probably not, no. Well? Aren't you horrified by me?"

"No." I chew my lower lip. "I suppose love is just that." I sit in the snow beside her. "I never told you about Thomas, did I?"

She shakes her head, eyes still on the grave.

"He was my only friend in the village. A few years older than me. It...it was a sort of jest among the villagers that we were meant to be married. We were inseparable. And I suppose we did fall in love. Or, I did. It was hard not to. He was handsome and intelligent and...kind. Kinder than I thought a person could be."

I twirl my finger through the snow. The movement calms me a little, gives me something to think of other than the confession brewing in my lungs.

"I used to bathe in the river, in the shadow of the forest. It was my one...excess, you might say. I didn't think anybody knew of my secret spot. But he found me there one evening last spring. He confessed he'd sought me out. And there I was, naked in a river, trying to hide my shame behind the rocks by the shore. But he...he had come for me."

I take my hand from the snow and rub my cheek. The heat there burns after the chill of the ground. "So, we tumbled in the water, and he said we'd marry one day. But then he left for Harvard instead."

Kit sighs. "That's quite sad."

I wince. "I'm sorry. I didn't mean...obviously it's not the same as losing the person you love to..."

"Death," she supplies. "No, but I do mean it. I'm sorry he left you. And, I suppose, you being you, you see that as some horrible sin you've committed."

"It is a sin."

"Even though everybody is bloody well doing just that, all the time, married or no." She smiles. "Lizzy's father had a few women he tumbled besides his wife. So, I wouldn't go feeling too badly about yourself."

I shake my head. "It's one thing to know it, and another to...to forgive myself."

"You don't need to forgive yourself. Any more than I do. You said it yourself. Love is just that."

I peek over at her, my face warm once again. "Do you think you'll love again?"

She blinks. "I...hadn't thought about it. Ask me when it stops hurting." She snorts. "No, that's not right. It'll never stop hurting. Ask me when I'm not so angry, then. When I've stopped wanting to tear the world apart."

I hope you do, I think. *I hope you find yourself able to love. And maybe I will, too.*

I try to bury these hopes, but they're out now, loose in my chest, looking for sunlight.

We stay in the snow. We sit, inches apart, not touching.

And I don't say anything.

19. The Devil I Can Be

I leave Kit to mourn and wander back to the path. Snow falls now, catching the moonlight like stars tumbling from the sky. I think of Revelation, of a blood red moon, but those stories feel so far away now.

If I'm honest, they always have.

I make to turn toward home, but something catches my eye. A line of prints in the snow, leading deeper into the woods. I edge closer.

Cloven feet.

I look back in the direction of the clearing. The prints are moving away from Kit, but I have no idea how quickly this demon can move. I have no way of knowing if we're being hunted. If this is a trap.

Beast whines, ears flat against his head. But all at once, his demeanor changes, lips pulling back over teeth, a snarl ripping from his chest.

I follow his gaze, and there, in the distance between two trees, is a figure, draped in a dark cloak, obscured by shadow.

A faint laugh reaches me. It slithers along my spine, bringing me up to my full height.

"Who are you?" I shout.

"Who would thou have me be?" comes a slithering whisper. It seems a mere part of the wind.

"Be gone," I say, though my voice is weaker. "I—I rebuke thee."

His laugh is sharper now. "Yet it is thou who sought me."

"I sought no congress with the Devil," I say.

"Am I the Devil, then? Good, good. The Devil I know. I can be him, yes."

"Liv?" Kit's voice rises at my side, and a moment later, she's bounding through the trees, at my side. She grabs my shoulders and turns me toward her. "Liv. Calm down."

I realize then that I'm shaking, that my voice is dead in my throat. I whirl away from her, but the cloaked figure is gone. Only the cloven prints remain.

"The Devil is in these woods," I tell her, grabbing her hand. "We must away, before he comes back."

"The..." Kit turns to where my gaze is locked. In a breath, she breaks away from me and bounds toward the trees, her own footprints crossing the cloven ones. She kneels by the very tree where the figure had stood, and my guts twist in fear. She seems transfixed, her hand hovering above a small reddish scrap in the snow. Carefully, I go to her side.

And that's when I see the book—her book. Love notes and copied poems, all in French, all in secret. The little red leather book has been dropped in the snow, left—it had to be—by the creature who stood here only a moment ago.

"How did it get here?" Kit says, her hand inches above the book. She wants it, but she's afraid now, too. "You said the constable took it, yes?"

I nod. "Aye. I cannot figure how it got here."

But of course, I can. There's some dark magic in the village now. An evil leaking into every corner of the woods.

And I spoke with it.

Kit takes the book, burying it in the pocket of her cloak and holding it close. I walk alongside her, telling her of my conversation with the thing—the man—the Devil.

"Do you suppose it was the constable?" she asks.

"The constable hasn't got cloven feet," I say. "Last I checked, anyhow."

"Nobody's got cloven feet, Liv! Do you actually think the Devil is about, luring women into the woods, saying odd things, and stealing books?"

"What else could it be? I know you don't believe as I do, but I've been told my entire life that the Devil walks the earth, looking to trap souls. Every good Christian he corrupts is a victory in his eyes."

"Aye, then he met his match." She nudges me. "Sounds like you stood by your godly values quite well. And me, I have none to begin with."

"Don't jest," I say. "The Lord gave me strength. And you're a perfectly decent person."

"Aye, well, I still say this Devil of yours is naught but a man." She touches the book through her cloak pocket. "And I think him the man who killed my Lizzy."

We step out of the woods. Even in the full dark of night, I note the glimmer of inky wings and glowing eyes on the gatepost.

"That way," Beaky caws as we approach.

"Not now, Beaky," Kit says. "Liv's had enough adventures."

"Murder-murder."

I shudder. This damned bird is going to haunt my nightmares for years to come, I know it.

"Yes, good boy. Murder." Kit holds out her hand, and Beaky leaps onto her wrist. "That's what you call a group of your friends, isn't it? Aren't you a clever boy?"

"Are you *nuzzling* it?"

Kit glares at me. "He's earned affection for being such a smart little bird, hasn't he? Yes, he has!" She gives his neck a tickle.

"Oh, Lord have mercy."

Kit sticks her tongue out.

I open the door quietly, assuming Abel will be asleep. The chair by the fire is empty, however, the bottle of cider half-drunk on the floor. I check the next room and find Uncle's bed empty, too.

"Abel?" I call out. "Abel!"

Kit checks upstairs, but descends a moment later, shaking her head.

"Might he have gone to tend the animals?" she asks.

"Nay, I told him I was bedding the animals down. Unless...oh, God, I don't know."

"Calm down," Kit says softly. "I'm sure he's all right. We—we were gone a while. Perhaps he went to look for you?"

In the forest? My heart stutters. No, no, I just got him back. And my foolhardiness may have led him into that forest, with that *thing*.

"Come on." Kit ushers me to the chair and makes me sit. The fire is fluttering out, mere embers clinging to the buckling wood. "Sit tight. I'll get more firewood. And stay calm. Your cousin can't have gone far."

I stare into the flickering embers, like stars in a dull sky. "What's happening, Kit? First my uncle, then the ghost, and now... My family is cursed, I swear it."

"Sit tight," she orders. "Don't move."

I don't want her to go, but it feels childish to say that. So, I curl my legs against my chest and stare into the dying fire. I try to set my heart to the rhythm of Beast's steadily thumping tail. The night has been too shocking, too strange. I shut my eyes and press my forehead against my knees.

"Deliver me..."

My eyes open. I dare not raise my head, dare not turn toward the source of that cold voice. But I know it—I can fill the room with the memory of her face, her curdled eyes and her bleeding mouth, the rings around her neck purple and blue like a dusk sky.

"Deliver...me..."

"I don't know what that means," I whisper.

"...from evil..."

I blink. Could it be...? I scramble from the chair and turn, but no ghostly figure greets me. Nothing stands in my way as I break for the stairs and climb to my room.

A small trunk sits at the foot of the bed Mem and I shared. It holds our few belongings, the things we don't use daily anymore but found too precious to part with—straw dolls and idle sketches. And there, at the bottom of the trunk, the horn book on which I learned my letters and the Lord's Prayer. Mem used it after me, but it's since sat useless in this box.

But there, on the lower half of the wooden paddle, the Lord's prayer in its entirety. I scan the penultimate sentence.

And lead us not into temptation, but deliver us from evil.

But what does it mean? If my mother is a spirit, how can I deliver her from evil? Does she mean to tell me she's in hell? Or in some horrible purgatory?

I couldn't save her while she was alive. I watched as my uncle strangled her. How will I ever deliver anyone?

"Oh, God," comes a voice downstairs. "Liv?"

I scramble up, bringing the hornbook with me. "I'm here! Here." I thump down the stairs under Kit's steely glare.

"I told you to stay put." She frowns at the hornbook. "What? Forgot your letters and needed a primer?"

"Did you hear anything? Ghostly or otherwise?"

She blinks, shakes her head. "Nay. Was it your mum again?"

"I think so..."

"We ought to talk to her. Properly."

"What do you mean?" I ask, following Kit as she goes to rummage through the cupboard.

"Have you any shears?"

"Aye, in the toolshed. Why...?" And then I see what she's pulled out of the cupboard. "No."

"Oh, come off it." She hooks the sieve on her finger and rocks it back and forth. "You're already talking to a ghost. Is it so horrible if you make it easier?"

"It's witchcraft! Conjuration!"

"Have you a better idea?"

I open my mouth, shut it. I cross my arms and stare moodily into the fire.

"Perfect." Kit shoves the sieve into my hands. "I'll get the shears."

20. Sieve and Shears

Kit takes my perfectly good sieve and stabs a hole in it.

At first, I think she'll only balance the sieve on the tip of the shears. But no, she stabs right through the mesh.

"I hope you know you're paying for a new one," I say.

"Of course, Deliverance. Here." She offers me one handle of the shears. I take it grudgingly.

"Now what?" I ask.

"We make a request of the spirit. Such as...well, here, I'll start. Oh, what's your surname?"

"Ashe," I say.

"Right. Goody Ashe, Goody Ashe, by Saint Peter and Saint Paul, if thou be among us, let this sieve turn around."

We wait. Nothing happens.

"Well, go on," Kit whispers. "Maybe she's waiting for you."

"I—what do I say?"

I take a breath. Despite the cold of the room, sweat slicks my palm where it grips the shears. This kind of simple magic seems innocent, yet I've had years of Uncle telling me that even a little slip is all the Devil needs to get in. Yet here I am, with a Quaker girl who loved a girl, and her talking bird, attempting folk magic to speak to my murdered mother.

I feel my last slim hope of Heaven slip as I say, "Mother? Mum? By Saint Peter and Saint Paul, if thou be among us, let this sieve turn round."

And it does. The thin metal strands of the sieve groan against the rusted metal shears as the whole thing turns once, slowly.

I gape at the sieve, unwilling to believe it fully. "Did you move it?"

"Nay." Kit grins. "Ask something else."

"Mum," I say. "If you want me to...to tell what I know, by Saint Peter and Saint Paul, turn this sieve around."

This time, it spins so quickly and furiously that the sieve flies off the shears with a thin metallic scream. Kit ducks as the thing scatters across the floor to bump into the far wall.

"Well, then," Kit says.

I shake my head. "She wants me to turn my uncle in? He's already in jail."

"Aye, for witchcraft, which they have barely any evidence of. An accusation of murder would put him away, though, wouldn't it?"

"I can't do that to Abel."

Kit frowns. "How good a father can your uncle be to Abel? If the man beats you and torments your sister, what's he like to him?"

"He's never touched him. They've...they've always been close." I shrug. "I suppose it's different when it's a son."

"Aye, well. Think not that you're doing it to Abel so much as for your mother, and for yourself and Mem."

"But he'll hang."

Kit tosses her hands. "Would that be such a bad thing?"

"I thought Quakers were against hanging."

"For some of the asinine reasons the English do it. Not for *murder*. Blood of man shed, and all that."

"He's my uncle!"

"He's a horrible person."

I open my mouth, hoping a rebuttal will fly out, but I'm spared arguing when the door bangs open and Abel fills its frame for the second time in a night.

"Where were you?" he says, and for a moment, his voice is so like Uncle's, like a coming thunder cloud, that I cower into myself. Kit steps between us, still holding the shears like it's perfectly normal.

"Sorry, my fault," she says. "I lost track of the time, and Liv was worried for me. She came to bring me back."

Abel frowns at the shears. "What are those for?"

"I thought I'd make it up to you by trimming the vines growing along the barn. Those things can crush a house if you let them get too big."

She lies so easily, with such conviction, it makes me wonder what sort of life she's had to lead up till now. What horrors did she weave her way out of with that tongue when she served in Lizzy's house?

Abel quirks an eyebrow, his anger visibly diminishing. "Aye, well...please don't bother tonight. It's dark, and there's barely a moon in the sky."

"Of course." Kit sets the shears by the door. I glance at the sieve still thrown against the wall, and, taking after Kit's quick thinking, go to Abel's side and guide him back toward the chair.

"Here, sit. I'm sorry I made you worry. Let me restoke the fire."

He sits heavily and takes up his abandoned cider. I add branches to the hearth and watch in the edge of my vision as Kit gathers up the sieve and quietly replaces it in the cupboard.

"Why don't you have proper firewood?" Abel asks.

"Oh. Well, Uncle wouldn't let me near the axe. So, I just gathered branches."

"Why didn't my father cut the firewood? It's man's work."

Kit makes a sound like she's choking on something. Abel, thankfully, doesn't notice.

"He...was busy with other things." Like drinking, and drinking, and hitting me, and drinking, I don't say.

"A lot of moldering branches hardly makes a good fire." Abel sighs. "I'll cut some properly in the morning. And you'll tend to the housework. I don't want you wandering those woods for shriveled branches."

"Yes, Cousin, of course."

Kit makes a face across the room, something between a sneer and a hanged man's contorted face. I cover my abrupt laugh with a forced coughing fit.

"You're not ill, are you, Livy?" Abel asks.

"Nay. Haven't dusted in a while, is all."

He nods, finishes his cider in one last long pull. I hope he won't get the taste for it the way Uncle has. I hope he'll stay Abel, and not become a monster.

"I've had a long journey," Abel says, "and at this point, a longer night. You don't mind cleaning up?" He eyes the remnants of dinner still scattered across the table.

Kit starts to say something—nothing good, I imagine, so I cut in with, "Of course not. Go, sleep. We can take care of this."

He thumps off to his and Uncle's room at the far side of the house. As soon as he shuts the door, Kit turns to me.

"Helpful, aren't you?"

"What's that supposed to mean?"

She shrugs. "He's not in charge of you, is he?"

"In a sense, he is," I say tightly. "With Uncle gone, he's the man of the house."

"Who says there has to be a man of the house?"

"The Bible."

"Chapter and verse?"

I glare at her. She sticks her tongue out.

"Fine," I say. "I'll look it up later."

"Don't bother. It won't change my mind."

I shake my head. "How can you be so flippant about the Word of God?"

"Well," she says. "There are plenty of gods, and they've all had things to say over time. Who's to say we've just so happened to land on the right one?"

My jaw hangs on its hinges. "You—you can't—that's just—blasphemy."

"The Greeks," Kit says, ticking off her fingers. "The Romans. The Egyptians, Babylonians, Assyrians, Macedonians, Persians, Chinese—"

"Speak plainly," I cut in.

"They've all got their own religions! They've been around as long as anybody. Why are they wrong and we're right? Doesn't that bother you?"

"Maybe it does," I whisper. "But it's not for me to question."

"Why? Why do you owe such loyalty to a god that doesn't even promise you the salvation you work yourself to death over? How many hours have you prayed and begged forgiveness for something as trivial as an idle thought?"

"Stop it," I say.

"Tell me you're not miserable."

"Of course, I am!" I snap, and immediately turn away. Tears prick at my eyes and crawl my up throat, but I won't let her see me break. "Life isn't meant to be *enjoyed*, though."

"What if it's the only one you've got?"

I suppress a shudder. "You're blaspheming again."

"Apparently, that's what I do."

I rub the heels of my hands into my eyes, scattering the pent-up tears. "Is that how you justify it? Living the way you do?"

She's quiet, and I turn slowly around to find her eyes hard on me.

"I don't need to justify it," she says at last. "I loved a girl who loved me back. There's nothing sinister about that."

"You're really not afraid," I say. "Of God, or Hell, or...any of that?"

She nearly smiles. "Liv. I lived my life afraid of so many things here on Earth. There's no fear left in me for things of other worlds."

"When you first knew you loved her," I say, "were you afraid then?"

"Yes," she says. "Terrified. But love is a frightening thing. And some things are worth a little fear."

"But she's gone," I say. "Isn't that...aren't you miserable now?"

"Yes," she says. "What's the point?"

"The pain," I say. "How can you...how are all right with that agony? That nightmare always returning when you close your eyes? How can you stand it?"

She takes a careful step closer to me. Her eyes are the soft light of a long-burning candle. "I can't. It kills me. There are moments I'm not sure I can keep breathing. But then, I do. And once I've caught my breath, I remember…I'm just glad I knew her. I'm glad I had her. For as short a time as it was, she was mine. And that can't be taken from me." She smiles. "Misery is a choice, Liv. And it's a shit one to make."

I nod, looking down. "I'll try to remember that. Well." I clear my throat. "I need to clean."

"*We* need to clean." She reaches out and, with her thumb, swipes a stray tear from my cheek. "I wouldn't leave you with all the chores."

And then, I know. I know the thing I can't say, but also can't bury. I know what my puddling heart, the fire in my stomach, the tingling her thumb left on my skin—I know it means I'm lost, can't go back, find no way forward.

This happiness must surely spell doom.

21. A Witch Among Us

I manage to fix a paltry breakfast in a sleepless haze. I barely slept last night with Kit beside me, too aware of my body and hers, determined to keep those few inches of spare mattress between us. She slept perfectly fine, snoring and still.

She's outside now, milking the goats and plucking up the eggs left by the hens. Abel rose with the dawn and headed out to the forest with the axe. And I'm here, in the kitchen, cooking eggs and dicing bits of venison to go with it.

All's well, isn't it? Aside from the strange happenings of the past few days, a bizarre sense of normalcy has returned to this house. Maybe, if Uncle is convicted, it would even be safe to bring Mem back. I'm sure the Wilsons would release her to me, knowing Abel has returned.

The back door bangs open, and Kit enters, holding a pail of warm milk in one hand and a basket of eggs in the other. She stamps her snow-crusted boots on the threshold. She let me braid her hair this morning, but she refused a coif.

I hate how pretty she looks, the few loose locks of hair stamped to her cheeks from the snow, the blackness of her eyelashes stark against her blue eyes.

I turn quickly back to the stove.

"What are you making?" Kit asks, shedding her cloak and hanging it by the door. I spare only a brief glance her way. I lent her one of my black waistcoats, but rather than making her look dour, she seems sharper, more confidant than I could ever be.

"It's only eggs," I say. "I ought to make proper food today. Bread, cheese...butter. Abel loves his butter."

"Maybe I'll go hunting again," Kit says.

"Nay, don't," I say, too quickly. I clear my throat. "Not with that thing out there."

"I'll have my crossbow," Kit says.

"What crossbow?"

"It's back in my hideout," she says, shrugging. "Where...where Lizzy and I lived. It was just a little lean-to, but..."

I nod. I know what she would have said. *It was home.* In a world like ours, even a home of sticks and mud can be more freeing than a huge gabled mansion.

"Anyway," Kit says, "if I see the Devil, I'll shoot him between the eyes. Promise."

"We've plenty of venison left," I say. "At least put it off a while."

"I just want to make sure I'm earning my keep." She tugs on her braid. "I know your cousin doesn't like me."

"He's like everyone in the village—wary of strangers. Give him time."

I take the eggs off the fire and begin scraping them onto plates. Beast nearly tumbles down the stairs in his haste to join us for breakfast. Just when I'm beginning to worry we'll have to wait for Abel, he shoulders the door wide, pink-cheeked and winded, but smiling.

"I've a surprise for you, Livy," he says.

"Oh?" I look up and nearly drop the plate in my hand.

Another figure steps into the house behind Abel. Dressed in a fine black doublet and breeches, his face partly obscured by a folt hat is—

"Thomas?"

My belly pools with warmth while my heart trickles ice. The muscles in my stomach clench, as though I were back in the river, naked and cold but burning as he came to me. I opened for him so easily. It seemed so right. There was pain, yes, but he was gentle. He kissed me and whispered promises in my ear.

Those promises died when he left. They were only whispers after all, wind before a storm.

But here he is, his curling dark hair a little long, his blue eyes bright with joy, his mouth lopsided in its eagerness to smile. And here I am, gawping like I've witnessed a hanging.

"Hello," I manage at last.

Thomas laughs, a little nervously, I think. "Yes, well. After my family, you were the first person I hoped to see." He grows somber. "Abel has told me of the trouble with Goodman Ashe. I hope you know I'll do everything I can to see him freed. My father doesn't hold with baseless accusations of witchcraft."

My breath snatches in my throat. Thomas knows what Uncle has done to me. He's seen the bruises. He kissed them and told me he'd take me away from the bastard.

I tell myself he is only saying this for Abel's sake. But I can't be sure, can I? I once thought he's stay. He proved me wrong.

"I... Thank you, Thomas. That's good of you."

A dense silence falls in the house. I know I ought to do more to hide my unhappiness, but somehow, I find I'm not up to it.

"I've been home, of course," Thomas says after a moment. "I was surprised to find Mem there."

"How is she?" I ask.

"She's well. My mother says she's a good servant. Only...should you ask, of course, we would gladly release her back to you."

Abel claps Thomas on the shoulder. "We thank you, friend. I hope only to see this family reunited soon. Of course, unless I'm mistaken, we'll all be one large family soon, eh?"

Thomas makes a show of blushing, bumbling his way through a weak denial. I press my forehead into my hand and sigh.

"Are you all right?" Kit whispers. I subtly shake my head, more for the uselessness of it all, but she walks right up to Thomas and says, loudly, "Hello! I'm Katherine."

"Oh, yes." Thomas gives a short bow. "I'm sorry, I should have introduced myself. Thomas Wilson. Are you a friend of Liv's?"

"You might say that." There's an edge to her smile that I like. "And no need for formality. Consider me a friend." I wince at her subtle word play, but Thomas seems not to notice. "You're the reverend's son?"

"I am."

"And what are your intentions toward my Livy?"

A laugh bursts out of me before I have the sense to control it. Thomas, for his part, seems utterly dumbfounded.

"I—I—" He looks to Abel for help.

"Katherine here is new to the village," Abel says, eyeing Kit.

"Call me Kit," she says. "I insist."

"Well." Thomas looks to me. "Actually, Liv, I was thinking—"

"We should go see Mem," I say, before he can suggest else. "I promised I'd visit again soon. I'll get my cloak."

"I'll stay here," Kit offers. "Tend to...things."

I nod. It's dangerous enough that Abel, and now Thomas, know of her existence. I don't want to drag her through town while whispers of witchcraft are floating around.

"Right," Thomas says, his voice faint in the sudden bustle. Abel gamely goes to find his overcoat while Beast leaps around, delighted by the prospect of a walk. I kneel before him and scratch behind his ears to calm him.

"Stay with Kit, boy. Keep her safe."

"I'm safe," Kit says. "But I appreciate the company." She wraps her arms around Beast and plants a kiss on his nose.

I nod to her once, something happy and scared all at once twisting in my gut. She'll be here when I get back. Whatever happens, whatever nonsense Thomas spouts to excuse his abandoning me, I have Kit and Beast to come home to.

"Livy?" Abel calls from the door. I offer a final smile to Kit and follow after the men.

Abel—somewhat purposefully, I think—outpaces me and Thomas, leaving a cloud of tense quiet between us while we trek toward the village. I keep my eyes forward, but the edge of my vision catches Thomas's false starts, his mouth opening and snapping shut without so much as a word passing between us.

Finally, he manages something. "So. Where does Katherine hail from?"

"Ipswich," I say.

"Ah. Lovely place."

"You've been?"

"I—no."

"Of course." I clear my throat. "But Boston—it's lovely, isn't it?"

"Oh, yes. Lovely."

"Truly. I miss it very much."

"Oh, of course, you...you lived there. Before." He smiles. "I confess I forget that you've not always been in my life."

"Oh," is all I manage in response. After a long moment, taut as thread on a loom, I ask, "What brings you back so soon? I thought you'd be gone, well, years."

"I'm only back for a short while. Really, um, there's only one thing... It's what I wanted to say to you before... Only, I'd thought your uncle would be around. But even if he can't, um, I still wanted to ask you, at least, if—"

"*Witch!*"

The cry fills the late morning with a sudden hum, a murmur of interest and a low current of fear. I glance up to see Abel stopped at the beginning of the village, holding out his hands in a calming gesture to a man and woman facing off in the road.

"She-devil! Whore!" The man spits in the dirt.

"Take it back, Goodman Brown," the woman hisses.

"Or what? You've already cursed me! Fie, devil, and be gone!"

"Please, Goodman Brown," Abel says over the shouting. "Goody Nash."

Goody Nash tosses her hands and stomps back toward her house, a sad wattle-and-daub thing even smaller than the home Uncle built for us. I walk closer, eyeing the property jutting up beside hers. Only a thin fence divides the land between Goodman Brown and Goody Nash's homes. Their lands are nearly identical, the houses differing only in size—Goodman Brown's being significantly larger. But as I watch the properties, another difference stands out to me. Animals walk along the Nash property, energetic in the cold: Goats butting heads, sheep huddling close, chickens chattering to one another. Goodman Brown's land is empty and silent.

"What's happened?" Abel asks, though I think I know.

"She's cursed me," Goodman Brown says. "The old witch accused me of letting my livestock graze her land, and she laid a curse upon me. I woke this morning to find every one of my animals dead. Bellies bloated and tongues black."

"Surely it's a coincidence," Thomas says, frowning. "It sounds rather more like an illness has taken your livestock."

"Nay, else hers would be affected, too," Goodman Brown says. "She's cursed me. Hateful wench!"

"Hold thy tongue, Goodman Brown," Goody Nash shouts over her shoulder, "or worse will find thee and thine yet."

"Ah! See! She curses me again! *Witch*!"

"Calm yourself," Abel says, but it does no good. Goodman Brown charges forward, and both Thomas and Abel have to hold him back, their shoulders bunching with the effort. I cast about, searching for anyone who might help. The figure I find approaching the scene, however, is the last man I hoped to see.

"What's the trouble here, eh?" Constable Walsh tugs Goodman Brown back from Abel and Thomas, eyes slowly taking in the scene. "Well? Speak up, lads."

"Goody Nash has cursed me," Goodman Brown says first. "She's killed my livestock and means to murder my family yet."

"Oh, the old codger's full of it," Goody Nash says. She's posted against her fence now, watching the scene with a twitch of amusement to her lips. She reminds me a bit of Kit.

"I see." Walsh lets Goodman Brown go and marches toward Goody Nash. "Is this true, woman? Have you cursed this man?"

"Constable, if my curses worked, he'd have keeled over ages ago."

Walsh's eyes narrow. "I see." He takes another step forward. "You understand, woman, that I take accusations of witchcraft quite seriously?"

"Oh, aye?"

"*Aye.*" And with that, he snatches her by the elbow and drags her forward. "You shall answer my questions, and respectfully hence forth, Goodwife Nash."

"Constable!" I step forward. "She didn't do anything. You can't possibly think—"

"You'd do well to mind me, girl," Walsh says, eyes dark. "Lest you forget, your uncle faces similar charges. I wonder if he didn't learn his craft from a wicked little niece." He drags Nash forward, stopping only to address the curious spectators leaning out of homes and the tavern. "Hear me well. If there be a witch among us, I will find her out, and she will face the hanging tree. Do not test me on this."

And then he's gone, dragging poor Goody Nash after him. I only look away when Thomas touches my arm, bringing me back to myself.

"Are you all right?" he says.

"What will happen to her?"

"He'll question her," Thomas says, not meeting my eyes.

"Question her," I say. "With what, thumbscrews?"

"It's not your concern," Thomas says gently.

"It may yet well be," I say, and I know that, more than I know anything in this moment.

Constable Walsh isn't done with me.

The town is alive with whispers as we walk to the parsonage. Goody Nash's arrest marks the second public declaration of witchcraft, and I fear such accusations will spread, quick as a sickness and just as deadly, until we've lost too much of ourselves.

Witches are always a fear, prowling the back of our minds like an unfulfilled promise. And yet never has my village actually had so much as a whisper of the Devil's maids among us. Until I found Lizzy in the forest, I never had cause to believe witchcraft might truly visit us.

And now, its spreading. The suspicions and the terror are touching everyone, and now, every stray look, every ill word, every wrong action, will take a darker meaning.

I'm afraid we'll never come back from this.

"Liv?"

I look up, realize I've stopped in the road, with the path to the parsonage just ahead. Thomas frowns, worried.

"What is it?" he asks.

"Nothing. I... My mind wanders."

"Aye, this I know." He laughs. "You always were my daydreamer, Liv."

Irritation slices through me. Why does my every quirk, every mood, have to be *his* somehow? What right has he to me, since he left without a word?

I follow him up the path to the parsonage, where Abel waits. Thomas lets us inside, and soon, the busy, noisy house drowns out my bitter thoughts and quiet fears.

"Back already?" Goody Wilson says from the loom. Her eyes land on Abel. "Oh! Abel! Happy day." She rises, sidestepping her younger daughters to wrap my cousin in a hug. "God bless you, dear. We were so worried."

"I thank you, Goody Wilson." Abel bows his head. "By God's grace, I'm returned."

"And on the same day as my Thomas." She takes her son's hands. "He surprised his old mother with a visit. Isn't he dear? Of course, I don't pretend to think I'm the only reason he's returned." She drops me a wink, and I wish for a dreamless pagan death.

"Is Mem about?" I ask. Of the many girls scattered in the main room, Mem is not one of them.

"Oh, she's in the gardens again," Goody Wilson says. "She loves those gardens, though I can't imagine why, in winter."

"Thank you," I say, and break away toward the kitchen. I find Tace there, boiling vegetables in a large pot, her face unusually pink.

"Tace?"

She looks up and swipes at her eyes. "Oh, Liv. I suppose you've seen Thomas?"

"Aye. Are you all right?"

I think for a moment that she's going to say something. Her lips part, her eyes darken—and I'm sure something sits on the edge of her tongue. But she shifts her face into a smile and shrugs. "Oh, aye. I just hate the smell, don't you? Boiled cabbage."

I nod, but still say, "Let me know, though. If you need anything."

Her smile stiffens, and she nods, but a moment later, she's returned her eyes to the boiling pot. I go through the back door, and there's Mem, stationed by the well like last time. She scrapes a fingernail across the thin layer of ice accrued on the water's surface.

"Mem?"

"I can't see her now." My sister looks up. "The Blue Lady. She didn't come last night. Was she with you?"

"Mem." I kneel beside her. "You can't say such things. Not anymore. There are rumors flying about the village of witchcraft. Any little thing will raise suspicion."

"It's no *witch*," Mem says. "It's a ghost."

"And a judge would hardly see the difference," I say. "I know Constable Walsh won't. Please. We've got to keep...your *ghost*...a secret."

"But what if she comes again tonight?"

"Ignore her. Plug your ears and whisper the Lord's prayer. But speak not to her."

Mem looks ready to argue, but her eyes catch on something, and then she's running, her small figure darting after nothing toward the barn posted farther back against the woods.

"Mem!" But it's useless. I chase after her, gathering my petticoat and apron to free my feet. I skid into the barn just in time to see her duck behind a towering pile of hay.

"Mem, this is ridiculous," I say, coming around the pile after her. I find her tucked in the corner of the barn, holding....

A kid goat. I swear I saw nothing before her, and yet here she is with her prize, the thing that apparently lured her away from me in the first place. A little gray kid with big, watery eyes and a stout, trembling tail.

"Can I keep him?" she says. She prods one finger at the kid's stubby horns. "I think he wants me to."

"Nay, Mem, he must belong to someone. Probably he's escaped from another's farm."

"Nay." She frowns. "He told me he came for me. He said he's my pet and we're to stay together."

Ice creeps along my spine. This may be just childish fancy, or a petulant lie. And yet the Devil may take the forms of animals, and I know, his favorite figure is that of a goat.

"Let him go, Mem."

She only hugs it tighter. "No."

I'm about to tell her off, to yank the kid from her arms, when a clatter of voices sounds at the entrance of the barn. I duck behind the hay with Mem, unsure why my first instinct is to hide. I peek out to see Reverend Wilson, with Thomas and Abel, gathered in the doorway.

"Now," Reverend Wilson says. "What's this about?"

Thomas and Abel exchange looks. Abel nods. Thomas speaks.

"I wanted your counsel, Father. How seriously do you take these claims of witchcraft?"

The reverend sighs. "At first, I thought it only Walsh's...over-eagerness. He fancies himself a witch finder general, I thought. And yet..."

"Yes?" Thomas prompts.

"Goody Nash is not the only one."

"My father," Abel says.

"Him, too," Reverend Wilson says. "But also... Goody Baxter, the old crone found dead by the woods? The constable and I, we searched her camp on the edge of the village after. She had in her hut poppets, stuck through with needles, and strange poultices and potions. And upon her hand, when the constable found her, there was a strange, carved mark. All signs point to it—she, too, was a witch."

Thomas shakes his head. "Then what killed her?"

"Likely, her own folly. Else the Devil had enough of her nagging tongue."

A deep anger boils inside me. Goody Baxter is dead, and here our own reverend is mocking her for speaking out against villagers who didn't care if she lived or died. What he calls nagging, a charitable person might call *asking*—begging, when she was desperate. A poor woman, fallen on hard times, and she's remembered as a nag for wanting a crust of bread off a full family's table.

"That's three witches, then," Thomas says.

"Nay," Abel cuts in. "My father is no witch. If it's true, and he held discourse with a spirit, it was only to cast it away. He would not break his covenant with God."

"I'm inclined to believe you," Reverend Wilson says, and of course he does. Of course he believes my uncle over Goody Nash, over the memory of the slain beggar woman.

"What has brought this upon us?" Thomas says at last. "I leave for a year, and the town's descended into chaos. What changed?"

"There's that girl," Abel says, and my heart plummets.

"What, the one at your house?" Thomas says. "Katherine?"

"Aye. What do we know about her, truly?"

"Deliverance vouches for her," Thomas says, and I feel a reluctant warmth toward him for trusting me so completely. "That's plenty for me."

"You're lovesick, friend. Livy can make mistakes, same as any woman."

I grind my teeth. I've known plenty of men to make dire, deadly mistakes, yet folly and fancy remain an accusation slung only at my gender.

"Do you mean to say," Reverend Wilson asks, "that there's a new girl in the village? I haven't seen her."

"She's been staying with Livy," Abel says. "Apparently since my father was arrested."

"But whence did she come?"

Thomas shrugs. "Ipswich?"

"Who *brought* her? A young woman cannot have travelled alone and undetected." The reverend shakes his head. "God have mercy. This girl may be the source."

"She's harmless," Thomas says.

"We'll know that when we've questioned her." The reverend sighs. "I shall leave Constable Walsh out of this, for now. Knowing how…eager he is to find witches. But I need to speak to this girl and ascertain her origins."

"Of course," Abel says. "We'll go now."

And with that, the three of them leave the barn. I turn to Mem, her arm still slung around the tiny goat. I no longer have time to worry about the creature's provenance. I can only hope it's benign.

"Go back inside," I say. "Help Goody Wilson. Do *not* step outside."

"I can keep Billy?"

I roll my eyes. "Aye, but he stays in this barn. You'll not bring him inside the parsonage."

She nods eagerly, pleased.

"I have to go." I kiss her forehead. "I'll be back soon."

I rise, and I run. I run to Kit.

23. Questions

I cut through the forest to head off Reverend Wilson, Thomas, and Abel. I run like I might take flight, like a true witch upon a broom. The trees whip and scrape and tangle, but I know the way, and my mission frees me. No pain finds my skin even as the wilds must surely dig at my cheeks and hands.

Soon, I find my road, and the gate, and I'm tumbling through the door. Kit looks up from a boiling vat of tallow on the stove.

"Liv? God, what's happened to you?"

I blink. I know she's only making candles, yet I can't help but picture a woodcut of an old crone bent over a cauldron, fixing up a potion.

She smiles. "'Bubble, bubble, toil and trouble.'"

"What?"

She sighs. "I wish I could introduce you to Shakespeare. Now, why do you look like you've just run through the woods in a mad dash?"

"Because I have. The reverend is coming here to question you. They mean to discover if you're a witch."

"Bloody Puritans," she mutters. "Fine. What do I do? Make me a respectable lady after your likeness."

"Well, first." Her hair covers her brand, but only if she holds her head just so, with that sly tilt of her chin. Seeing as how it's the most damning bit, I need to make sure the reverend doesn't see it. I go upstairs and hurry back with a coif. She snarls at it, but doesn't protest as I fix it over her head.

"There." I tuck her braid demurely between her shoulder blades.

"Is that all?"

"Don't be so forward with the reverend," I say. "Cast your eyes down. Speak clearly but softly. Now, we need a story of how you got here."

"I've got it."

"Well?" I wait. "What is it?"

"It's a surprise. I'm a fine storyteller, Liv. Don't worry. Anyway." She nods to the door, where voices now cluster. "They're here."

Indeed, the door flies open a moment later, Abel in the lead. He frowns when he sees me. I try to mirror his surprise.

"Abel? What are you doing back?"

"I should ask you the same."

"I felt guilty, being idle while Kit was here alone with the work."

"What about Mem?" Thomas asks, entering after Abel. The reverend follows behind.

"I saw her. Only, she seemed... I fear she's still angry with me, in truth. I thought it best not to press her."

Thomas nods, a faint smile of understanding on his lips. Abel, meanwhile, turns his focus back to Kit, cold and appraising.

"I hope you don't mind," he says, "but we've brought the reverend. Strange things are happening about town, and with you being new here—"

"I'll handle this, Abel," Reverend Wilson says, putting a hand on my cousin's shoulder. He smiles down at Kit. "Katherine, isn't it?"

"Yes, sir," Kit says, in a voice entirely not her own. This Kit is shy, a little skittish, yet eager to help the reverend. "Though some call me Kit."

The reverend nods. "Whence do you come, Katherine?"

"From Ipswich, sir."

"And what brings you hence?"

Kit looks at me and gives me a small, watery smile, as though we're sharing a secret, a story we both know. "I followed my true love, sir."

My stomach drops, but she continues, making the story palatable for the reverend.

"We wed back in Ipswich and came hence to find land to build a glorious farm. Only, on the way, he fell ill. I'm afraid he only got worse. T'was he knew the way to our destination, and without his mind right, we wandered. He sickened worse yet. And...and that was the end...the pox, you know..." She ducks her head. "He died. I wandered days in the woods, lost, until I spied this house. Deliverance took me in."

"That...is a harrowing story," Reverend Wilson says.

"Aye. But the Lord saw me through, and spared me so I might testify to others of his mercy."

I blink, and do my best to bury a smile. She's a proper actress after all. Maybe this Shakespeare fellow had something to him.

"Very well," the reverend says. He looks to Abel. "Are you satisfied? For mine eyes spy a Christian woman much afflicted, yet still worshipful of God and obedient even in turmoil."

"Aye." And yet there's something still in my cousin's eye as he watches Kit. He doesn't believe her. Or, at least, he's still suspicious.

Thomas, however, is sold. "You are very brave," he says. "Truly. Might I... I'm training to become a minister myself, and your story is inspiring, to say the least. Might I tell it someday to my flock?"

"Aye, good sir," Kit says. "I would be honored."

"We could make a book of it, really," Thomas goes on. "You could be the next Mary Rowlandson!"

"Oh, I..." Kit's cheeks go bright, but less from embarrassment, I suspect, than annoyance. "I wouldn't want *that* much attention. It's God who deserves the praise, isn't it?"

"Humble, too," Thomas says to his father. "How God has blessed our village with your presence."

"We shall see you tomorrow at meeting, then?" the reverend asks, and without hesitation, Kit nods.

"Aye. I look forward to your preaching." She dips her head in a small bow.

There are so many ways we might fail in this ruse, but Kit is holding herself together, proving capable of this deceit. And I should be horrified that we're lying to a minister, but I'm only relieved. Relieved, and a little queasy with admiration.

She's strong. I want to be strong, too.

"Let's away, Thomas," Reverend Wilson says.

Thomas casts one last, long look my way. "Liv. Good day. I'll...well, I'll see you soon."

I nod, force a smile for him. He's only leaving the house, not disappearing to Boston again. But I feel a dark rage brewing in my heart regardless.

We never had a moment alone. Perhaps he still means to explain himself. Or perhaps he'll never speak of it.

When Thomas and his father are gone, Abel turns to us. "Is all that true, Katherine?"

"Aye." She blinks, all innocence.

"Why did you not tell me yesterday?"

"I asked her not to," I say before Kit can answer. "I knew of the suspicions brewing in the village, and I feared anyone new might come under the constable's suspicion. Kit has been a good friend. I only wanted to protect her."

Abel shakes his head. I can tell he's angry, but also tired, ready to be done with this. "I suppose after my father's accusation, you had reason to be worried. Constable Walsh is eager to find more witches."

"Did the reverend say that?"

He didn't mean to tell me this—I see it in the tightness of his eyes, the curl of his mouth. But the words are out, between us. He has reason not to want to speak ill of the constable's hunt—denial of witchcraft is as good as a confession thereof. But blind acceptance of it is a condemnation of his own father.

"He worries," Abel says slowly. "There are stories from Boston, from England, even, of witchcraft spreading like plague. He thinks perhaps the constable has taken it into his head that the scourge has reached us here."

I nod, trying to keep a solemn demeanor. "Surely not? We're alone here. We lead quiet lives. What would the Devil want with us?"

"Exactly that," Abel says. "We're a righteous village, filled with godly people. The Devil would love to snatch that goodness away."

"So... *do* you think there are witches?"

"I think we're being tested. And we'll answer to God for what we do in these coming days." He clears his throat. "Now, there are chores to be done. We're pitifully short on candles."

I want to tell him the constable took what stock we had, but I decide it best to revert to obedience, to quiet. Kit's already got the tallow going. We'll make candles, soaps. We'll darn socks, feed the animals, sweep the hearth. Say our prayers and read the Scripture.

We'll be good girls.
We won't look like witches.

24. Meeting

We trek through the hard-frozen snow, slipping and cold, the dawn bright on the edge of the horizon. Abel leads the way, using Uncle's staff to punctuate each step, piercing the snow as he goes. He doesn't need a walking stick, of course. But I think he means to project some new authority. His father has been taken, and he's going to show the villagers that he's a man now.

The meeting house rises at the far end of the village, tucked into the southward stretch of forest. It's a large, simple building of dark wood, the two high windows on either side squinting like eyes in the dull, early light. The door is posted open as villagers trickle inside.

Kit stills as we approach. A tightness bends her mouth down and crinkles her eyes. I take her hand, ignoring the spark between our skin.

"You'll be fine. The reverend has already approved of you. And Thomas practically thinks you a saint."

"Yet Puritans don't abide saints," she says, smiling.

"You know what I mean."

Inside, the hard wooden pews wait to be filled. Narrow stairs lead up toward the gallery above, though our village has yet to see an excess of people which would require the extra seating. Kit eyes the high, secret seats hopefully, but Abel leads us to our usual places. Without a hitch, he takes Uncle's usual seat, third row, on the very end of the pew, aisle side. I sit beside him, and Kit practically falls in my lap in her clumsy attempt to avoid the nearby parishioners.

"Calm down," I whisper, though a laugh undercuts my words. "Nobody is going to even notice you."

She adjusts her borrowed coif and shrugs. "Can't be too careful."

Goody Wilson approaches then, Mem at her side. "Abel, Deliverance. Your sister wishes to sit with you for service."

My smile breaks free. "Thank you, Goody Wilson."

I make room between me and Abel, and Mem plops down beside me, a whisper ready on her lips.

"She's back, she's back!"

My smile flickers out. "Mem, not now."

"But the Blue Lady—"

"Not here," I hiss.

Mem scowls and turns her eyes forward, pretending to be fixated on the pulpit as Reverend Wilson takes his place behind it, holding a psalter.

"Our village is being tested," he says. "The Lord is asking if we are willing and ready to be righteous. I hope the answer is yes. But to be righteous, we must humbly ask forgiveness. Let us sing Psalm fifty-one."

Kit eyes me and mouths, *I don't know the words.*

Pretend, I mouth back. I'll just have to sing loud enough for the both of us.

We sing through the psalm, words of repentance and pleas for forgiveness. Kit makes shapes with her mouth that match well enough. We are singing David's hope for a clean heart when a shriek fills the room.

From the front row, Tace stumbles away from her family, clutching her throat and screaming.

"Nay, I will not!" she wails, and falls to her knees. Thomas rushes to her side and tries to lift her, but she strikes out, pushing him back. Reverend Wilson watches from behind the pulpit, wide-eyed and mouth agape, as his daughter wails at some unseen pain. She collapses to her side.

"She has my throat! She chokes me!" She gags then, twisting her face to the floor as spit and foam and blood gather on her lips.

"Who?" Constable Walsh shoves past the parishioners in his pew to get to Tace, writhing in the aisle. "Speak, girl! Who has you by the throat?"

"Goody Nash!" Tace manages between hacking coughs.

Walsh scowls and yanks Tace up off the floor by her arm. "I swear, girl, if thy words be false—"

Tace lurches in his grip. Her face twists as though she means to vomit all over the constable, and he frees her. She falls back to her knees, but the heaves wrack her body, moving her chest in rhythm with the violent sounds clawing up her throat.

When her mouth opens, it's not vomit that spills forth, but a huge nail, glittering with spit and bile. It clatters to the wooden floor. Silence follows. Even the constable doesn't move or speak.

"She means to kill me," Tace says at last. "I refused to sign her book, and she swore vengeance." She turns her eyes up to the gallery, and then the rafters, and issues another scream.

"Her specter sits upon the beams! Oh, God, she's come for me!"

Walsh unfreezes, then, and drags Tace up by the collar of her dress. "This girl is bewitched. Who among us is a witch? Speak! If thou consort with the Devil, give answer now. I'll find thee out and thou'll surely hang."

"Constable!" Reverend Wilson at last steps down from the pulpit. "Unhand my daughter. She is bewitched, not doing the witching herself."

Walsh reluctantly drops Tace's collar, and the girl collapses into her father's arms, sobbing apologies and fears. Thomas comes to take her a moment later, tucking her under his arm. He begins to lead her back to their pew when Tace shoves his arms away and stumbles back into the aisle.

"Another servant has fallen." She turns her eyes, hard and dark, to the constable. "She didn't do what he said. And so, he made her dead."

"*Who* is dead?" Walsh growls. "Speak thee of Goody Baxter?"

"Nay, that crone was only the beginning. Or the middle. And oh, if only we were at the end." Tace grins, and it's then I notice lines of blood tricking from the corners of her mouth. "You'll find her, good Constable..." She points like a drunk giving vague directions. "Behind the meeting house. Dead-like."

Walsh and the reverend exchange glances, and then both hurry toward the doors. It seems the entire congregation moves at once to follow, funneling toward the exit to see this finest rumor in person.

"Come on," I say to Kit. I grab Mem's hand, lest she slip away, and we go to Tace, who has once again been recaptured by Thomas. He holds her around the shoulders, but the fight seems to have slipped out of her. Her head lolls against his shoulder, her eyes half-open, her bleeding mouth split in a dazed smile.

"Tace?" I try, but the girl seems not to hear me. I meet Thomas's gaze. He's pale, wide-eyed. And for a moment, I see only my friend who needs me, not the man who broke me.

"Here, lay her down," I say, gesturing to the vacated pew behind the Wilsons. They, of course, remained, Goody Wilson standing with her other daughters huddled close. She watches her eldest girl with wet, blinking eyes.

Thomas gets Tace settled on the pew, where she seems instantly to sleep.

"Have you noticed anything?" I ask. "Has she seemed...different?"

"Distracted, maybe," Thomas says. "I thought little of it. I've only been back for a day. I...I wouldn't know how she is anymore, would I?"

"It's Mem's fault," Obedience pipes up. "She speaks to spirits in the night. She brought the witch!"

"She *is* the witch," Humility says.

"Hold thy tongues," Thomas warns. "Such accusations are serious, and your childish minds cannot comprehend what you say."

"I am no witch," Mem says to the other girls. "Mine Uncle is the witch. He killed my mother, and he kills these women now."

"*What?*" Abel says. His face fills with red, and I swear he'd strike Mem if I didn't stand between them.

"Mem," I hiss. At once I'm horrified and—curious. Horrified that, yes, Mem knows the secret I always meant to keep, and that she somehow learned it from a spirit. But curious, too, because...doesn't it fit? I know of only one murderer in this village.

But, no. He's in jail. It's impossible.

Unless he *is* a witch.

"We don't even know if Tace spoke truth," Thomas says, tired.

But, in that moment, the meeting house door flies open again, and a parishioner shouts, "The bewitched girl speaks true! A dead woman! Mercy Jones!"

Abel swings to action, storming toward the door. Kit, Thomas, and I follow, Mem still latched to my hand. Abel pushes through the crowded villagers spilling around the side of the meeting house, toward the thicker gathering at the back.

"Move aside, move aside!" Abel shoves shoulders and arms and clears a path. Kit grabs my hand and we sneak through in his wake. Thomas trails, offering quick apologies to the people we brush aside.

Sure enough, there's Mercy Jones, only...I might not have recognized her had I not known. Her face is drenched in what must be her own blood, and her neck is shredded meat, skin and tendons and throat a mangled, pink mess. The stench is iron and rot together, the snow and cold dulling the smell only a little.

A wolf, I think. A rabid wolf. No human could do this.

But then, the constable, knelt at her side, turns her right hand over. Carved clumsily into the palm is a crude skull, the blood a thin crust at the cuts.

"She hath been marked for the Devil," Walsh says, standing quickly. "Just like Baxter, then." He eyes the reverend. "I'll have to question your daughter, you know."

"Aye," Reverend Wilson says faintly. "Of course." He looks up. "You'll be fair to her. She rejected the Devil's bargain. You heard her, she refused to sign the book."

"Aye, I'll be fair enough." He cuts his eyes to the five of us, staring gape-mouthed at the corpse. "Get you gone. What business have you here?"

"You've accused mine father," Abel says, cutting his gaze to the constable. "It behooves me to see what mess you think he's in."

Walsh grins slowly. "Ah. Abel Ashe. I didn't realize you had returned. Your cousin had little to offer in payment for your father's confinement. Pray, did you have a good haul at trapping?"

"Nay," Abel says. "My party was struck down with the pox. I'm afraid you'll find little to take from me, sir."

"We'll see." Walsh looks briefly at me, his smile going small, secret. I tuck myself closer to Kit's side, our fingers twining.

"And who's this rare beauty?" Walsh says, nodding to Kit.

"Katherine," Kit says, her voice flat but her eyes direct. "And you are…?"

The constable turns a sickly shade between purple and red. "You should learn to address your betters as such, girl."

"My apologies. I suppose I forgot myself."

I begin to tug her away. Mem, still secure in my other hand, eagerly follows. We weave back through the crowd. I don't know or care if Abel and Thomas follow. I only want to get away from the body, and get Kit away from Walsh, and to take Mem home.

Home. What is that, anymore? The house? A mere building? How long will that even last? The constable has made it clear he wants more from us. Abel has naught to give. We may lose everything now.

Thomas weaves out of the crowd and joins us where we've stopped, at the edge of the forest, where it's quiet, cool.

"I'm sorry," he says. "That wasn't a sight for ladies."

"That wasn't a sight for anybody," Kit says. "You're a bit pale yourself, Thomas."

He smiles. "You certainly know how to handle yourself. I've never seen someone stand up to the constable."

"He annoyed me," she says. She seems to realize, then, that she's still holding my hand, and she quickly disengages. "Anyway. I don't like when men leer at me while threatening to take my friend's property. It's rude."

"They ought to add that to the manners books," Thomas says.

"They *should.*"

"Can I walk you home?" Thomas says, looking between us. "You are right, of course. This sight is a bit much for me as well."

I look down at Mem. "What about...?"

"We'll leave her with my mother."

"No!" Mem tugs on my hand. "Liv, you heard Obedience and Humility. They think I'm a witch, but I'm not. I only listened to the Blue Lady."

"I know, Mem, I know." I rub my forehead and glance at Thomas. "Your mother puts no stock in such tales, does she? She won't..." I look at the constable, now trying to direct the crowd away from the body.

"Of course not," Thomas says. "Children make up stories all the time. She knows that."

"I want to go home," Mem says.

"Soon," I promise, kneeling to look her in the eye. "After all this has settled, I'll talk to Goody Wilson. I promise."

Mem leans close and whispers in my ear, "Hurry, then. There's not much time left."

I startle and lean back, but Mem only smiles up at Thomas. "I'm ready now."

Thomas takes her hand and leads her back to the meeting house. I rise, meet Kit's eye.

"What's wrong?" she asks.

"I...suppose we're running out of time."

Kit and I follow Thomas back to my house, quiet but for the crunch of snow beneath our shoes. I have never left a meeting so early—usually, the sermon drags on for hours, then takes up again after lunch. Now, my Sunday is open and mysterious. It feels wrong, and that, somehow, is thrilling.

"I should be with my family," Thomas says at the gate, in a way that suggests he'd really rather not.

"You should," I tell him. "Kit and I will be fine." I push the gate wide, let Kit pass. "Tace is in our prayers."

He nods. Doesn't move.

"Go, Thomas. Be with your sister."

I let go of the gate, only to find my hand captured in Thomas's. His hands are slender, long, but the grip is total and strong.

"I do need to speak with you," he says quietly. "I know my mind should be elsewhere now, but..."

Cold creeps down my face. "You don't have to... What I mean is... Thomas, you don't—there's nothing to explain."

"There's everything to explain," he says. "How I left, it was...cowardly."

"I understood," I say. "I still do. I'm...well aware of my station, and yours. And what I did—"

"What *you* did?"

"I led you into sin," I say quietly, grateful that Kit has gone on to the house. She'd likely slap me for saying such, but she's not here, and it's the truth as I've always known it.

Thomas blinks at me. "Liv. Darling, do you hear yourself when you speak?"

"I...yes?"

"You—" He drags his hand down his face and blinks rapidly a few times more. "You blame yourself for everything. You never believe you're good enough, or quiet enough, or polite enough."

"Thomas," I say, a warning in my tone.

"No. I'm going to say it, because you need to hear it. Liv, you're probably the only truly righteous person in this godforsaken village."

"Thomas!"

"You berate yourself for every misstep." He cups my face in his palms. "And it's because you truly love the Lord, and worship him. You're good, Deliverance. You're..."

His words fail, and it's just as well. He kisses me. There is none of the clumsy hesitation of our youth, or the terrified fumbling of our last encounter. He presses his lips to mine and flicks his tongue between my teeth.

My body folds to his. His hands grip my waist and he presses his desire against me. I gasp, and the spell of our kiss shatters.

"I'm sorry," he breathes. "I...I'm afraid I'm still learning to behave myself around you." He gives me a weak smile that topples my resistance. I throw my arms around his neck and press my watering eyes shut.

"I thought you hated me," I say.

He holds me tightly to his chest. "I hated myself. I've only ever loved you." He pulls back just enough to kiss my cheek. "Marry me."

I lean back in his arms. "W-what?"

He grins. "Marry me, Liv."

For whatever reason, I turn my head. A figure flashes away from the single window in our sorry house. Kit. Watching our exchange? Had she seen all that?

Why does the idea bother me so?

I turn back to Thomas. "Well, you'll have to ask my uncle. Or...Abel, now, I suppose."

He slides a finger along my jawline, drawing a shudder from me. "And if they're agreeable?"

"Obviously yes," I say, blushing. All the cold in my body has been replaced by the old, familiar fire Thomas always left in me.

Thomas kisses me again, softer now. I feel I might fall through the world, adrift on desire and love, until a cracked, halting voice interrupts.

"Get thee gone."

Thomas and I leap apart. Beaky sits on the gatepost, glaring between us.

"Did that bird...just speak?" Thomas asks.

"No," I say. "Can't have."

"God save the king," Beaky squawks. Damned royalist betrayer.

"Of course," I say, "I've heard it said crows can, ah, mimic human speech."

"Fascinating," Thomas says. He reaches out to touch Beaky, who returns the gesture with a snap from his beak. Thomas barely pulls away in time.

"Get thee gone," Beaky repeats.

"I'm glad I don't need his approval," Thomas says. He kisses my cheek. "I should return to my family. We'll speak tomorrow?"

"Of course," I say.

I watch him walk back down the lane until Beaky snaps at my hand.

"Ow! What?" I stare at the bird. "What?"

"William the Third," he says, and flies off.

"Hell beast," I mutter. I let myself through the gate and into the house. Beast bounds up to me, delighted to find me home so early. He slobbers kisses on my cheeks.

I find Kit about the kitchen, furiously stirring a vat of lye.

"It's the Sabbath," I tell her. "We can't do work."

"I like work. And I'm not a Puritan. I can do whatever I damn well please."

I shake my head. "What's gotten into you?"

"Nothing. I'm splendid. You look pleased."

I touch my still-warm cheeks. "Oh. Thomas and I...we sorted things out, I suppose."

"Lovely." She bangs her stirring spoon against the rim of the pot, flinging hot lye. "He seems charming."

"He's—"

"Someone's killing these women."

My mouth pops open. "You don't think they're witches?"

"No." She sets the spoon aside. "And if they were, then what? The Devil's killing his own minions? No, somebody's taken to slaughtering women." Her jaw tightens. "And he started with Lizzy."

I think back to Lizzy's body, its cold, pale perfection on the snow. There were no wounds. Only later, when I returned, was her skin torn, and that was the work of scavengers. All signs point to the cold killing her.

Except for that mark upon her hand—the same one found on all the other women.

"We need to look at her body," Kit says at last. My jaw drops. "I know, I know. But we need an idea of what happened, don't we? I do. I can't just rest here never knowing what happened to her." She clenches her jaw. "And if she was killed, maybe—maybe her body will help us know how. Or who's doing this."

"Kit, I—I'm sorry. But the scavengers got to her. I don't know what could be left—"

"There's something," she says, brushing past me to don her cloak. "And I mean to find it."

"It's the Sabbath," I remind her, weakly.

"Hang the Sabbath! There's a murderer loose, killing women like me, and I really can't abide your goddamned rules right now, Liv."

My mouth snaps shut. I nod. "Right. Fine. Shovel's in the shed."

She tears off her borrowed coif and tosses her braid. "Thanks."

She starts toward the door. I should let her go. I *have* to let her go. But I'm already following her, and Beast is thumping his tail at the prospect of a new adventure.

"Wait," I say. "I'm coming."

Kit pauses in the doorway, smiles. "Look at you, Deliverance. Breaking Sabbath." Beaky alights to her shoulder and eyes me.

"God save the king."

"Shut it," I tell him.

The ice is thick, the dirt thin. The shovel breaks through the meager grave, and before long, we're staring down at Lizzy's mangled neck, her blue face. Kit brushes dirt and ice away from the face. Her fingers linger a moment on a red curl laid against Lizzy's cheek.

"I...I almost didn't believe it. Until now." She takes a shaking breath. "When I kept coming here, there was a part of me that thought she wasn't truly down there. I thought...it was a cruel joke. Because how can she be gone?"

She brings a hand to her mouth and tries to bury her sobbing. But it's useless, and she cries, and I can't help it. I kneel beside her and wrap her in my arms. Soon my collar is damp, chilling my skin in the deep cold, but I can't make myself care. Not with Kit breaking. Not in this terrible, mournful place. Beast whines and lays on his stomach before the grave, tail twitching sadly.

Eventually, the tears stop. Kit draws herself up and reaches again for Lizzy. She smooths the dead girl's curls, fixes her collar around the torn neck. She's strangely comfortable with the body, this most grim *memento mori*. She brushes her fingers over Lizzy's eyelids, but they're hard, forced open above their dull, sunken contents. Even so, she only drops her hand into her lap.

"Would it...would it help if we got her a proper burial?" I ask. "In the cemetery?"

"Nay." Kit shakes her head. "Lizzy loved the woods. Obviously, she'd have preferred to live in them, but if she had to die anywhere..." She sighs. "You may be right. She died of cold and then the wolves...well. There's nothing to say she was killed." She pauses. "Besides, they all died differently."

This is true. Lizzy was merely dead on the forest floor, partially frozen. Goody Baxter, by all accounts, died of drink and the cold she could no longer feel as she slept outside. Her throat was torn, but that could very well have been the work of scavengers after the fact.

Mercy's death could very well have been an animal attack, her throat ripped wide as though worked by jaws. Only the skull carved into her palm gave any hint that a human hand had touched her.

Maybe Mercy did it to herself—maybe she was a witch after all, and Goody Baxter, too. Maybe these women are dead thanks to their own mishandling of deadly powers.

But I knew Mercy. She was a grim girl, given to piety. She was solemn and good and loved God. I can't picture her signing her name in the Devil's book. She'd have died before that happened.

And her body, the placement behind the meeting house…it seemed purposeful. As though she had been tossed there for us to discover just as Tace fell into her trance.

The marks on the women's hands are the only definitive link.

"There was one thing," I say. "That I noticed before. On her hand."

Kit passes me the shovel. "I can't."

So, I dig. Kit wanders off to the edge of the clearing, Beast keeping her company, and I break the ice around Lizzy's body until I've uncovered her right arm. I tug the stiff limb free of the grasping dirt and turn her palm up.

"Kit?"

She shuffles back to the grave and looks over my shoulder.

"Did Lizzy have this before?" I ask.

I hold up her white, bloodless hand. The strange, grinning skull, so like our grave markers. *Remember you will die.*

Kit shakes her head. "Nay. We were only branded here." She touches her forehead. "And that's...that's been cut."

"The other women had them, too," I say. "Good Baxter and Mercy Jones."

She drops to her knees. "She was killed. Killed and marked."

"I saw prints," I say, remembering. "When I came back to bury her. Cloven prints, just like the ones we saw."

"So, the Devil did this?" Kit shakes her head. "Nay. This is the work of a man. And a man can be killed."

She shoots to her feet, and I realize too late that she means to hunt the creature down right now. She breaks through the trees, and I scramble after her, leaving Lizzy half-unburied behind me.

"Kit, stop! Wait! Where you going?"

"To my camp, so I can get my crossbow, so I can put a bloody arrow in whoever did this."

"Kit!" I grab her shoulder, but she shoves me away. My back hits a tree, and I'm too shocked to say anything. I only watch her, her shoulders shaking, her jaw trembling.

"We were supposed to have a life!" she screams at last, and all the pain is there in her voice. Raw as torn flesh and sheer as ice. "We were supposed to be happy. We did what they wanted and left. And all we wanted, all we dared do, was love each other. Why..." She drags in a hard breath. "Why don't we get happy endings?"

Her words cut into me, bury themselves to the hilt in my heart. And then I'm saying, "You still can," and the contempt that twists her beautiful face lances me.

"I'm not sure if you've noticed, but women like me and Lizzy are in short supply around here."

"That's not...strictly true," I say, blushing for a reason I don't care to examine.

She shakes her head. "Right, so, I should find myself a replacement? Is that what you did when your Thomas abandoned you?"

"*Kit.*"

"You moped around, wishing him back, didn't you? And he *left.* Lizzy was taken from me. And you got your perfect ending after all, so don't preach to me about finding someone else."

I stare at her, dumb and hurt. At last, all my addled mind finds for words is, "You were listening."

She rolls her eyes.

I take a step closer to her. "I know you're hurting. Believe me. I've lost people, too. I know what it's like to wake up empty, with a pain that can't go away no matter what you do. I live with ghosts. I live with guilt. I hate the world. Sometimes I think I hate God. But that...that would be too easy. To be able to blame him. Sometimes I think...he's not even there. That the world is ruined and cruel and stupid because there's nothing more to it. And that makes the pain even worse."

She flicks her eyes to me, and I see they're shining.

"So, yes," I say. "I know. And you can scream and claw at the world for as long as you need to. But don't take it out on me."

She twists her hands together, eyes fixed on the ground. At last, she says, "I'm sorry. Lizzy always told me I could be bullheaded when I was upset."

"She was quite right about that. But your apology is accepted."

She nods. I look down. She apologized, but there's still a tension between us, too thick for the knife of my acceptance. I stir my mind, trying to find something to say.

I'm saved from needing to come up with something by the snap of a branch nearby. Beast barks, his voice sharp between the trees. We weave through the woods toward his barking and find him on the main path, tail stiff, head low, a snarl ripping through his chest.

I turn slowly toward the thing that holds his gaze, but there's nothing. At least, nothing immediately obvious. I creep forward and see, however, the fresh cloven prints in the ice, leading deeper into the forest.

"Goddamn Devil," Kit says, and I catch her around the waist before she can storm off.

"Don't," I say. "We have no idea what that thing is, what it can do."

"Reckon it can bleed," she snarls.

"Kit!" I grab hold of her shoulders and look her in the eye. "I'm not losing you to this."

Her mouth opens and shuts. "Am I yours to lose, Deliverance?"

"I—you know what I mean."

"I don't, no."

I step back, letting my hands fall away. "We should get back to the house."

"Right." She nods, but her eyes drift back to the path. I know she won't let this go, not until she's avenged Lizzy.

But I won't let her go. Not if I can stop her.

26. Slaughter

I sleep better with Kit here. But still my ghost comes.

Tonight, she sits in the old broken-legged chair shoved into the corner of our loft. She doesn't rise, doesn't approach. She seems tired, too.

"Deliver me," she says.

"How?" I whisper. But I blink, and she's gone. I shut my eyes and whisper prayers that I'm not sure rise past my lips. I used to think of God as someone sitting before me on a throne, hearing my prayers as they came. But now, the words are dead on my lips. Nobody's listening. No one—

A distressed bleat stops my prayers. The sound comes from the back of the house. The barn?

I fly from bed, and Beast is at my heels. I forget my cloak in my haste and rush into the frozen night in only my shift. My bare feet slip on a patch of ice worn smooth in the path, but I right myself and careen around the back of the house. The small barn where the goats sleep stands open, lantern light spilling an orange glow across the hay.

I run toward it, but slip again at the entrance, something warm and thick and damp tripping up my feet this time. I push myself up and find my shift stained red, my hands, the ends of my loose hair—all dipped in the warm blood soaking into the hay.

I look into the barn only long enough to know for certain that the goats are dead, that this is their blood. And then I shut my eyes and hope to forget what I've seen—the ruined bodies, the empty eyes, the way flesh looks when it's opened.

The smell hits my panicked brain at last, and I add a stream of vomit to the gore. The iron and meat stench permeates everything, and not even the cold open air is enough to dispel it. I want to move, but I can't. It's the way I am when faced with my ghost. Frozen.

Someone, finally, pulls me back. I collapse into Kit's arms. She at least took the time to put on a cloak and shoes.

Beast edges toward the barn, then stops. He sits on his haunches and lets out a long howl. I realize I'm crying, too.

"Liv?" Kit smooths my hair as I bury my face in her neck. "It's okay, Liv. Hold on."

And then Abel is there, swearing at the night and hauling Beast back. He ushers us away, back to the house, and suddenly I'm sitting before a blazing fire, blanket over my shoulders, Beast nestled on one side, Kit on the other. She hands me a bowl of broth and I sip at it, feeling finally crawling back into my limbs.

"Who would do this?" I say at last.

"Our Devil, I think." Kit looks at me. "Who do you think he is? Really?"

"I used to think my uncle. He's the only killer I know. But...he wouldn't slaughter his own goats."

"And he's in jail."

"He could slip out. If he's actually a witch."

Kit's smile is small. "Do you believe he is?"

"Nay." I take another sip of broth. "A man needn't be a witch to be cruel."

"A man also needn't be a witch to slip from jail." Kit frowns. "It happened all the time back in Ipswich. The chains are loose, or the cuffs too large. People can just get up and walk away."

I think of our little jail, removed a ways from the village. It's a meager building, stone and squat and untended unless the constable goes there to check on the prisoners. And we've so infrequently had prisoners. Is the jail even fit to hold someone?

"I need to clean this blood off," I say, handing the broth back to Kit. I doubt my little washbasin will be enough, and I have a notion to go dunk myself in the river, were it not so deadly cold. "In the morning...what say you we investigate?"

"What, visit the jail?" Kit grins. "I knew I liked you, Deliverance Ashe."

Red water, smelling of old coins, fills my washbasin when I'm done. I run a cloth down my face and neck, trying to scrub away not only the water, but the slick feeling of the blood on my skin. Dawn creeps between the trees, threatening daybreak. I'm not ready, and though my sleep is haunted, I only want to fall back into bed.

Kit and Abel's voices drift below, low but tense. I wonder what my cousin thinks of this latest horror, if he sees the supernatural or suspects a real flesh-and-blood villain.

I descend from the loft to find Kit boiling oats for our breakfast. Abel paces before the fire, brow creased.

"I'll have to tell the constable. It's a crime. He'll investigate."

He's talking more to himself than either of us, but I understand the debate. He wonders if the constable will see this slaughter as further proof of my uncle's guilt, of dark things swirling around our forgotten farm. His desire to find who's responsible is dulled by that possibility.

"The constable won't help," I say. "He'll only find a way to use it against us."

Abel's steps pause. "Perhaps. But what other recourse is there?"

"None," I say. "There's none. We've lost our goats. But we'll lose worse if we involve him."

"You may not have a choice," Kit says, her eyes on the window. I follow her gaze, and sure enough, Constable Walsh pulls his cart up to the gate.

"I'll deal with this," Abel says, storming out the door, forgetting his coat on the way. I turn to Kit.

"What do we do?"

She takes the boiling oats off the stove and sets them on the table. "Is hiding an option? Running away?"

I smile. "That sounds almost delightful, given the alternative."

"Say the word," she says, and my stomach fills with quivering light. She goes to the window and peers out. "Your future husband is here."

"What?" My mind staggers drunkenly for a moment before I remember: Thomas. He proposed.

I join Kit at the window. Thomas rides up on a horse and halts his steed beside the constable's cart. He dismounts, and the three men seem to argue. The constable gestures at the house, and Abel shakes his head. Walsh blusters and flings his hands. Finally—uninvited, I have to assume—he bursts through the gate and stomps toward the house.

Kit and I peel away from the window, and a moment later, Walsh barges in, his red-rimmed eyes fixed on me.

"Your cousin claims he has not payment for his father's expenses."

"It's true, sir," I say. "We've suffered...unexpected losses."

"Oh, I've no doubt. Mischievous things are about. That's what happens, isn't it, when witches roam free?"

"Sir?" I say, and unconsciously back into Kit. She weaves her hand into mine.

"Your *troubles*," Walsh says, sneering, "are truly heartbreaking. But mine are practical. And, seeing as how Master Abel cannot pay with coin or good..." He grins. "I suppose you'll have to do."

He grabs me by the elbow and drags me forward, out of Kit's grip. He's got me over the threshold and halfway up the path when Thomas and Abel intercept him.

"What the *hell* are you doing?" Abel asks.

"Taking my due," Walsh says. "If you cannot pay for your father's expenses, I'll have myself a new servant to make it worth my while."

"Unhand me," I say with a cold confidence I don't feel.

"Your family owes me a debt, and you are the only thing worth taking anymore."

"You can't have her," Thomas says.

"Out of my way," Walsh snarls.

But Thomas doesn't move. He steps toward the constable. Thomas is slight, and at least half a foot shorter than the hulking man, but the constable flinches back. There's something sharp and cold in Thomas's blue eyes. In his voice, there is a dagger.

"Unhand her, now, or else I'll see you banished."

The constable chuffs a weak laugh. "You've no authority—"

"I've more than you, Walsh. I know my father finds your fervor for witchery suspect. It would hardly take more than a suggestion from me to convince him you've gone mad with power. In fact, I've heard it said that those who see witches most are likely perpetrators themselves."

The constable's already ruddy face blooms, patchy with rage. "If you mean to suggest—"

"I do indeed. Unless you take your hand off my future wife."

Walsh flings me forward, right into Thomas's waiting arms. I wilt against him and twine my fingers in his.

"I suppose congratulations are in order," Walsh sneers. "Forgive me, young minister. I was unaware you had declared your intentions." He cuts a glance at me. "I confess, I assumed you'd found better in Boston."

"Leave," Thomas says.

I turn in Thomas's arms. Just beyond the constable is Kit, standing with Beast by her side. She's holding a shovel as though she meant to bash the constable's head in. And, God, I wish she would.

Walsh presses himself close to Abel. "You owe me a great deal of money, boy. And I will find a way to take it."

"Of course." Abel smiles. "Good day, Constable."

Walsh shoves Abel aside and huffs back to his cart. Nobody moves or says a word until the rattle of his wheels fades down the road.

"Well, Thomas," Abel says sternly, though he's smiling. "You failed to inform me you had asked for my cousin's hand. Though I can't say I'm surprised."

Thomas who, a moment ago, had been a fearsome thing, flushes pink and casts his eyes down. "I—forgive me, Abel, I meant to—"

"I approve, of course." Abel claps his friend on the shoulder. "We'll celebrate, yes? Tonight?"

Thomas grins. "Indeed. Come to the parsonage for supper. My mother will be delighted to host you." Thomas looks over to Kit, who is still brandishing the shovel as though she means to injure someone. "You'll come as well, won't you, Kit?"

"I..." At last, she lowers the shovel. "I've had enough excitement for one day, I'm afraid. Besides, someone ought to keep an eye on things."

She's right. After the goats, and the constable's threats, leaving the house unattended seems unwise. We shouldn't even be celebrating. Our engagement now feels more like a trick, a convenient way to keep the constable from binding me as his servant. It's hardly the joyous day I imagined.

Thomas nods to Kit. "A wise idea. And I thank you, Kit. I'm glad my Liv has a friend such as you."

She nods, a quick jerk of the chin, and then she's gone, propping the shovel beside the house and going around to the back.

I begin to pull out of Thomas's embrace, some compulsion drawing me toward Kit. But he captures my hand and tugs me back, a gentle smile on his lips.

"I'll see you this evening? I ought to go tell my parents of our plans."

"Aye." I nod. He kisses my forehead, chaste and polite.

He wanders off, back up the path, through the gate.

I have the strangest thought, that my future was once a lot of threads, made into nothing but pure potential. And now...those threads have woven, tightened, and bound me to Thomas. The thing I always wanted and expected.

And yet, as I turn and go into the house, I feel those other futures that might have been seams in my life unweave and leave me frayed.

Kit?"

I hurry around the house and check the paddock, grimly empty this morning. But she's not here. I quickly tend to the chickens clucking their hunger, my stomach sinking. Where can she have gone?

Back at the front of the house, I find Beast waiting for me, wagging his tail. He darts toward the gate, drawing my eyes up to the gatepost, and Beaky perched upon it.

"Oh, God, grant me strength," I mutter, and start toward him.

The bird eyes me a moment, suspicious.

"Well?" I say. "What have you to say? More royalist propaganda?"

"This way," he says, and takes flight. He moves, sleek and black, toward the forest.

I look back at the house, but Abel isn't in sight. I doubt he'll notice my absence. He has much to rejoice, now. I'll be wed to a good family and my future secured. With Mem bound out, he'll only have himself to worry over.

I follow Beaky, keeping my eyes trained to his shadowy body as he flies. He lands every so often to glare back at me.

"Oh, sorry, am I too slow for you?"

"This way," is all he says, though I swear with a touch of impatience.

He takes me off the path, along a little trail stamped smooth by the feet of animals. I walk slowly, awkwardly in the tight space. Beast's nose bumps my ankles as we go.

Finally, Beaky swoops to land on a neatly aligned tent of branches and sticks, packed with mud and now sprinkled with snow. Kit sits just outside the structure, before a small fire, crossbow in her lap.

"Bad Beaky," she says, with no conviction.

"Sorry," I say. "He told me to follow."

"Aye. He thinks I need company. What I need are more arrows." She checks the sight on the crossbow, aiming it blessedly away from me.

"You...you didn't come here to hunt the Devil, did you?"

"Nothing better to do."

I sit beside her on the cold ground. "Would you like to come with us this evening? To the parish?"

"I would rather mine eyes be gouged out and fed to a cat, Deliverance."

I frown. "You dislike Thomas?"

"No. He's sensible and dull. Your perfect match."

I open my mouth, ready to chastise her, but she tosses the crossbow away. It clatters on the frozen ground.

"You don't need to say it," she says. "I'm being cruel again. I just..." She pinches the skin between her brows. "I would like to finish this, Liv. Find this Devil, make him pay his due, and be on my way."

"On your way?" Alarm flitters in my chest. "Where will you go?"

"I'll find my way to Pennsylvania. There's a large community of Friends there now. I'll be safe." She touches the mark on her forehead. "More so than with your lot."

"I...shall be sad to see you go."

"Think then of how much happier I'll be, away from Puritans. Away from this wilderness." She barely smiles. "Away from Devils who walk the world."

"I wouldn't let anything happen to you."

"Aye. If you keep me as safely as you keep your own heart, there will never be another mark on me."

I bristle. "What is the meaning of your talk?"

"Your face," Kit says, "when they talked of your future with Thomas. You looked not like a bride, but a woman attending her own funeral."

"You said you'd stop being cruel."

"I'm trying to be kind." She shrugs. "I think it's possible to love someone and not want to be possessed by them."

"Thomas does not own me."

"Nay, he doesn't. Keep it that way." She reaches again for her crossbow. "I do hope you're happy."

"I'm not," I say. My body moves without my mind's prodding, drawing me into her sphere. Our lips meet, clumsily at first, slipping and searching, but then, in a moment, there's warmth, and we fit, we go together like we've been waiting for one another. Her breath is warm, but her lips are cold. Her fingers lift to curl around my neck, and my pulse beats in her palm, rapid and scared but still so overjoyed.

She pulls away before I'm ready to give her up, color high in her cheeks, eyes unfocused and gleaming.

"Well. You *are* full of surprises."

"I'm...sorry, I...I shouldn't have—" But Kit closes her hand over mine before I can finish.

"Liv, you're beautiful and brilliant. Infuriating, too. But...I feel like I'm betraying her. She's barely gone." She nearly smiles. "But can I be honest? When the preacher's son asked for your hand, I wanted to chop his off."

A startled laugh cracks from my pulsing throat.

"I need time," she says, more softly, "and I have to assume you do as well?"

"Aye." I nod. "I don't...I love Thomas, but...the idea of marriage is suddenly...a bit horrible, somehow? I don't know." I look down at my hands. I've twisted them together, clutching myself. "And I like you an inordinate lot."

She grins. "Then let's say someday, maybe."

"Someday, maybe." I look out across the trees. The forest at once seems infinite and compact, endless and yet cloistered. Yet I don't feel stifled here. The closeness of the trees feels like an embrace. The leaves rattle like a skitter of laughter. Branches bend like smiles. And I could swear, in this moment, the wind sighs, *Safe. You're safe.*

"We could run away," I say. "See if the world is bigger elsewhere."

"England." Kit smiles. "I've wanted to go back to England since I lost my parents. We came here because my father was looking for—I don't know, freedom? But we don't belong here. The land isn't ours, and it knows it. Even Pennsylvania, I think, will stifle. I want a city. You can disappear in a city. Sink into the bones of a street and stay there. That's what Lizzy and I meant to do. We were going to sneak aboard a ship bound for London. I was going to hear a play, like my grandmother talked about."

"London, then." I take her hand, squeeze it. "Someday, maybe."

She grins. "Have you ever been?"

"We lived there when I was very young. But I don't remember it well. I was too young when we left for Boston."

"You'll love it. It smells, mind, but once your nose has dulled to it, the city is incredible. The churches, Liv—they're gorgeous. Oh, and the palace. I don't know why we ever left."

I remember by own family's reasons. My father raging about the ousting of Cromwell, the newly minted Charles the Second and the return of the monarchy. That all happened long before I was born, but it seeped into my childhood. Defined it. And when I was too young to know what it meant, my father said we were only leaving a country that didn't love us.

And I loved Boston. I loved that my parents were finally happy. I didn't know what it meant to be there, that we'd forced other people away, slaughtered those who had ancient claim to the land. And when I was old enough to know that, I had to believe God wanted us there.

Now, I look around at the forest, the trees chattering in the wind, brief flurries of snow striking music against the leaves.

It's beautiful. But it's not ours. The wilderness belongs to itself. And it seems it's grown teeth to chew us up, and claws to defend itself.

The forest has always seemed a thing looming at the edge of the village, dark of intent and frightful. But our village, our wattle and daub homes, our brooding meeting house and sinking jail—those things don't belong. They sit as a scar upon the wilderness's expanse. We've settled like a fly on sweet flesh. Sometimes, I expect we'll be flicked away as easily.

"Why Maine?" Kit says, breaking me from my trance. I look over at her, and I don't know how I didn't realize sooner. She's beautiful, dark hair falling loose from her braid, pale skin stained with a cold flush. Lips chapped, eyes bright.

"My uncle wanted to hide from the law, I think. Boston was organized. Maine is wild. He knew of this village, and they allowed him to settle here without many questions."

"Do you think he could be the killer?"

"Aye. He killed my parents, didn't he?" I rest my chin on my knees. "But I don't know how to prove he's doing this."

"We investigate, of course." She smiles. "You promised me a trip to the jail, no?" She rises and holds out her hands for me. I let her haul me to my feet, and she surprises me with a kiss on the cheek.

"Lead the way, Deliverance."

I lead Kit through the forest, giving the village a berth. I don't need anyone seeing what we're up to. If we're caught, I'll say I only hoped to visit my uncle. But even that...knowing what he's been accused of, the villagers might then think me a witch.

I step out of the forest on the village's eastern edge, past the meeting house and the scattered homes. The path here is thin, barely wide enough for a horse cart. People only go this way for one purpose, and then, in shackles, in the back of the constable's cart.

We walk the path silently, our hands clasped. Beast stays close to my side as though nervous, but also protective. He won't let anything befall me.

"There," I say, nodding. Kit stalls in the path.

"That's it?"

The building off to the side of the path juts from the forest like a tooth, its roof tapering and tearing into the branches above it. The building itself is a square of brick, worn by the weather and dark with stains. A single window, barred with iron, looks out. The door, too, is iron, and seems sturdy enough to my untrained eye.

A quiet sorrow hangs over the place, like the misery within bleeds onto the air and crawls through the bars. I expected to hear something—shuffling or moaning or cursing. But the jail is silent, the air dense with the lost hopes of those within.

"I can look," Kit offers, but I shake my head.

"We go together," I say.

Hand-in-hand, we walk to the window. I have to get up on my toes to see inside, the bars cool against my fingers as I tug myself up to peer into the dank cell.

The smell hits me, waste like acid and rot together on the air, soaking into the hay spread like a pathetic covering over the ground. Goody Nash is who I see first, her ankles bound in shackles stamped to the wall. She's muttering, her words barely audible over the eager buzzing of flies finding warmth and sustenance from the refuse strewn across the hay. She glances up, barely acknowledging us before tipping her head back down.

"You've a visitor," she grumbles.

My eyes follow her weak gaze to a huddle of dirty clothes farther along the curved wall. Uncle Ezra, shackled at the ankles, too, lays along the bend of the wall. His beard is dirty, and I spy fleas jumping off his skin, blurring the air around him. He pushes himself up onto an elbow and glares at Goody Nash.

"Silence, she-devil. I'll fall not for your tricks."

"Oh, just look at the goddamn window," Goody Nash says.

Uncle turns his eyes carefully toward the barred window. His face curls when he meets my gaze.

"Come to gawk at your uncle, reduced so low?"

"Nay, Uncle. I've come to ask you—"

"This is your doing. You sent that specter to me. You are the only true witch among us."

A shudder trips down my spine. "You truly communed with a specter, then?"

"Aye, because it confronted me! Your whore mother never knew when to keep silent."

Anger boils in my gut and finds its way up my throat. "Hold thy tongue, Uncle. You are in no position to accuse a godly woman of sin when you are lying in your own shit."

Kit grins. "I like you more and more, Liv."

"If my mother visited you," I say, relentless now, "it is because you murdered her before my eyes. Deny it not," I snap when he opens his sore-encrusted mouth. "I remember. You thought a girl my age would forget, that the terror would erase my memory? But I've thought of what you did daily. There is no forgiveness for murder."

"A brave speech," my uncle growls, "from a stupid girl. Your mother deserved what befell her, and your father, too. They were not godly. They meant only to live a life of pleasure, not of devotion. Do you know, Deliverance, that your *godly* mother longed to return to England? Aye, she wanted to be under the rule of a damned king, faithful to a corrupt church, so she might have the comforts of the world. She meant to turn you and your sister into little she-devils. I spared you that. Now, tell me again how she was a righteous woman."

"Wanting a good life is no sin," I say. "Murder, now..." I shake my head. "This is all I needed to hear. Tell me, Uncle, how do you do it? Do you slip your bonds in the night to kill these other women? Does the Devil help you? And why?" I'm angry now, boiling, and I can't stop. "Do you only like to hurt? Does it make you feel *righteous*?"

"What the devil are thou talking about?"

"Goody Baxter! Mercy Jones! And Lizzy, too—the girl in the forest? Don't deny it. You killed them all, didn't you?"

"You see the shackles about my legs, girl? Do you think I managed to slip away from here?"

"You might have."

"Nay, if only that were true," Goody Nash says now, looking up. "I might have reprieve of his presence, then. Alas, he's been here all the time I have."

Goody Nash arrived at the jail after my uncle's arrest, but before Mercy's murder. That still doesn't prove anything. He might have bewitched her. He might have slipped away with magic or the Devil's hand.

"Are you done here, girl?" Uncle lays his head back in the filthy hay. "This place is rather more pleasant without your presence."

Kit tugs at my arm, guiding me away from the window. My fingers slip from the bars.

"I don't know, Liv. It seems secure enough. And Goody Nash—"

"He could have still done it. With the Devil to guide him—"

"Liv..." But Kit doesn't say anything more. I know she doesn't believe. But I do, at least a little. Maybe my faith in God is wavering, but devils I know to be real.

What else explains such darkness in the world?

Cruelty, my mind whispers. Uncle killed my parents believing he was doing righteous work. He needed no Devil to whisper to him, then. Only his own hate.

"There must be something else," I say. "Some evidence."

Kit raises one eyebrow. "On the bodies, you mean?"

My face blanches, leaving me colder than the iced air ever could. "Perhaps."

"Would Goody Baxter and Mercy..." She pauses. "Be in the ground yet?"

They couldn't be. The land is too frozen, the cemetery's ground impossible to break. I wonder if they'll even bother for poor Goody Baxter, if anyone will carve her a headstone or inscribe the dates of her life.

I shake my head.

"Where might they be, then?"

I wince. "There's a dead house, out by the cemetery. They've probably been left there."

"All right." Kit smooths down her petticoat. "And where's the cemetery?"

"You can't be serious."

"I'd like a closer look at these markings, personally. Somebody means to make this village think the Devil has come. I say a man is doing this, and I'd like to know why, before I take his heart from his chest."

I nod back toward the village. "There's a path beyond the parsonage."

"All right, then." Kit turns on her heel and stalks away. Beast nudges me with his wet nose, a look of joy on his ragged face.

"You like these adventures too much," I say, scratching his ears.

Branches heavy with snow and the clinging threads of dead leaves give way to an open space north of the village, a clearing repurposed to make a small cemetery. A low gate is slung around the area, and a few headstones peek from the snow, the grinning skulls and empty-eyed skeletons peering through the ice.

These headstones used to terrify me, the way the dead faces seemed to mock the living, their whispers insistent: *You'll join us one day, too. Memento mori*, my uncle called it. He loved to remind me that one day I would die, but seems to have forgotten it of himself.

Beyond the uneven spread of headstones sits little more than a shack, a building of weathered wood and flimsy thatch. The door hangs slightly off its hinges, as though it's been recently opened and carelessly forgotten. I start forward slowly. Kit barges ahead.

"It's only a body," she says.

I shudder. I don't mind the idea of death, as a concept, but there's something grim about the notion of facing it, being with it. Lizzy felt different, maybe because I didn't know her, maybe because she came as a surprise. Goody Baxter has been a fixture of my life for years. Mercy Jones once braided by hair. And now, I'm going to trespass on the place where they rest, waiting for a proper burial that might never come.

Kit pushes open the door to the dead house and winces. "They're here."

Something in her voice tells me she's not as brave as she's putting on. I join her in the doorway. Wrapped in a shroud and shoved in a corner like a spare sack of grain is Goody Baxter, still and cold in this waiting place. The slimmer form of Mercy Jones lies nearby. A rusty stain blooms about where her neck would be.

My stomach lurches, but I swallow down the wash of vomit that coats by tongue. I have to be stronger than this.

We move forward together, and as one, kneel by the cold form of the old beggar woman.

"We could...say a few words," Kit says.

"You didn't know her."

"All women share certain things. I didn't know her, but it's not hard to imagine." Kit places a hand on the woman's shrouded head. "The world was unkind to you, but you lived in it anyway. You were strong every day, because you had to be."

Tears sting my eyes. Kit is more correct than she could know.

"I always liked you," I tell Goody Baxter now. "I thought you were funny and clever, and I hated that my uncle wouldn't give you food when you asked. I wish I could have been a better neighbor to you."

Kit smiles. "There. That was nice."

I nod, even as my good feelings fade and dread hits my stomach like sickness. Now comes the unpleasant part.

Without saying anything, we get to work, unwinding the shroud. First the face comes free, blue with death and cold; her throat, ripped by wildlife after she died; her dirty clothes, the same ones she wore daily. At last, we have an arm free, and I carefully draw out her hand.

I study the skull marking on her hand. I only glimpsed it before, but it is indeed the same crude, lined marking Lizzy received. The work of a knife on newly dead flesh.

Kit stares transfixed on the mangled throat. "Liv, you said Lizzy was...not, um... That the scavengers came after."

"That's right."

"I agree. I mean...this looks different." She hovers her fingers above the torn throat. "It's not...tidy, do you see that? A wolf makes clean work. This is..."

I chance a long look at the torn throat. My stomach protests, my throat cinching against another pulse of vomit. But I manage to look long enough to understand what she means. The woman's throat is open, and flayed, but somehow *wolf* doesn't come to mind when I examine these wounds. There's something clumsy and blunt about them.

"Right," Kit says. "Mercy, then."

We rise together and go to the second shrouded form. We unwrap her, out frigid fingers stiff in their work. At last, we have the young woman freed. I should take time to say some words for Mercy, as we did for Goody Baxter, but we're intent upon our investigation now. Kit examines the mangled throat. I have an easier time with my stomach. I hate to think I'm becoming used to such gore, but so it is.

"They weren't scavenged," Kit says after a moment. "Not by anything with big, sharp teeth."

I swallow the taste of bile. "Are you saying..."

She points to one strong, clear marking, bruised and clotted with dead blood. "A wolf's mouth is rather larger than that."

"It's a...person," I say. "Or...if the Devil is about—"

She sighs. "Do you think the Devil has teeth like a man's? All blunt but for a few? I don't know why, but I pictured him with a neat row of fangs."

"Someone's chewing throats out?" My stomach threatens to give up its newfound strength. "That's asinine! They'd fight back, surely. There would be...a struggle, or..."

"Perhaps he poisons them first," Kit says. "There are plants and draughts enough to kill the whole village in these woods." She shrugs. "Or he strangles them first. They lose consciousness, and he comes back to tear out their throats, to cover the markings."

I look down at Mercy Jones. "Does she look like she's been..."

"I can't honestly tell." Kit sighs. "How badly do you think the constable wants a big witchcraft trial?"

"I don't know. Why?" I blink. "You don't think *he* did this?"

"It would certainly bolster his case. You said your uncle was terribly in debt to nearly everyone in the village. Perhaps the constable is willing to make him look like a witch so he can collect his property after he hangs."

"But this is madness. To kill three people just to frame my uncle?"

"He'll get Goody Nash's property as well. And he'll come to collect on the Jones family, no doubt. Perhaps say her mother is a witch, too."

"This is madness."

"It's certainly insane, but then, so is the constable."

I'll grant her that. "We should go, before someone finds us here."

"You have an engagement celebration to get to, too."

"Oh, hell." I shoot to my feet. "I forgot. Oh, *shit.*"

"Deliverance," Kit says. "A kiss and a curse all in one day?"

"Help me with the bodies!

We rewrap Mercy Jones and Goody Baxter, and I say a quick, silent prayer over them. They deserved better. So many women do. But we live in a cruel world. Sometimes, I wonder if it's right to hope, or foolish, a waste.

Back at my house, I find Abel already waiting for me at the gate.

"Where have you been?" He looks between me and Kit. "Have you been idle all day?"

"We..." I look to Kit, whose dread expression quickly shifts to a beaming smile.

"Please don't be angry," she says. "We wanted to celebrate the engagement. We walked through the village, that's all."

Abel sighs. "Regardless, good news is no excuse to be idle of your chores all day. I certainly hope Thomas knows what he's getting into."

I blink at him. Where I'm supposed to feel shame, anger instead creeps in. Does he truly think me so wild and unkempt, because I spent an afternoon away? Because I was out of his purview for a few meager hours?

And if my cousin is like this, God, what will a husband be like?

"Well, we need to go." Abel nods toward the village. "A supper of celebration awaits you at the parsonage, in case you've forgotten."

"Of course not." I think I manage a smile, though it feels mangled, bent by my cooling anger. "Let me don something fresh."

Abel wrinkles his nose. "Aye, you look as though you've been digging graves."

Kit manages to turn a startled laugh into a cough. Abel frowns.

"You're not ill, are you? I've had enough of sickness for a lifetime."

"Just a tickle," Kit says, smiling.

We hurry inside, up to my loft. I choose my nicest pinafore, a subdued, deep blue. I wonder, wildly, what it would be like to wear something other than Sadd colors. Something bright that scraped attention from the world and onto me.

I wash the dirt from my hands and face. Kit idles by the window, staring down at the snow-crusted world.

"What are you pondering?" I ask as I pull on my pinafore.

She hums. "Oh, that the world is this big, wild thing, and we try to make it so small. We carve pockets into pieces of land and call them kingdoms. But there are so many things we'll never see."

I stare at her. "That's..."

"Sad."

"Lovely, too. Some people never think such things."

"I can't help it." She turns to me with a smile. "I want to see the world, Liv. I want to take a ship to every port. I want to taste wine in Morocco and eat dates in Jerusalem. I want to climb a mountain." She grins. "In Africa."

"That sounds dangerous."

"Living is dangerous. Dying is inevitable. Might as well enjoy one while laughing at the other."

"You're..."

"Mad, I know." She smiles.

"Wonderful." I tug her away from the window and wrap her in my arms. "Entirely too wonderful."

She rests her cheek on my shoulder for too brief a moment. "I'm growing accustomed to you as well, Deliverance." She kisses my cheek, a swift peck, there and gone. "Now, away with you. Enjoy your celebrations."

It hurts entirely too much to leave her behind in that loft.

I meet Abel at the gate. Beast does a twisty little dance when he sees me.

"The dog stays." Abel wrinkles his nose. "It smells."

Beast barks once, offended, and trots back to the house. He nudges the door open with a defiant wag of his tail.

"It shouldn't be in the house," Abel mutters. "It's—"

"It's cold, and he's my friend," I say. "Now, shall we?"

Abel smiles tightly in response and starts off down the path. He's got Uncle's walking stick again.

I look back at the house. Beast looks out at the from the window. Kit, up in the loft, is no doubt back at the small window, pondering the bigness of our suffocated world.

As we walk, I think of Uncle, of the accusations I flung at him. Finally, with bars between us, I felt safe enough, strong enough, to tell him what I knew, what I thought. Things Abel would never forgive me for. His faith will never waver that his father is a good man.

I wonder if he'll become like Uncle. If drink will slowly warp his mind and body, if he'll start seeking Scripture for the cruelest bits, if he'll beat his children with that staff he's holding now.

I wonder if it's in their blood, these men of mine, to hurt.

But, no, my father was kind. He could be hot-tempered when it came to royalists and taxation. He could be thoughtless when in deep pursuit of his interests. But he never struck me or my mother. He never got joy out of causing pain.

I hope Thomas will be a good husband. I hope we'll be happy.

We near the parsonage, the village a grim spread of winter gloom at every edge of my vision. Goodman Brown works outside his home, chopping wood on a block. I wonder if he feels anything for Goody Nash, if he thinks of her in prison. The small smile that creeps along his mouth as he looks up and regards her empty home tells me no.

Abel leads the way up the thin, tree-lined path to the parsonage. A cluster of villagers stands outside, selectmen and clergymen, the betters among us milling together. Constable Walsh is among them, and he gives me a dark smile as we approach.

"The woman of the hour," he says. "I'm afraid young Tace has decided to rob you of your due attention."

I'm about to ask what he means when a scream tears from one of the upper windows. *Tace.*

I hurry past the clustered men and find their wives gathered inside, gossip like wind on the air. The Wilsons' many daughters flock amidst the petticoats, seeming lost as the screams continue.

"What has happened?" I say. The women regard me with creased brows, but offer no explanation.

"Liv?" Thomas descends the stairs, his handsome face ragged. Shadows hang from his eyes. In just the few hours since I've seen him, I swear he's aged a year.

"Thomas, what's happened?"

"It's Tace. She's gone into another fit. Or...I don't know what to call it."

"Where are your parents?"

"Father is upstairs with Tace. He fears to stop his prayers, methinks. I cannot find my mother. She was preparing supper, and the guests started to arrive, but then Tace—and since then I haven't seen her." He rubs his forehead. "I'm sorry. This was supposed to be a celebration."

"Think nothing of it," I say. "Your sister is what matters now."

"Liv, Liv!" Mem bounds in from the back door, joy in her blue eyes. "You've got to see!"

"Mem, not now."

"It's important," she sings, and vanishes back out the door.

"Shall we?" I say, and Thomas follows me, seeming grateful to be out of the house, where Tace's screams have become a constant ringing.

We find Mem at the well, tracing cracks in the ice. She smiles when we approach and points to the cold surface.

"See?"

I creep closer, but there's nothing, just the creased flow of ice creeping across the well.

"Nay," I say. "What do you see?"

"A memory," she says softly. "I wasn't supposed to remember. But she whispered it to me, and now I know. That's why you named me Remembrance, isn't it? So I could remember her one day?"

"Liv?" Thomas puts a hand on my shoulder. "What is she talking about?"

"I—nothing. Childish fancy." I take Mem's hand and tug her away from the well, from Thomas. "You can't keep talking about this sort of thing. Not with what's happening about the village."

"But that's why it's important," Mem whispers. "She told me to remember her, so I could remember what Uncle had done." She lowers her voice to a mere breath. "He's doing it again, isn't he?"

I open my mouth to deny it, but God, I'm tired of lying. "Perhaps. But if he is, if this is all a ruse—Mem, is doesn't matter to them, to the constable. If they hear you speak of specters and visions, they'll think you a witch. They're more ready to believe this is the Devil's plot than our uncle's."

"What's happening to Tace?" Mem asks, switching topics in that ready was children do.

"I don't know. But you must pray for her."

"Something's broken inside her." Mem glances up, her eyes on the high window where the screams are a thin noise trapped in glass. "You only scream like that when your soul hurts so much."

I stare down at my young sister, this child I once thought so naïve, so lucky in her blissful ignorance. How old she seems now, how grimly wise in the face of these terrible things.

"Let's go inside, hm? We'll find Goody Wilson."

"We'll not find her," Mem says.

"Why would you say such a thing?"

"The Blue Lady told me. *Mother* told me."

I press my lips between my teeth. "When?"

"Last night. She whispered it. She told me..." Mem's gaze tips over her shoulder. "*Look not in the barn, child.*"

"Thomas?" I call, and he rushes to my side. "How long has it been since you saw your mother?"

"An hour or so. Why?"

At that moment, the screams crescendo, leaving the walls of the house and filling the air behind me. Tace stumbles out the back door in nothing but her shift, chased by her helpless father. Abel and a few of the other men appear around the side of the house, drawn by the shouting.

"He comes again!" Tace braces herself on the well, arms shaking. Her father tries to grab her shoulders, but she slaps his hands away. "He's been here. Death comes again."

She crumples in a screaming, writhing heap on the ground. I don't wait for her to say more. I run to the barn, knowing already what is there, praying I'm wrong.

The doors are barely open, a sliver of light piercing the shadowed hay, and I push them wider. That old-coin stench, that syrupy warmth, hits the back of my throat, too familiar now.

Goody Wilson did not die like the other women. She hangs from the rafters, strung up like a witch twitching in the wind. And I wonder what came first—the hanging, the slow strangulation—or the bloody mess that is her chest. The front of her dress is torn away, as is the skin that once hid beneath it. I see a glimmer of bone, ribs curving against the ripped red innards. Her heart lies on the barn floor, its once-pulsing blood long soaked into the hay.

"Liv?"

"Thomas, no!" I turn back, rush the doors, try to bar him out. But he's already seen, and now, his screams echo Tace's. He pushes against my embrace, claws the air like he can draw himself forward. I don't let him go, no matter how he writhes to get away.

I lie. I tell him he's all right. I tell him to look away. I tell him I'm right here, will always be here. And eventually, like a candle striking the end of his wick, he burns out and falls away from me, collapses against the barn door. I finally look up to see Abel standing there, his face impassive. He looks from the hanging body to me.

"What is it?" Reverend Wilson's voice comes from somewhere behind Abel. "For God's sake, what was he screaming about?"

"You don't want to see, Reverend," Abel says. "Please. I'll tell you, but you need to step away."

"Oh, God. Rebecca!"

Abel manages to hold the reverend back. I somehow get Thomas back on his feet and out of the barn. The constable, of course, waits just outside.

"What happened?"

"See for yourself," I say, shoving past him. I don't care that I spoke out of turn, that I've angered this possibly dangerous man. Nothing seems to matter anymore.

All is madness here.

30. Confession

I get Thomas into the parsonage, to the kitchen table laid out with bread and butter as though a perfect dinner would soon join it. He's crying, but shaking his head, unbelieving and broken all at once.

"What's happened?" Humility asks, yanking at my petticoat. Obedience is at her side, staring slack-jawed at her brother.

"What's wrong with him?" she says.

"I asked first, Di." Humility flicks her sister's nose, and the girls dissolve into a tussle of hands and arms. I use their distraction to slip away and find Thomas a bottle of cider.

Thomas's crying has dried to a helpless panting, his breaths hard and ragged and quick.

"There, there." I rub his back, trying to steady his breathing, but I may as well try to coax a stone from the earth. It's like I'm not even here. After what he's seen, I'm not surprised.

A moment later, what paltry peace I've managed around Thomas is shattered.

"It's Mem!" Obedience is back, Humility at her shoulder. "She's a witch, and she bewitched Tace, and now our mother is dead!"

"You brought her here!" Humility flings herself at me. The girl is only a few years older than Mem, but the sudden, severe motion, her narrow fists balled, startles me. I stumble back and trip over a chair that's been left askew. Humility leaps atop me and lands a few weak slaps. Obedience yanks against my braid like she means to tear it from my skull.

"What are you *doing*?" The second eldest girl, Temperance, catches her younger sisters by their collars and hauls them off me. "Get away from here. Now. Go!"

The two girls scatter, and my heart seems to shatter. Temperance is only fifteen, and yet here she is, seamlessly taking on the role of eldest in Tace's madness and Thomas's catatonia. She moves to herd her younger sisters to a corner of the room while a chaos of adult feet pounds back and forth between the house and the barn.

I get back on my feet. Thomas, in the madness, has somewhat awakened.

"What devilry has come to the village, Liv? It was so peaceful when I left."

"I don't know." I sit beside him at the table, take his hand, though it doesn't fit mine.

"I know you won't want to hear this... But are you certain about your friend?"

"Kit?" I tear my hand away. "Thomas, she's no witch."

"This all started right when she arrived, didn't it?"

"Yes, but..." I try to find the right words. "Things happening at the same time doesn't mean they're related, does it? If I sneeze, and it begins to rain, do I then control the skies with my nose?"

He only shakes his head. "I'm not saying I believe it. I just—"

Whatever he wanted to say is cut off my Tace's screams. I shoot up from the table to find Constable Walsh dragging the girl by her hair into the main room. Reverend Wilson follows at a close pace, but doesn't try to stop the constable manhandling his daughter.

"What is this?" Thomas is on his feet, kept away from the constable only by the cage of his father's arms. "Unhand her."

Walsh throws Tace to the floor. "She hath confessed to signing the Devil's book, and cavorting in the wilderness with him. Her madness is a symptom of his displeasure when she tried to return to her godly ways."

"No," Thomas says. "Tace would never—"

"We will get to the bottom of this," Reverend Wilson says. "We'll try the accused witches tomorrow. We'll snuff this out of our village, whatever it takes."

"You can't be serious," Thomas says. "She's your daughter."

"Watch how you speak to me," the reverend says, his voice shaky but low, filled with the anger he doesn't know what else to do with. "Your sister will answer for what she's done. Look what it's led to."

"Mem, too!" Obedience tries to escape the corral Temperance enforced, but her older sister holds her back. "Mem started this."

"Hold thy tongue," I say. "My sister has done nothing."

"She is a witch," the girl says, "and so are you if you deny it!"

"Quiet!" The reverend storms toward Obedience and snatches her up by the arm. She screams as he wrenches her off the floor to hold her up to his gaze. "I'll have no more madness in this house! None!"

He lets her drop, sobbing, to the floor. Humility drops to her sister's side and tries to soothe her with whispers. Temperance stares between her injured sister and the father she seems to barely recognize.

"Take her," Reverend Wilson says at last to the constable, who, smiling, hauls Tace to her feet and out the door. Thomas watches with a dead gaze.

"We'll find them out," the reverend says. "We'll find the witches and they will hang. It'll all be fine, after that."

"Father..." Thomas shakes his head. "How could you?"

"You didn't hear it," the reverend says. "But she confessed."

"She wouldn't," Thomas says.

"Since she hath confessed, and resisted the Devil since, there will be mercy for her." The reverend holds Thomas by the shoulders, staring square into his face, and I'm surprised to see they're now the same height, Thomas a little sturdier in the shoulders. "We need her now to tell us who else met the Devil. Who else is a witch."

"You didn't believe it before," Thomas says. "You said Constable Walsh was merely eager for a case like the Goodwins, that he was seeing the Devil in everything."

"That was before I found my wife hanging in my barn," the reverend says, and Thomas crumples at the memory of his mother.

A deep, ringing silence ensues. The room is crowded with the men and women who had come here, thinking a celebration would ensue, thinking of a fine meal and an idle evening. Now, they're shuffling their feet, darting their eyes, unsure whether to go or stay.

"Where is Mem?" I say at last. "I should bring her home."

"You'll do no such thing," the reverend says. "If my daughters speak true, I'll find the truth out myself. Remembrance stays here, so I might observe her behavior."

"But—you can't keep my sister."

"You bound her out to us," the reverend says. "She is my servant now, not your sister. And I'll witness it myself if my servant is a witch."

I search the room, hoping to find Abel, needing an ally in this moment. But he's nowhere to be seen among the wide-eyed villagers.

"I'll ask everyone to leave now," the reverend says loudly. "Begone. Leave my family to its grief."

The parsonage empties, quiet footsteps and low murmurs the only sound.

"I'll take you home," Thomas says.

"Where's Abel?" I ask, falling into step beside him.

Thomas only shrugs. We leave the parsonage, the beautiful home suddenly a grim shadow at our backs.

"I never told you," I say, "about my mother, did I?"

"Nay," he says.

"My uncle killed her. I saw it happen."

He's quiet a long time, and I think I shouldn't have shared, shouldn't have intruded on his pain with my own. But then he says, "Does it get any better?"

"It hurts the same," I tell him. "Just...less often. There are longer moments between the memories."

"Why have you never told anyone? He should hang for it."

"He should. But he was all I had left. Besides, I felt as though I had to obey him, and he bade me not speak of it."

"I'm sorry. That you had to carry that."

"I'm sorry, too."

"I think perhaps I'm dreaming," Thomas says after a pause. "This can't be real, can it?"

There's nothing to say to that.

Back at my house, I find Kit outside, scattering feed for the chickens. Beast bounds around the paddock, following Beaky's flight above and barking happily at him. The scene is too peaceful, too wholesome, compared to what we've just witnessed.

"I should go," Thomas says. "Will you be all right?"

"I—yes, Thomas. Are you sure you won't stay?" I can't imagine him going back to the parsonage, to the horror of what's waiting in that barn.

"My father will need me," he says.

I nod. "If you find Abel there..."

"I'll send him home." He smiles, but it's lifeless as a winter leaf. He turns and moves like a walking dreamer, unaware of where he is and where he's going.

"Did you break his heart?" Kit comes up beside me. "I've never seen someone so dejected."

Exhausted, I let my head drop against her shoulder. "There's so much I need to tell you."

31. The Short Drop

We need to leave."

Kit paces before the fire, tension coiled up her spine, making her motions hard and quick.

"I can't leave. What about Mem?"

"We'll go get her, and then we'll leave. The three of us. I have a map, I can find the way to Portland. We'll board a ship—"

"We haven't any money."

"We'll *sneak onto* a ship," she corrects.

"So, you want to venture through the forest for weeks, months, maybe, with an eleven-year-old child, a dog, and a crow. Oh, and a goat, Mem's got a bloody goat, now, hasn't she? All in pursuit of a town neither of us has ever been to, to board a ship we have no passage on and cannot guarantee will be docked."

"This village is full of mad people, Liv. They'll hang anyone, won't they? They've already accused your sister. What if you're next?"

"I haven't done anything!"

"Nor has anyone else! There's no witchcraft about. There is, however, a murderer." She nods toward the back of the house. "Think you the goats were just an accident? Someone's coming for you."

"Why me?"

"I don't know, and I suggest we don't stay to find out."

I cross my arms on the kitchen table and drop my head against them. "What about Abel?"

"Do you trust him?"

"What do you mean?"

She tips her head back and considers the ceiling. "I mean," she says, "do you trust him, in light of whose son he is? Where his loyalties, when pressed, will no doubt lie?"

"Abel wouldn't choose Uncle over me. Not once he knows. I—I need only tell him."

"You think he'll accept his father as a murderer based on your memory alone? Liv, he's...he's very much of this village. He'll never truly understand you."

"I'm not running away," I say. "I'll not leave what's left of my family behind."

Kit drops into the chair before the hearth. "Fine. Let's just stay here then, shall we? Wait for the witchfinder to come to us?"

"You're paranoid," I say, just as the door bursts open. A flurry of snow scatters across the scarred floor, and Abel steps in, shaking out his hat and propping his walking stick against the wall.

"Where have you been?" I say, rising. "I've been out of my mind with worry."

He gives me a weary look. "Goody Nash's trial."

"What, already? It was only announced hours ago."

"Aye, and, understandably, the reverend wants answers."

"But how? Who served as jury? Who was judge? How did they—"

"Enough, Liv. Suffice to say, the old crone is guiltier than sin. Her denials proved it, as did the testimony of Goodman Brown's daughter, who has seen her specter since the arrest. She'll hang at dusk."

"What?" I say.

"Told you," Kit mutters.

"And you'd be smart to come with me," Abel says. "It'll do you no good to seem sympathetic to the old witch."

"She's no witch," I say. "She's just a quarrelsome neighbor."

"Reverend Wilson and Constable Walsh have said she is a witch, and so, she's a witch. Speak no more of this. We must be at the gallows soon."

"No," I say. "This is madness, and it must stop. Goody Nash was accused by a neighbor who never liked her, and now we're to believe she's the cause of all this death?"

Abel rubs at his forehead, clearly done with my questions but suffering through them anyway. "She proved herself guilty when she denied involvement with the Devil."

"So, a claim of innocence is proof of guilt? Is that how the law operates?"

"Enough!" He grabs my arm and shakes me once, hard. For a moment, it's not Abel's tired, pocked face staring down at me, but Uncle's, weathered and sneering. Enjoying the pain he causes. "I'll not have you tear this family apart with your sympathy for witches." He flings me away from him and turns to Kit. "Your name has been mentioned. The reverend and the constable are suspicious."

"No," I say, clutching my bruised arm. "They'll not take her, too."

"That's why I'm warning you." Abel sighs. "They'll come to question you eventually, and I'll not protect you nor harbor you. Be gone by the time we're back."

Abel grabs his walking stick and shoves open the door. "Come, Liv."

I look to Kit. She smiles.

"You know where to find me," she whispers.

"The woods are dangerous," I say.

"For them." She takes my hand and gives it a gentle squeeze. "Not us. It protects us." She slips her hand away. "I'll be fine."

I nod, and follow my cousin out into the cold, sleeting snow.

Our village is small. In terms of punishment, we have only the grim little jail and the stocks set a few yards from the meeting house.

For the gallows, we use a tree.

Nobody has hanged in my village since we arrived, and I doubt anyone had before then, either. The whole thing seems a shoddy affair. We gather at the meeting house in the fall of gloaming, and listen as the constable's cart creeps closer, the wheels rattling little stones in the path, crunching ice gathered at the side of the road.

The crowd hisses as she comes into view, Goody Nash bound at the wrists and bent low in the back of the constable's cart. I wonder if he even bothered to bring her out of jail for the trial, if he'd already decided her fate. Does she know she rides now to her death?

The constable drives his cart past us, up toward the northern road leading to the parsonage. The north woods, then, near enough to the cemetery and the dead house to save the constable a second trip.

"Murderer!" a man—I think Goodman Brown—calls from the crowd.

"Oh, hang you all," Goody Nash spits. "I'm no more a witch than Walsh here is fit to be constable."

"Watch yourself, witch," the constable growls.

"Or what? You'll hang me twice? Get on with it and leave me be, for God's sake. Can't you drive any faster?"

The crowd follows the cart, a grim procession, a funeral for a woman not yet dead. There is a memory, more a feeling than true recollection—black clad people waiting on a smooth street, a horse and cart rattling toward me. And I...stepped into the road. But a hand snatched me back.

Hold thyself together.

Uncle, hissing. Abel, too, watching the cart with bored, cold eyes. In my arms, a baby—Mem, days old. Saying goodbye to our parents as they clattered past on a Boston road, on the way to a cemetery.

Will I see them in Heaven? I wanted to know.

And Uncle only said, *None is guaranteed to be among the elect.*

I blink back to the present and look up at Abel. His face is the same now, smooth with disinterest.

"Do you remember," I say, "my parents' funeral?"

"Barely," he says. "We were quite young."

I frown. I was twelve, already with my first blood, and he was nearing fifteen. That's hardly too young to hold a memory. And yet maybe he's right, because I had forgotten it until now, had tucked it away as another terrible thing I didn't want to dwell on.

"Did you like them? My parents?"

"Of course." He looks down at me. "Now, this isn't really the time, is it?"

The forest gives way to a small clearing where we cluster, a mass of anger and hate against this woman who cannot have done anything to deserve this. There is a large tree, a knotty branch coiling from its trunk, and a noose ready upon it. In the near-dark the thing looks like an arm reaching from the forest to snatch us one by one into the shadows.

I feel something on the trees, a pressure like unexpressed anger. Something lurks all around us. My breaths come with difficulty. I tug the tie of my cloak away from my throat.

The trees groan around us. The wind whispers curses.

"We shouldn't do this," I whisper.

"Quiet," Abel says.

The constable hops from his cart and sets a rickety ladder against the tree branch, then hauls Goody Nash from the cart and onto the ladder. He climbs after her to fit the noose. She turns and spits in his eye.

The crowd takes up a long, cold hissing. The constable wipes the spit and descends the ladder.

"Goody Nash, thou art a witch, as found by this court. By the laws of God, I sentence you to hang this night." A smile creeps into his cheek. "Confess now, and pray God forgive you, and you may yet find mercy."

She looks directly into his empty eyes as she says, "I am no witch. And thou art no man, Farewell Walsh. Thou art a sniveling beast." She casts her gaze now on the crowd, and it pierces trough me, a shard of ice meeting flesh. "If you let this deed happen, if you condemn me as a witch and claim to walk in righteousness, God will answer thee in kind."

"A curse!" Goodman Brown—God, what is *wrong* with him?—wails, pointing to the condemned woman. "She hath cursed us! End her breath before she makes another!"

"Here's a curse, Jacob Brown." Goody Nash smiles. "May you drown in the fires of Hell."

Walsh knocks the ladder out from under her feet, and she drops. Her neck doesn't snap—she wasn't up high enough—

and so she dangles there, alive but gasping, her feet kicking against the air, seeking purchase. And we watch. As a crowd, as a village, as a collection of godly people, we watch an innocent old woman suck at the air, gathering what breath the rope will allow. It takes too long, and I'm faint in my head and sore in my feet by the time she finally stops dancing on the air.

Full dark has fallen. Stars glitter between the trees. The woods are watching us. They saw all.

Walsh replaces the ladder and climbs up to cut Goody Nash down. Her body thuds heavily on the dirty, hard snow. Only now does the crowd disperse. All but me. I'm fixed to the spot, staring at the corpse of a person I used to know, used to say hello to.

"I'll have that grazing land at last," Goodman Brown mutters to another villager. I spin on him, but he's already walking off, a smile obvious and unashamed on his face.

"Deliverance." Abel only uses my full name when his patience has long since broken. I look back at Goody Nash. The constable drags her by the noose back to his cart. Another one for the dead house.

"*Deliverance.*"

I turn to my cousin. I follow him up the path. I don't know what else I can do.

"Aren't you worried," I say when I reach him, "that your father will be the next victim of this madness?"

Abel shakes his head. "That won't happen."

I want to ask how he's so sure. But I don't.

Tonight, I will feign goodness and obedience. I follow my cousin home.

Kit is gone, as I knew she would be. Beast sits mournfully at the door and whines his curiosity. Abel shoves past him, into the house, and takes the seat before the fire.

"Fetch me a cider," he says.

I bristle at the lazy command, but do what he says, bringing him his drink. I'll bring him as many ciders as he can swallow tonight.

Things would go much more smoothly if he passed out drunk.

I light the tallow candles, filling the house with their stink. I roll dough for bread. Neither of us speaks of dinner, of reading the Scripture. Abel slowly sinks into a doze, his pitcher of cider askew in his lap.

I take my opportunity and throw my cloak on. Beast follows, his padded footsteps the only sound in our small home.

Outside, rain breaks the snow already collected on the ground, pocking the ice and filling the world with a secret chatter. My boots slip against the mushy ground, but I trudge on, into the canopied protection of the forest.

I take the path to the little deer trail, remembering each turn somehow in the dark and damp woods.

I find Liv in her clearing, the tented sticks crusty with snow, a small fire fluttering out under the beat of the rain. Beaky sits on a low branch nearby, eyeing me as I approach.

"Murder-murder," he says, and I wonder if he knows, if he saw what my village did to Goody Nash.

"There you are." Kit ducks out from beneath the branch-house. She doesn't ask me how I am, what happened. She only pulls me into a hug and kisses my temple when I start crying against her shoulder.

"She didn't deserve it," I say. "But they killed her anyway."

"I know, I know. I've seen it, too."

"They had no *proof*."

"They want no proof." She squeezes my shoulders tight. "They want someone to blame."

I nod against her. "Well. Let's give them someone to blame."

She ducks back, lowering her gaze to mine. "Who?"

"The Devil, or whoever it is who wanders these woods. He's hiding, and he let a woman hang for murders he committed. So, let's bring him to light."

"The truth will out," Kit says, and smiles. "I'll get my crossbow."

We set out west, following the sun as it ducks beneath the trees and settles for the night. Soon only a blue haze of light remains between the trees. Kit holds aloft a lantern she'd kept hidden in her camp. The tallow candle within drips fat tears of wax and bleeds its stench through the glass.

We tread in the footsteps of animals, squeezing between trunks and branches. Snow sloughs away from our steps and reveals damp patches of moss beneath.

"Why are we going this way?" I whisper, afraid, somehow, that someone will hear me.

"There's a river this way."

"And...?"

"The Devil's got to drink, too, hasn't he?" She shrugs. "If someone is living out here, I figure he'd stay close to a source of water."

I nod. That makes sense, and Kit had been living out here for months, undetected. My fear of this place, my unease at losing the well-trod path, is my simply my fear of the unknown, the secret world my village pretends isn't out here.

We settled this small space and called it ours. To creep to far beyond those borders is to see, truly, that we could never claim this world.

Soon, the murmur of the river joins the chorus of rainfall. Kit holds up a hand, and we stop. There, on the river's bank, a huge buck laps at the water. A few scraps of velvet still cling to his antlers, their many points sharp and casting patterns on the slushy snow.

In that moment of watching this happy, peaceful animal, I feel a sudden gutting sorrow that I've ever eaten venison before, that I've taken the flesh and muscle of something else to sate my own body. He seems so right out here. And what am I? How, really, am I different than him, except that I'm clumsy and lost in this world, and he's free?

"Liv," Kit hisses, and nods across the bank. She tucks the lantern away, throwing darkness over my vision, but I can still make out the thing that's caught her eye.

A cloaked figure, obviously human in shape, emerges from the woods opposite us. The figure bends toward the water and gathers palmfuls of river, drinking like he's been deprived too long. The deer watches this interloper, still in a way that speaks of danger. At last, the figure rises and wipes his hands on his cloak. He takes lurching, wobbly steps away from the river, back the way he came.

Once he's been gone a long time, we creep out from the trees. The buck stiffens at the sound of our footfalls and careens away. His hoofbeats make a frantic music to match my heart.

"Follow me," Kit says. "Careful now." She finds footholds on river rocks and hops across the snarling water like it's nothing. Beast hops right into the water and swims after her. I take a deep breath and make careful, halting progress the way Kit went, only I can't understand how she made her stride long enough for some of these leaps. I nearly fall twice, but finally stumble onto the opposite bank.

"Here." Kit points to the clumsy pattern of bipedal cloven hooves in the snowmelt. "He didn't look so sure on those feet, did he?" She loads her crossbow and smiles. "Let's go pay the Devil a visit, shall we?"

"Be careful," I tell her, falling into step beside her as she marches after the prints. "He's obviously quite good at killing people."

"Yes, well. That's why we're going to surprise him."

I hope she's right. But now I feel the woods watching, knowing us in a way we can't know it. And if the Devil is part of this place, won't he always have the advantage?

The prints wind west, then north, drawing a path where I wouldn't have seen one otherwise. The trees grow tighter, the brambles grow wilder. Beast whimpers at the inhospitable path, and I try to hold the thorny plants aside so he won't snag his fur. But the world around us is thicker and darker and not meant for visitors. I'm beginning to think the Devil truly is a specter, and, apart from his feet, has made himself a shade to pass through this place.

But then the forest opens onto a clearing, and in that clearing is a cabin.

It's ruined, the siding falling away, the roof buckled beneath years of snowfall. Boards strike out like broken teeth. The one window is shattered, the glass long buried in snow. The forest behind the house seems eager to reclaim its territory, brambles and vines crawling along the walls as though to tug it down into the dirt.

The cloven hooves lead up to the door. Booted feet lead away.

Kit levels her crossbow. "I knew it."

"What?" I say, though I think I understand now, too. I follow her to the door. I nudge it open so she can keep her weapon aimed, just in case. But the door swings into an unoccupied room.

Kit lowers the crossbow and steps inside. I follow her, sickness clawing at my stomach. A pain settles deep in my mind as I scan the room. A single rotted mattress, a crumbling fireplace, a scalded cauldron for cooking. Spoiled hanks of meat sit out on a low table, writhing with the dark bodies of flies. The head of a bull moose sits rotted off to the side, the skin dripping away from jaws and puddled eyes, the antlers raw with frost.

Somebody once stayed here. But not recently. They've clearly let the place go.

"Look."

I turn back to the door, where Kit stands. On a peg by the door hangs a black cloak, wide enough to hide a huge man. Beneath the cloak are the severed hooves of what must be that same slaughtered bull moose, straps nailed into the bone, as though...

As though somebody had been wearing them like shoes.

"He's no Devil," I say. "He's only dressing as him."

"Aye. And he slaughtered some poor moose to do it."

I feel a rush of vomit crawling up my throat, but swallow it back. I back away from the hooves until my back strikes the table. The flies rile up and swarm around me at the interruption of their meal. I stifle a scream as a maggot twitches onto my wrist.

"Let's go," I say, shaking the little demon off. "Please."

Kit takes my hand and leads me out of the cabin. Beast shakes himself and rolls in the snow as though he, too, wants the rank smell and atmosphere of the place off him.

"Vomit if you need to," Kit says.

"I'm—" I mean to say *fine*, but I end up spewing bile onto the snow instead. Kit rubs my back as I gag.

"Better?"

I nod and cram a mouthful of snow into my mouth. I swish it around and spit it back out. "He's dressing as the Devil. But why?" I look at her. "I'm the only one who's seen him."

"Maybe not," Kit says. "Perhaps he went to Goody Baxter, and Mercy Jones. Perhaps..."

"That's why he killed them." I swallow; the taste of bile is thick on my tongue. "So, I'm next?"

"No." She shakes her head. "He could have killed you already. I think he's..."

"What?"

"I think he's taken with you, Liv. You told him off, when you met him. You refused him."

"And that *pleased* him?"

"Perhaps. Or perhaps not. But I don't think he's done with you."

"Oh, God. That's worse." I bury my face in my hands. "I can't do this. This is...this is just evil." I drop my hands. "People can't be this evil."

"They can, Liv. You saw it today."

Goody Nash. The constable giddily ripping the ladder out from under her. The crowd hissing. My own cousin with a contented smile on his face.

There aren't too few people who could be this Devil—there are too many. Too many people cruel enough to dress in hooves and a cloak and kill women forgotten by the world.

"We have to tell the reverend of this," I say. "At least to put a stop to these senseless trials."

"Right." Kit helps me up, and we walk hand-in-hand away from this terrible place, back to my village.

Which, maybe, isn't much better.

33. Oyer and Terminer

The night hangs like a shroud around us as we hunt for the path back to the river, and from there, to Kit's camp. The tallow candle in the lantern makes fitful shadows as it gutters down to the last of its wick. Kit doesn't stop moving, guiding me through the clinging woods until, lantern spent, we stumble into the clearing of her camp.

I say an automatic prayer of thanks for our delivery, though I'm less certain than ever that somebody is there to hear it.

The rain has cleared the snow away from the ground growth, letting the greens and browns of the earth rise back up. The sweet rot of moldered leaves floods my nose.

Kit ducks into the tent and comes back with a bundle of mostly dry branches. She sets to making a fire.

"We'll to the reverend in the morning," she says.

"No." I kneel beside her as she builds the fire. "I want you to stay here. Stay hidden. Just in case."

She frowns. "I'm not letting you go alone."

"You heard Abel," I say. "They're looking for someone to blame, and there's no one but me in the village prepared to vouch for you. I'll tell the reverend what we found." I squeeze her hand in mine. "He'll believe me. He wants answers, too."

"What about the constable?" she says. "He has no fondness for you."

"I only need to convince the reverend," I say, though even I don't fully believe that. The constable is eager and ready to hunt witches. And I'm about to spoil his fun. I have to hope he's as eager to find a murderer as he is witches.

"All right." She cups the back of my neck and pulls me close. Our lips meet, cool and chapped, in the briefest of kisses.

"That wasn't goodbye," Kit whispers, pulling away.

I nod. "I'll be back tomorrow."

I rise, turning away before I can think too much of what that might mean. Beaky flutters past my eyes and lands on a branch in my path.

"Murder-murder," he says.

"I know," I say. "I know."

Abel is still asleep when I get back to the house. He's still in the chair, the mug of cider empty in his lap. Large snores rip from his throat.

I haul my exhausted body up to my loft. I manage to shed my boots and soggy pinafore before falling into bed. Sleep closes over me like a gripping fist, and releases me too soon to the daylight.

I groan. Though I must have slept hours, it feels as though only seconds have passed.

Downstairs, I find some leftover venison for Beast's breakfast and force a few bites of dry bread for myself. I go to scatter feed for the hens. I don't look toward our empty barn.

By the time I'm back inside, hair damp from the clinging mist, Abel is awake, rubbing his face and muttering about a pain in his neck.

"Is it late?" he asks, checking the watery light at the window.

"Nay," I tell him. "The sun has only just risen."

"Good. We must go to the meeting house this morning."

"Why?" I ask, dread filling my gut.

"My father's trial begins today, and I mean to witness it. I don't trust the constable."

I swallow the taste of bile. My uncle's trial. I knew it would come eventually, but already? And knowing how Goody Nash's ended so abruptly, and with her death…

I want my uncle to face justice. But I need him alive if I'm going to get answers. I'm not convinced he isn't involved in these murders. If the constable kills him for witchcraft, these terrible things might remain a mystery forever.

"I'll get ready," I tell him, and head to the loft.

I change into a clean shift and find my second-best set of clothes: a soft blue kirtle the color of a bruise. I dress quickly, clean my hands and face in the washbasin—I feel the forest clinging to my skin even now—and meet Abel downstairs. He's looking as respectable as he can in a clean doublet and breeches, his folt hat well-worn but still fine.

"Ready?" He takes up Uncle's walking stick. I fall in step beside him.

Beast makes to follow, but I tell him to stay, even as his sorry whine pierces my heart. "I'll be back," I promise, and somehow, those words feel too heavy. Too much to guarantee.

I follow my cousin to the village and wonder if anything will be the same after this day.

The village is alive with whispers.

Rumors and hissing tongues crowd the air as we make our way toward the meeting house. Everybody, it seems, has come to watch my uncle's trial. After the end of Goody Nash's trial—and her life—I suppose they don't want to miss the spectacle.

Abel scowls at the many people trying and failing to bury smiles beneath solemn frowns. They're enjoying this. This is the closest thing we get to entertainment. There are no plays or concerts, no bear baitings. Death is our amusement. Doom is our greatest show.

Abel cuts the crowd confidently, leading us to our usual seats at meeting. I crane my neck to check the Wilsons' row and see Mem's blond head squished between Temperance and Prudence. Humility and Obedience cast sharp looks her way every few seconds. Mem ignores them.

Goody Wilson's absence is a raw gap at the end of the pew. I feel it in my heart, scraping my bones.

Thomas paces before his family. Tace, too, is not here, and I fear the constable has thrown her in that dank, stinking jail. Thomas's eyes flick occasionally to the place where his sister should be. Where his mother should be. Finally, I catch his eye, and he comes over.

"How are you?" he asks, voice low, clutching Abel's shoulder.

Abel gives a jerky shrug, dislodging Thomas's hand. "Fine. And you? I—I didn't get to say so yesterday, but I'm sorry. About..."

There's no good way to say it. He doesn't.

Thomas manages a weak smile. "It still doesn't feel possible that she's gone. And Tace... I feel I should have been here for my family." He shakes himself a little, coming out of his melancholy. "Well. Stay strong, yes? Your father is innocent of this. We all know it."

A rabble rises at the meeting house doors. Parishioners crowd close, then skitter away as the doors fling wide and the constable steps into the room. He hauls my uncle forward by a length of chain connected to his wrist shackles.

"Stay strong," Thomas whispers, and returns to his family's pew.

Walsh leads my uncle forward, past the crowded pews, the hissing parishioners. He shoves my uncle toward the front of the room, where the pulpit has been replaced by a long table with three chairs behind it. Reverend Wilson sits in the center seat, his eyes bloody and narrowed with exhaustion. Beside him is an old white-haired man whose pointed beard pokes at the collar of his doublet. I've never seen him before, but he's too clean, too put-together to be from my village. Perhaps he is come from another settlement to serve as a judge, to give this farce some credence.

The constable takes his seat on the reverend's other side. With the three men assembled, the white-haired man rises.

"Ezra Ashe, thou art charged with the crime of witchcraft, of holding congress with spirits, and of bewitching persons of this village. How dost thou plead?"

My uncle tips his head just enough to glance at me from the corner of his eye. A smile twitches beneath his crusty, unkempt beard.

"Guilty, your honor."

Hisses and jeers, shouts and cries of triumph fill the meeting house until it's too much, until I think I'll suffocate on the frenzy. The white-haired judge bangs his palm against the table to bring order back to the room.

"You have made a contract with the Devil?" the judge asks.

"I have," my uncle says. Beside me, Abel shakes his head and mutters, "No, no, you haven't."

"How did the Devil appear to thee?" Reverend Wilson asks.

"As a tall man in fine clothes, with a high-crowned hat and a staff carved of dark wood."

"And how came the Devil to you?"

"I was...told to meet him."

The furor starts up again, and the constable pounds his fist to silence the crowd. "Enough! Goodman Ashe, who told thee to meet with the Devil? Was it Goody Nash?"

"Nay. Goody Nash was there, always, at the sacraments we took. The Devil fancied her, yes. But no. I was brought into the coven by another witch."

"Another witch?" the old judge says over the growing din of the crowd. "For God's sake, man, who?"

My uncle lifts a shackled hand and points behind him. "My niece, Deliverance Ashe."

Shouts rise and hands find me, trying to push me or yank me, I don't know. One woman brushes her fingers against my arm and shrieks as though the mere touch of my sleeve has burned her.

Through the shuddering, twisting bodies, I find Thomas's face. Resigned, drawn.

He mouths one word: *Run.*

I push past Abel and bolt for the doors. I'm outside, free, nobody stopped me, too shocked by my flight. But my feet have only just struck the road home when large arms scoop me up and haul me back. The constable wrestles me down into the muddy ground.

"Guilty as they come," the constable murmurs in my ear. "Let's see your betrothed save you now." He grabs the back of my neck and presses my face down into the dirt, just to be cruel, just to humiliate me further.

"To the jail with you, then." Walsh hauls me back up and swings me into his cart waiting alongside the meeting house. The crowd has moved outside by now, more interested in my arrest than my uncle's confession.

I find Abel's eyes in the crowd, but he looks away, his jaw set. He believes his father, I realize. He thinks I'm a witch, that I led Uncle into sin. I shake my head, trying to bring his gaze back to mine, but it's pointless. He shoves back through the crowd into the meeting house.

"Liv!" Thomas rushes forward, battering parishioners aside. He clutches the side of the cart, his face inches from mine.

"Find Kit," I say. "In the woods. A lean-to. She'll help. She—she knows what to do."

"Liv—" He grabs my hand. "You're innocent."

"I—"

"Probably the only one." He kisses my palm. "I'll see this made right."

"Thomas—"

Thomas is ripped away, dragged back in his father's grip. Walsh hops onto the cart and whips his horse into motion.

"We're going to get to the bottom of things, Deliverance," he says, throwing a terrible grin over his shoulder. "Mark me."

The day crawls to dusk, and the dusk lurches into night. The jail goes dark, and no one comes to light the lantern hanging by the window. I didn't expect they would.

I'm not alone. Tace lays huddled on the other side of the cell, muttering and twitching, but otherwise not acknowledging my presence. I'm achingly aware of the people not here: Goody Nash, who has taken up residence in the dead house; and my uncle, who seems to have gone free after his false confession.

They were never going to punish him, were they? My uncle is hated—a drunk, a debtor, a vile and unruly neighbor. But he doesn't fit the picture these men have of *witch*. He's wrong for the story the constable means to write.

So, now he's free, and that means he can kill again. I can't prove he's killed anyone since my mother, but my claws are in my own story, and I've begun to believe him the killer entirely.

The jail is cold and stinks of the waste left behind. I shiver and retch until, somehow, my body begins to still. Perhaps I'm dying, the cold stealing what's left of me. My eyes flutter. The night sinks into my shut eyelids.

"Deliver..."

I squeeze my eyes tighter. "No. Not now."

"Deliver...us..."

I shudder a breath. "Deliver us from evil. For thine is the kingdom, and the power and the glory—"

"None."

I open my eyes. The bloated, blue face hovers above me. She looks less substantial, somehow, less a corpse and more a shifting figure with bone beneath translucent skin. Her wide eyes flash and the sockets of a watching skull stare down at me.

As usual, I cannot move. I only watch as she lifts a boney hand, tendrilled with the suggestion of flesh, and caresses my cheek.

"None...righteous. *None.*"

I know, I want to say. *I see that now.*

"Not...even...you."

Tears drop from my eyes. *I'm sorry, I failed you, I let him kill you.*

"Deliver...thyself," her bone-mouth says. "From evil."

My body releases, and I scrabble to sitting. My ghost is gone, leaving me with only the pale cloud of my own breath before my eyes. Tace sleeps away on the other side of the jail, only obviously alive by the occasional hump of her breath.

I draw my legs to my chest and prepare for a sleepless night in the cold, rank dark. But then, footsteps approach outside. I dare to let hope flare that it's Kit, or Thomas, that my rescue is nigh. But the wood door creaks open and a huge shadow slips over me.

"Are you ready to confess?" Constable Walsh says.

"I haven't done anything," I say. "My uncle lies."

"You go frequently to the woods, no? Your cousin said as much." Walsh shuts the door, closing us into the dark together. "He also said you have been idle of your prayers and Scripture."

How quickly Abel has turned against me. It shouldn't shock me, truly. He has always had more respect for our ways than for any one person practicing them. But I'm not prepared for the betrayal.

"He told me, too, that he found his goats slaughtered. Did you do that, Deliverance? Did you make a sacrifice to the Devil?"

"I'm the one who *found them,*" I say. Tace twitches at the clamor of my rising voice. "There's a madman," I go on, quieter.

"He dresses in a dark cloak and wears a moose's hooves upon his feet. He wears the Devil's skin like a costume. He's the one killing these women and doing these terrible things."

"Have you proof?"

"Yes. We found his cabin in the woods."

"We? Ah." Walsh smiles. "Your mouthy little friend. Abel has asked we find her, too. He's quite certain she's the one who led *you* to witchcraft. A terrible chain, isn't it?" He steps forward and kneels in front of me. "One foolish girl to another foolish girl. And then you tried to bring down a righteous man."

"My uncle is not righteous," I say. "If you ask me, you've just let the murderer go."

The constable rises and turns to light the lantern dangling by the door. "So spiteful," he says as he strikes flint to the wick. "And ungrateful. He took you in, when you became an orphan."

"He *made* me an orphan," I say. "He killed my parents. My mother, right in front of me."

"Would that I could believe you. But the Devil speaks lies through his witches."

"I'm no witch," I say, but it doesn't matter. With the small, stinking jail cast in dim tallow light, the constable turns to me.

"I will get a confession out of thee." He stoops to lift an object I hadn't noticed with him in the darkness, a three-pronged metal device. As he brings it closer, the raw divots of a screw become clear, and the pronged horizontal bars along its axis.

A thumbscrew.

"You can't torture me," I say. "It's...it's illegal."

"When we're through here, Deliverance, you won't be telling tales of torture. You'll only be speaking a confession."

I scrabble away in the waste-soaked hay, but the constable grabs for me, capturing my flailing right arm. He shoves my fingers and thumb between the toothed metal bars. I jerk away, loosening my fingers a little. With a roar of frustration, Walsh pins me down on my stomach, his knee sinking into my spine as he works my fingers back into the device and twists, guiding the bars closer together along the screw, crushing my fingers between.

I scream. There's no dignity in the sound, but why save that when I have nothing else left? My knuckles make sick, easy popping sounds as he twists the metal down harder, working the beams closer together despite my smashed flesh and straining bones between.

Walsh leans in to whisper into my ear, "Speak, Deliverance. I am thy confessor."

"Nay." I bury my face in the hay and let it absorb my scream. He twists the thumbscrew harder, fiercer, and a splintering groan echoes the terrible pain that crawls like lightning up my arm and into my heart. My whole body cries now in response to the agony that is the broken bone and shredded meat of my hand.

But I don't confess. And soon, it seems, the thumbscrew won't go any farther.

Walsh gets off of me and unscrews the device, letting my pulped hand drop. The feeling is less in the ruined hand now than it is in the rest of my body, mourning its numb and possibly dead part. I pray he's given up, that he knows I'll never claim witchcraft no matter what he does. But then he comes forward with a length of rope and begins winding it in a pattern around my head.

"No, no, wait, please!"

He yanks in either direction, and the rope squeezes my face, my skull. Skin tears where the raw piling of the rope moves quickest. His arms strain out to either side as my whole head rings at the pain twisting my face, my mind. My neck cries out, bones creaking. I'm sure this will kill me, and for a moment, I hope for it. I'll die, but I'll never give this bastard what he wants.

"Speak, Deliverance! Speak! I am thy confessor!"

I can't speak, not with my head straining on either side, my mouth a warped line against the rope's pull.

"Speak, I say! I am thy—"

The pain vanishes with a wet, windy sound. A moment later, Constable Walsh collapses at my side, an arrow piercing his heart. His mouth works even as blood puddles beneath him and coats his tongue.

"Confess," he garbles.

I tear the ropes still clinging to my head away and throw them down. I look him in his dying eyes. "I am no witch." I get to my feet. "And you're no man."

I kick his face, relishing the pop of his nose as it caves into his skull. He makes a last, garbled noise, a judder of breath that ends in a spray of blood. Then he's dead.

"Liv?" Kit clutches my elbows, crossbow slung at her side. She reaches out like she means to touch my face, but drops her hand just as quickly. "What has he done?"

"He tortured me. Thought I'd tell him I was a witch."

"Liv!" Thomas scrambles into the jail next, Beast quick at his heels. He takes my face in his hands. I don't want to know what he sees, what tears and burns are left in my flesh.

Thomas at last turns from me to the constable's body leaking blood into the hay. "You killed him," he says.

"Aye, well, I thought he was killing *her*," Kit says.

"I think...I killed him, actually," I say. "I broke his nose. I think it pierced his brain."

Thomas exhales, a sound like a laugh and gasp all at once. "Well done, both of you. I hated that arsehole."

Beast barks from the door, then rushes into the jail to sit before me, whining. I wrap my arms around him and bury my face into his musty fur, and that's when, finally, I cry. In the warm love of my dog. That's what breaks me.

"Thomas," Kit says quietly, and nods to Tace's huddled form. He blinks, understanding coming to his face, and he hurries to his sister's side. She goes on making nonsense sounds, even as he tries to coax her to waking.

"Liv?" Kit touches my shoulder, then drops her eyes to my right hand, limp against the hay. "Oh, God."

"I'm all right."

"No, you're not."

I look, and she's right. My hand is mottled blue and corpse white, broken veins and killed flesh. I understand, distantly, that I might lose the hand, that the dull absence of feeling in my fingers is worse than the pain had been. But I can't seem to care. I just cling to my dog while Kit rubs my back.

"We'll get you fixed up," she says.

"You don't have to lie."

"Well, I'm going to."

"I'm not going to have a hand."

"We'll get you a hook. A lovely silver hook. And we'll become pirates and sail the seven seas."

I blubber laughter into Beast's fur. "I don't want to be a pirate."

"You haven't given it a proper chance, yet, have you?"

I finally glance up at her. "I knew you'd come."

"Given the chance to rescue you and put down that rabid constable...well, I couldn't resist."

Movement comes from the other side of the jail. Thomas finally gets Tace to sit up, though she moves rather more like a corpse than a girl. Her dull eyes scan the room, and I see the burns of rope on her face, too. Walsh tortured her before me.

"We need to go," Kit says, helping me to my feet. Thomas tries to get Tace to stand, but she flops like a limp poppet in his grip. He catches her and lifts her into his arms like a child.

"Where can we go?" he asks, and I see it on his face, the realization that everything he knows is ending.

"We'll go to my camp," Kit says.

I shake my head. "Mem. I can't leave without Mem."

Kit swears, but nods. "We'll find her. She must still be at the parsonage, right?"

Thomas nods. "Tempe took the girls home after the trial."

We leave the jail, and the cold, winter-scented air scrapes my throat and nose like it's cleaning the rot of the jail away. We walk slowly back to the village, aware of every small noise, every possible danger. It's late, and I hope we find the village asleep. I hope we can take Mem away and never see another soul.

But as we approach, I realize that's not going to happen. Despite the late hour, houses are alight with candles. Lanterns swing in the dark. And, a little ways distant from the meeting house, a crowd is gathered.

"Murder!" Goodman Brown cries, rushing into the road. We duck against the trees to avoid his frantic eyes. "Murder! Where is the constable? There's been a murder!"

We exchange looks as we wait for Goodman Brown to shuffle back to the crowd. They're gathered around the stocks. I wrack my mind, wondering who else might have died, who is left that my uncle might hunt and kill now that he's been assured his freedom.

"Wait here," Kit says. I catch her arm with my good hand and shake my head.

"I'm not letting you go alone."

"You're supposed to be in jail," she says. "Stay with Thomas. I'll see what's happened."

I watch with sinking dread as Kit takes to the path and joins the crowd around the stocks. She vanishes into the crush of bodies. Soon, I catch sight of Reverend Wilson trying to disperse the crowd, calling for the villagers to make room. His authority seems thin without the constable's angry bulk, but most people scatter at last, leaving the sight clear for me to take in.

"It can't be," I say, and crash to my knees. It's too much. The impossibility. The senselessness. If this is true...then I don't know what else is.

My uncle is bound in the stocks like any prisoner, neck and wrists trapped between the wood. But he's not there for a public humiliation. His throat is open like a grinning mouth, and his blood stains the stocks, soaking into the wood beneath his neck.

The villagers have left the spectacle, yet one figure remains. She is even paler now, just a blue flush against the darker night. But I see her skull smile, and her empty eyes seem filled with glee as they catch my stare across the expanse.

Deliver me. She lets her ghost hand fall upon and through my uncle's head, and she's gone.

Kit rushes back to my side. "I take it you saw."

At first, I think she means my mother. But neither Kit nor Thomas wears the slack face of one who's seen a specter. I shake myself back to the present problem. "Who would have done this?" I ask. "The constable?"

"Nay," Thomas says. "The constable was pleased with him. He wanted you to be a witch, didn't he? And your uncle gave him the exact story he wanted. They sentenced him to a day in the stocks, but...whoever killed him..."

I nod. "Whoever killed him later believed him a true witch, and unrepentant." Or knew what he'd done to my parents. My mother's pleased, skeleton smile flashes behind my eyes.

"Liv. We need to go." Kit takes my unbroken hand and nods toward the parsonage. We hurry along the edge of the forest and come out at the back of the parsonage. Thomas opens the back door slowly, gripping the handle and pressing the wood forward so it makes no noise. We creep into the kitchen.

Temperance shoots up from the table. "Liv?" She shoots her gaze to Thomas. "Thomas what—is that Tace?"

"Shh," he hisses. "Is father home?"

"Nay, he's out. What are you doing here with them?"

"Tempe, listen. Liv is no witch, and neither is Tace." He goes to the nearest chair and sets Tace into it, positioning her so that she's resting safely with her head on the table. "Where is Mem?"

"Her cousin came to collect her," Temperance says. "After the trial."

"Abel was here?" I say.

"Aye," she says. "He said he needed her back. Said he had to...to make sure the witchcraft didn't get to her, too."

"Oh, God." I cover my mouth.

Suddenly, it's there. The truth, and it makes a sick kind of sense. Abel is his father's son in so many ways.

35. Into the Dark

I don't really believe it, don't think I can let myself know what Abel is, until we step out of the parsonage.

A warm gust of air cuts through the winter. Ash skitters across the air. Smoke settles heavy on my tongue, acrid at the back of my throat. The wind carries the taste of fire, coming from the direction of my house.

"Mem," I say, and take off running. Beast matches my speed, always by my side, and Kit and Thomas hurry behind us. The path from the village has never felt so long. The woods loom, laughing with their wind, whispering with their leaves, mocking my pointless hurry.

When I get there, it's too late.

The house wears a crown of flames. Smoke gutters from broken windows. The chickens—our only surviving livestock— walk dazedly around the property, clucking and flapping their useless wings.

Beast barks at the fire as though it's an intruder, and maybe it is. Or maybe this is what was always in our home— destruction, death. I think of my nights pinned to my bed while a specter tugged at me and whispered a twisting of my name. *Deliver me.*

I couldn't deliver anyone, couldn't save a single person who mattered. All those murdered women—Goody Nash—my mother. And Mem. Is she inside?

I stumble toward the house at the thought, but Kit wraps her arms around my waist and hauls me back. Thomas skitters into my path and holds up his hands.

"Liv, wait. She's not inside."

"How do you know?" I say.

He points to the thin trail leading into the woods. Prints in the snow-damp mud. Tiny, hesitant feet. Mem's.

And beside hers, guiding her, a pair of cloven hooves.

As soon as we enter the woods, Beaky flutters onto a branch in our path.

"Murder-murder," he caws.

Kit sighs. "Where have you been? Don't scare me like that." She holds out her hand and the crow hops onto her wrist.

"Murder-murder."

"Why does he keep saying that?" I ask, meeting the cool black gaze of the bird.

"Think nothing of it," Kit says. "He's just...talking."

I wish I could believe her.

We funnel into the woods, the smoke from my house coiling through the trees. Ash and snow fall together, a quick flurry of cold and heat brushing my skin. The cloven feet lead Mem's tiny prints off the path. Thomas ducks into the trees, leading the way. Snow crunches under our feet and twines with the sound of distant, cracking flames, a strange melody.

We pass close to Kit's camp, but the footprints go around it, on a twisted route that even a deer might stumble along. The trees shove close, and I brace myself with my unbroken hand as we wind our way into hidden corners of the forest.

Finally, the woods open up and the sound of the river rushes forward. I realize, of course—the prints will lead us to the cabin. The cloven feet stop at the river's edge and take up on the other side, clumsier, wider with the damp spray of water. Mem's little feet vanish on the other side. Did he carry her? Or...

"Where is she?" I ask. "What did he do to her?"

"I'm sure she's fine," Thomas says, but how can he know, how can any of us believe anything is fine? Danger and misery and pain, that's all that's left, that's all anything is anymore.

"Liv?" Kit grips my shoulders, and I realize my breaths are hard and fast, clouding on the air. My chest is clenched, my heart a writhing, quick thing inside.

"I can't lose her," I say. "Not her, too."

"You won't." Kit cups my face and lifts it so I'm looking into her eyes. "Everything will be all right."

At that moment, a growl rumbles through us, sending ripples through our skin where it touches. Kit turns her head slowly just as a huff of warm breath stirs her hair.

The wolf is lean, snarling, a glint of hunger sharp in its eye. Kit turns slowly, her arms out as if to protect me, but we're just thin limbs of meat to this monster. It pulls back its lips and flashes stinking yellow teeth.

"Liv?"

"Hm?" I whimper.

"Run."

Kit twists around, shoves me back. I collapse into Thomas's arms, and that seems to jolt him into action. He hauls me away toward the river as Kit ducks from the wolf's swiping claws and gathers her crossbow.

Beast splashes across the water beside me, and it's only his presence, his fear, that keeps me from tearing myself away from Thomas and going back for Kit. She rolls away from the wolf and aims her crossbow. The wolf snarls. I don't see what happens next, because Thomas pulls me along, deeper into the trees on the opposite bank.

"We have to wait for her!" I shout.

"What about Mem?" Thomas shakes his head. "Liv, Kit will be fine. But we need to keep going."

"You're mad if you think I'll—*Beast*!"

Beast, having caught the scent of something, tears off into the woods. And I can't lose him. Not my oldest, truest friend, my shadow and my constant. I don't even think. I follow him, praying for Kit, crying for her, but knowing I'll never let my dog go off alone.

"Beast, come back! Beast!"

Whatever has his attention is too sharp, too important. He ignores my desperate commands and scrabbles forward, over brambles and thorns and arched roots. My feet catch on these obstacles, but I right myself and plow ahead. There are no footsteps behind me, and I think Thomas must have stayed with Kit. I'm glad he did—and yet, as I begin to recognize the twists of branches like beckoning fingers, and the gap in the trees like a smile, spilling moonlight, I wish I wasn't alone.

The cabin is just ahead, and Beast stops a few yards off, whining. He sits by a puddle and howls.

"Beast." I kneel beside him and wrap my arms around him. "Don't run off like that. Ever. Beast?" He continues to whimper, and now he twists in my grip, trying to get away from the puddle at my knees. "Beast, what?"

Clouds scatter just then, freeing the eye of the moon to glare down on the clearing, and in the glittering shards of light, the puddle beside me shines red.

I'll never know why, but I reach out and touch it. It's thick, cooling but still warm, bright on my pale fingers.

"God," I whisper, but I can't pray, or even think in this moment. There's so much blood. I didn't know any one person had so much in them. I watched a doctor bleed Abel once, when sickness had settled too long in his chest. There had been a cut at the crook of his elbow and even that thin stream of blood seemed too much as it gathered in the bowl. *This*—this is a whole person. Maybe two people.

"Liv?"

Thomas's voice, distant in the trees. I manage to call out, "Here," but part of me wishes I wouldn't be found. Part of me wants to lay down and die here, where...where Mem must have died.

Thomas finds me curled by the blood, sobbing into the knees of my cloak. "Liv? What...what is that?"

"He's already killed her," I say.

"We...we don't know that."

"Look at it, Thomas! Look at how much there is!"

"You don't know it's hers." He crouches at my side and tries to lift me, but I realize, then, that he's alone, and what that means.

"Kit."

He looks away. "I—I tried, Liv. I went back across, but..."

I search his face, his body, and there's a scratch across his doublet, the four-pronged slice of a wolf's paw. Blood beads on the wound. Not enough to truly injure. But Kit...

"She's dead?"

"I tried, I *tried*, Liv," he says, pleading.

No. She can't be. There can't be no one left.

"I'm here," Thomas says. Did I speak aloud? I shake my head, but he presses. "And Mem could still be alive. We'll find her." He nods to the cabin. I don't want to go inside. I can't imagine what's inside.

But I rise. I walk with him, haltingly, toward the cabin. When we reach the door, I'm the one who pushes it wide.

The stench of old coins, of raw and rotted meat. The chorus of flies and the slick shuffle of bugs feasting. The moose's head that was here last time has been shoved aside; the hanks of spoiled venison are thrown to the ground.

On the table now is Abel, his doublet cut open. His bare chest is a mess of peeled skin and exposed muscle. His ribs are snapped up, shoved aside, dark with gore.

His eyes are open, his mouth wide as though he died screaming.

Someone pulled him apart while he was still alive, rooted around in him, looking for...what? And who could have...?

I turn to Thomas. He doesn't look surprised.

He doesn't look scared.

He meets me eyes and smiles.

36. Blood to Drink

Thomas?" I swallow the bile creeping up my throat. "How did you get away from the wolf?"

He steps closer to me. "It was already dead. I'm sorry I deceived you."

"Why did you?" I take a step away.

"Because you needed to see." His smile spreads wide, flashing teeth. "You needed me. I fixed it, Liv. I took away all your pain, and mine. Now, there's only us."

"Only..." I'm pressed against the table where Abel's body is laid out like an experiment. Was Thomas searching for something? Or was this a mere frenzy?

"You're the Devil, aren't you?"

"If I am, I'm not aware."

"Then why?" I let the tears waiting in my eyes loose. I let the sobs rip out of me. "Why kill all these people?"

He sighs. "I can see...what they truly are. I left this village, you know, to examine my own guilt. I couldn't abide what I'd done to corrupt you, all for the pleasure of my own flesh. I went to Harvard with a humble heart. Like Saul on the Damascus Road. I wanted to repent. I thought the presence of godly men would enlighten me."

He sighs. "And yet all I saw was hypocrisy. Proud men and foolish youths. I prayed and prayed, either that God would show me my own hypocrisy, or guide me down the path He intended. And I saw my way clear." His face hardens in the shadows. "God wants nothing to do with false prophets. He cannot tolerate those who praise His name in public but condemn it in secret."

"Did you...did you kill someone at Harvard?" I'm shaking, my entire body strumming fear. "Is that why you came back?"

"Nay. I wanted to. I wanted to smite the hypocrites. I wanted to do God a favor and cut Increase Mather's tongue from his mouth."

My mouth drops, but I snap it shut. How is it that this boy I've known for so long, who I spent every day with, is now talking so passionately of maiming the president of Harvard? What happened in this one year?

Or, rather, what did I miss in all those that came before?

"I had to come back," he continues. "To get away from those false prophets. But I—I felt this thing too strongly. I knew it was my mission. But God told me...He said the villagers wouldn't understand. That in their ignorance, they would think I did the Devil's work, and not His.

"So, I lived here for a time. And God showed me a way to choose the unworthy."

"*What?*" I say.

He gestures to the black cloak hanging on its peg, the discarded hooves. "I wear the guise of the Devil, and any who follows me has rejected God. I claim to make the same promises Satan gives his witches." He grins. "Only, they don't get quite what they hoped."

My hands grip my hair. I think I'll pull it out, tear myself apart. "You tricked them? Goody Baxter and Mercy Jones—"

"They accepted the bargain of the Devil," he says a little louder.

"They were lost! Scared! Goody Baxter had no home. Mercy was beaten by her parents. They only accepted because...they wanted to escape."

"Escape God's will for their lives," Thomas spits. "If they wanted better situations, pray, why not live better lives? Goody Baxter might have done an honest day's work. Mercy might have minded her tongue and held off on the slutty looks she cast the men around her."

"Be quiet," I say. "You cannot blame them for wanting something to change."

"You refused me," Thomas says quietly, the smile returning. "I needed to know, of course. If you were to be my bride still, I needed to know you would refuse the Devil at every turn. And you did."

That day in the woods, when he whispered to me from the trees. He was testing me. Seeing if I would be the next girl he slaughtered. Thomas would have killed me. He was prepared to.

"It's as I said, Liv." His smile is heartbreaking in its radiance. "You're righteous. You're innocent. And together—"

"What about Lizzy?" I cut in.

"Oh." Thomas frowns. "The girl in the woods, you mean? I saw her witch's mark. She didn't want to come with me. Claimed she knew I was no Devil. But I knew she was guilty, because she'd been marked. She was the first. I didn't know how to go about it yet, so I only slipped poisoned berries into her basket while she foraged. It was a dull way for a witch to die. I refined my ways the next time."

I'm glad Kit cannot hear this, but then I remember...

"You said Kit was dead. Did the wolf kill her?"

He laughs. "She's quite resourceful, actually. She had it felled when I returned to her."

"Oh, God, no."

"Did you know, Liv? About her witch's mark? I might have let her live if it weren't for that. I know she's dear to you."

"I love her!" I scream. "You stupid monster, you pretend Devil."

Thomas blinks at me. It takes him a painfully, idiotically long time to understand. "That's...unnatural."

"*You* are unnatural. Killing innocent women. Your own mother. Did she go with the Devil, too?"

"Aye, she did. Followed me for promises of rest, of time only for herself." He clenches his jaw, shakes his head. "Why is it so hard for women to behave?"

"Behave?" I laugh. "You slaughtered people! You—" I remember the bodies in the dead house and my stomach twists in understanding. "You chewed out their throats like a rabid wolf."

"It needed to hurt," he said simply. "And look like an animal attack. I think it was rather sensible."

"Go to hell," I snarl.

He lunges forward then and grips my throat in his hand, pressing my spine hard against the table. Beast barks, frenzied, but Thomas pays him no mind and presses his fingernails into my jaw. "You were put on this earth for me, Deliverance. I possess thee. I was promised thee."

"Was I the reward?" I say, my voice thin and strained beneath his grip. "Did God say that? That you could have me once the killing was done?"

"It's no more than I'm due," he says.

"I will never be yours," I say, and shove my knee hard between his legs. He crumples in pain and I break away from him, out of the cabin. Beast follows hard at my heels, a low whine constant in his throat. I suck clean air into my body and ready a scream. "Mem? *Mem, where are you?*"

Footsteps clatter behind me. And I have no choice.

I run into the woods.

The forest is shadows and teeth, claws and cold breath on my face. I plow through the trees, heedless of my direction. My panting breaths burst white on the air. Beast stays evenly by my side. Behind me, Thomas's footsteps smack hard on the path, close, closer—

I swing madly to the left and crouch to get beneath low branches. A huge, mossy boulder, slick with ice, rises up ahead of me, and I find the hard parts of the stone to grip and haul myself up with my feet and one good hand. Beast bounds up ahead of me with greater ease and watches anxiously as I climb. Twigs and brambles snap behind me as Thomas struggles through the too-small space to follow.

I scramble up the boulder and pause at the top to breathe, letting the cold air wash through my throat and nose. The stink of the cabin leaves my tongue, but not my memory. I choke down a sob. Abel, Kit, both gone. And Mem. She wasn't in the cabin. So where is she? What has he done with my sister?

A frustrated roar rises from below, and Thomas's footsteps smack the forest floor. He's free, getting closer. I hurry down the other side of the boulder, onto a rising hill. I grip the trees to haul myself faster through the tangle of darkness, my shattered hand held close to my chest. But still, I hear him behind me. Still, he doesn't give up.

I crest the ridge of the hill and look down. More forest, more nothing, lies before me. Moonlight scattered below glints on the tail of the river. I must have gotten turned around, confused in my haste. I thought I was heading south, but no. I could go down, follow the river southwest and come out at my house. My burning house, I remind myself. I could go on to the village, but who would believe me, the accused witch, over Thomas? My uncle has been killed, my cousin slaughtered, my sister missing. Will anyone believe I had nothing to do with it?

The snap of the forest behind me tells me I have no choice. I run down the side of the hill, my feet loose beneath me. I trip and end up rolling the rest of the way down, bruising my body on poking roots and sharp rocks. I scream when my broken hand falls trapped beneath me. Beast is at my side in a heartbeat, nudging me into a sitting position.

I scan the river, trying to gauge the best way across. It's wider here, rushing madly. To my left, a twisted heap of deadfall makes a hummock across. I run to it and clamber over the gathered branches and pines. Beast bounds ahead of me and waits, tail twitching anxiously, on the bank.

"Liv, Liv, Liv," Thomas sings, and I whip my head around. He's gracefully stepping down from the hill, not far, not far enough for me to make it. I scramble over the deadfall, but he only laughs.

"I thought you the godliest among them," he says. "I thought you better than this."

I jump down on the other side of the river and run along its uneven shore, heading west. Thomas follows calmly, not hurrying, like he knows I can't truly escape.

"You are better than this," he calls after me. "Repent."

I push my legs harder, faster, but too soon I grind to a halt. The wolf from earlier is in my path, a heap of mottled fur and still muscles. Arrows stick from its body, the killing shot buried in the animal's heart.

Beast sniffs at it, interested, but I shoo him forward. At the last moment, I double back and tear an arrow from the wolf's haunch. It might do me no good, but at least I have some defense now.

I wonder where Thomas left Kit. I expected he killed her here, near the slain wolf. But she's nowhere. A glinting path of blood tells me she wandered somewhere close. And it's as good a path to follow as any. I snap my fingers for Beast and he follows me along the wake of bloody footprints.

For a while, the woods are quiet, echoing my breath back at me. I don't hear Thomas anymore. There's only the sound of my feet, and Beast's. Our labored hearts. The chatter of the river.

And then a shadow bursts from the trees. I scream, battering away the touch of cool feathers against my skin.

"Went that way," Beaky shrieks.

I finally focus on the crow, hopping along a branch right in my path. He waits until I meet his gaze before taking flight and leading me through the trees.

I hurry after, hoping I'll find Kit. Dreading it. If she's alive... But Thomas said she wasn't. Did he only mean to torment me?

My eyes never leave Beaky. Not until someone steps in my way.

Thomas, panting, bleeding from cuts and scrapes along his face, smiles. An axe rests against his palm like he's cradling the head of a child.

"Are you ready to repent?" he says.

My muscles sag. My body droops. It wants me to give up.

But I can't. I can't let Thomas continue on this way. How many more people will he kill if I don't fight?

I take a step away from him and point the arrow I ripped from the wolf at his chest. "Stay back."

"Liv." He smiles. "Please."

He gives the axe a lazy swing, and I scream, throwing myself backward. My broken hand strikes a tree and pain lances through my whole body. Thomas laughs, rich and delighted.

"Tell me, Liv, who will save you if not me?" He slinks closer, the axe hanging at his side. "I am thy salvation, thy mercy. I'll forgive you."

"I don't want your forgiveness," I say, and I hate how my voice shakes. But it doesn't matter, because my left hand is steady on the arrow. I focus my hate, the pain ripping through my chest, into the muscles of my hand. When Thomas surges forward, I do, too. My arrow finds flesh, finds purchase, but— *no.* I scurry away. The arrow sticks from his right arm, just below the shoulder. He winces, but there's a smile buried there, too.

"That," he says, "was truly pathetic." He snaps the arrow, leaving the head buried in his skin, and throws the tail away. "A godly woman wouldn't hurt her husband."

"You are not my husband."

"How did you go so wrong?" He walks toward me, the axe loose in his grip. "Was I away too long?"

"I've always been this way," I tell him. "You just couldn't see it."

"You have abandoned God."

I throw my hands out, as though a single gesture can encompass everything horrible and wrong about this moment, this week. "He abandoned me! I tried to be what you wanted. What my uncle wanted. But why?"

"You might still be among the elect," Thomas says softly, like a prayer. "You'll find out soon enough. I'm sorry, my love."

"Thomas—"

"As Abraham sacrificed Isaac, so I will give you up to the Lord's will."

He swings the axe. I stumble back, but not quickly enough to avoid the edge of the blade. The sleeve of my left arm tears, and the skin beneath it. There's blood, quick and hot, and I don't feel the pain, even though I should.

My wound sends Beast into a frenzy of barking and lunging. He claws at Thomas, snapping his jaws. He manages to get one of Thomas's ankles, and Thomas tumbles forward with a roar. The axe doesn't leave his grip, though. I dive forward and try to grab it, tug it from his hand while he's distracted. Beast rips at his ankle like he might tear the foot away, but Thomas kicks with his other foot, striking Beast on the nose. Beast whimpers and scurries back. Thomas gets to his feet, a slight limp in his right side now, and whirls on Beast, axe raised.

I tackle Thomas from behind and send both of us spilling down a gully. He lands on top of me and quickly gets his bearings. The axe is pressed to my throat in a breath.

"Repent," he begs. "I want not to send thee to hell. Please, Liv. Repent."

I say nothing. I won't give him that. I want to fight, but the axe is cold against my throat and ready. I shut my eyes. Beast barks above, distressed, furious, but he's safe, and I hope he stays safe. Maybe Beast will find Mem out here. Maybe they'll find a way at life together. As for me...

I don't say a final prayer. It seems pointless.

I take one last breath.

But the axe suddenly slips away, leaving only a shallow cut at my throat. Thomas makes a stiff choking sound and falls off me. I sit up and see why: An arrow sits between his shoulder blades, buried deep beside his spine.

I look up the gully, and I laugh, cry, scream all at once. Kit scrambles down the side of the gully, keeping the crossbow aimed at Thomas. She's moving wrong, staying hunched, and I notice at last the deep bloom of red across her blue waistcoat. He stabbed her stomach, must have assumed she'd die from the wound. But she's here.

"*Kit*," I say, because what else can I say? It's her. *Alive.*

"Liv." She smiles, but there's pain twisted through her features. "God give you good morrow. *Stay down*," she barks as Thomas makes to rise. "I've got sight on your heart and I'll gladly pierce it if you move."

"Stubborn one, aren't you?" he gasps through the pain.

"Oh, aye." She looks to me. "What should we do?"

Kill him, I want to say. But no. Mem is still missing. And beyond that, we need him. We need to show the village what he is, what he's done. It's the only way to clear our names, to get some semblance of life back.

I kneel by his side. "Where is my sister?"

He spits blood. "Go to hell."

I grip the arrow in his back and twist. He screams into the dirt, his face washing pale. "*Where is Mem?*"

"She got away from me," he says through his teeth. "When we reached the river, she ran from me."

"And you didn't give chase?"

"She wasn't important. She was only the trap, to get you to follow." He twists his head against the forest floor to smile at me. "I wish it had worked, Liv. I wanted to spend eternity with you."

I look away from his eyes, so blue in the night. "Why did you kill Abel?"

"'Create in me a clean heart, Oh God, and renew a right spirit within me.'" Thomas grins. "Abel was a good man. He had a clean heart. And God showed me how much more I could be with all that holiness in me." His smile dims a bit. "I took out my mother's heart, too, but it wasn't clean. I could see the sin in her veins. There was nothing righteous left in her. So, I left it for the scavengers."

I rise, stomach churning. I need to be away from him. "You're...*mad.*"

"More than that," Kit mutters.

"And my uncle?" I turn back to him. "Did you feast on his heart, too?"

Thomas makes a disgruntled face. "I didn't kill your uncle. How could I have?" he goes on as I make to interrupt. "I was busy with Abel all this day, and then bringing your whore friend to rescue you. I'd no time for that old drunk, nor the desire. He was worthless to my plans. His heart is probably black and running with liquor, besides."

"Then who—"

"Liv." Kit touches my shoulder gently. "He's a lunatic. His words mean nothing. Let's find your sister."

I gesture at the forest, despairing. "She could be anywhere."

"Maybe she found her way back?" Kit says, but not with much hope. Mem is just a child. She's never been in the woods;

I never let her venture out here. How might she have gotten home in this impossible dark?

"Perhaps Beast could track her," Kit says.

"Aye." I nod. "But what do we do about him? We have to bring him to the village."

"Will anyone believe us?" Kit says. I shut my eyes. I truly don't know. Here I am, an accused witch with a family entirely dead and missing. The constable is dead by Kit's and my own hands. And the only person with true authority left is Thomas's own father. The reverend will surely choose his own son over us.

"Will you confess?" I say now to Thomas. "Your plan has failed. If we take you to the village, will you admit what you've done?"

"As I have only done God's will for my life? Gladly."

Kit and I haul Thomas up. We push him up the gully first, Kit keeping her crossbow aimed at him. I pause, considering the discarded axe, and grab it, tucking it under my arm.

Between Kit's wounded stomach, my broken hand, and Thomas's mangled ankle, we're slow getting up the slope. Beast waits, snarling at Thomas's approach. Beaky waits on a nearby branch.

"Murder-murder," he says.

"Quite," I agree.

Kit kicks at Thomas's ankles, urging him forward. "Go on. You know the way."

"I am glad to be a martyr for God," Thomas says as he walks.

"You are no martyr," I say. "You killed women who knew not what you were."

Kit stiffens. Her finger twitches on the crossbow. "Did he...Lizzy?" is all she manages to say.

I shut my eyes. "Aye. I'm so sorry, Kit."

She breathes hard through her nose. "If the village won't kill you, Thomas, I will."

He laughs. "Would that not make you the murderer you claim me to be?"

"I don't pretend I'm doing God's work. Killing you would be entirely for my benefit."

Thomas stops in the road. The arrow in his back moves with his breaths. "Katherine," he says. "I wish I had thought to kill you sooner. How well you played a godly woman."

"Keep moving," she says, but Thomas turns to face us.

"This last thing I can do for God."

He lunges at her. She fires an arrow, but it crests over his shoulder and sticks uselessly in a tree. He takes her down in the thin snow, and she screams. I think of the wound in her gut. Her pain fills the air.

Thomas pins her, hands on her throat, and squeezes, trying to choke the air and life from her. My hands move without my mind fully understanding the motions, the way my fingers coil around the axe, the way my muscles bunch as I lift it. The way the air feels smooth beneath the blade, and his flesh a hard punctuation to the swing. I blink, and the axe is buried in his back, on the other side of his spine. And somehow, that's enough. His hands go slack. He spits blood down his front. Kit shuts her eyes against the spray and shoves him off. He hacks and twitches, but he never says anything again. After a moment, he goes still.

"Thanks for that," Kit says.

"Of course." I shake my head. "Now he can't confess."

"He never planned to, methinks." She takes my shaking hand. "We'll find Mem. I promise."

I look out at the forest, the trees like reaching fingers, the snow like pale skin, the sliver of moon a blinking eye. We're inside the monster that ate my sister. Thomas was only the beginning, a shadow servant of this endless place.

The wilderness is not finished with us.

38. The Woods

Kit slows the farther we go. She doesn't seem to notice. But her eyes flutter and her steps lurch. I stay close to her side, ready to catch her if she falls, to carry her on if need be. I'm not losing her now.

Beast sniffs the path, and I hope he's leading us toward Mem, but I don't know if she's even out here. Perhaps she found her way home.

There is no more home, I remind myself. Our home is likely naught but a pile of ash and splintered beams.

Would she go back to the parsonage? And if she did, would Reverend Wilson welcome her? His own daughters threw accusations at Mem. I can't imagine he'd accept her story of being spirited away by his own son, dressed as the Devil.

Kit stumbles, falls. I drop to her side and feel her face. It's cold, colder than it should be even in this winter chill.

"Kit? What's happened?"

"It...it should hurt," she says, touching her hand to her stomach. "But I stopped feeling it a while ago."

I shake my head. "No. Stay with me, all right? You cannot leave me."

"I'll try not to," she says with a smile. "But..." She coughs, and I flinch when flecks of blood scatter on the snow. "Do you hear that?"

"Hear what?" I say, my eyes fixed on her chapped, bloodstained lips.

"Singing," she says.

I take a breath, listen. And when my heart finally calms, when I manage to banish the image of Kit's blood on the snow, I do hear it. A verse caught between the wind. A flat voice thin through the trees. A woman's voice, singing a song I've only heard from one tongue.

She made the words herself. She strung them together in the moment. Her songs only existed once, never to be heard twice.

"Mother?" I scan the forest, and then—a flash of white, of pale yellow. It's quick between the trees, too fast to follow. Yet the voice stays with me, guiding me forward.

"Can you walk?" I ask. Kit locks her jaw and nods. I help her up, taking as much of her weight as I can. We walk through the forest, a single entity, Beast a step behind. I'm not letting her go. I've lost enough for a lifetime.

The pale figure flashes through the trees every once in a while, but it's her voice that guides me, the strained notes of a song my mother once whispered to me as I drifted off to sleep. A lullaby from her mind.

Deliver me, she said. Have I done that? Have I done enough? If I save Mem...maybe then. Maybe my mother can rest if her girls find their way back together.

The voice fades, then, and my heart pounds in terror. My guide cannot leave me now. But a new voice takes up the song. A child's voice, soft and proud.

I step out from the thick darkness and find myself at Kit's camp. A fire burns in the clearing, and Mem sits before it, murmuring the same verse of a song over and over.

"Sleep, girl, eyes a-shut, thine waking will come soon enough."

"Mem!" I scramble from the forest. My sister rises, fear melting into relief as she runs to meet me.

"Liv! Liv, he told me he'd kill you." She buries her face in my stomach and cries. "But I couldn't stay. The Blue Lady said, 'Run, run,' and I did. I'm sorry, I—"

I smooth her hair down, whispering assurances. I'm not ready to tell her about Abel. I think Mem already knows somewhere inside. But it's a hard word to say, killed. When you're a child, that word seems impossible. You fancy there are ways to cheat it.

I'll let her have those fancies a while longer.

Kit steps out into her camp. "How did you find this place?"

"The Blue Lady led me." She stares off into the trees. "She looks different, now. I think she's going away."

I try to find the figure of my mother in the darkness. There is the merest flicker of blue light, and no more.

"She said you delivered her."

I take Mem's hand in mine. The fire illuminates our pale skin, and the russet stains we share.

"Mem?" I frown. "How come you to be covered in blood?"

She blinks at me. "I remembered," she says. "And he was just stuck there. She said...hell was waiting for him."

I stare down at her, mouth open.

"I honored my mother," Mem says. "And now she's sleepy. She'll leave you alone now. Both of us."

I shut my mouth and nod. "No more nightmares. Promise me."

Mem grins. "Only dreams."

Kit makes a faint noise behind me, and I turn to see her sinking next to the fire. Mem's eyes catch on the wound at her stomach. "Liv, Liv! She's bleeding!"

I hurry to Kit's side. "I know, love. Kit? What do you need?"

She gives me a smile that teeters close to agony. "Nothing now, Liv. Just...stay close."

"Kit. No, we'll—"

"I wanted to see everything." She tucks a loosened strand of hair behind my ear. "Plays most of all. You'll go to London for me, won't you? Hear a play. Drink wine. Have candies, all you want."

"You're coming with me," I say.

"You've got a stubborn streak yourself." She rests her head against my shoulder. "Stay until I'm asleep. Then see the world for both of us."

I cry into her loose, dark hair. She smells of smoke and blood, earth and winter air.

Her breathing slows.

"Please, no," I whisper to the ground, to the broken branches and the crawling ice. These woods always seemed alive to me, realer than God or Heaven. So, I pray to them now. "I'll do anything to keep her."

"Anything?"

My head snaps up. Behind me, Mem grabs my sleeve.

"Liv? Who's that?"

The woman standing before me is clothed in darkness, jeweled in moonlight. Her skin is the bark of the trees, her hair their snaking vines and leaves. Her eyes are the ever-moving blue of the river. She lifts an arm of woven branches and Beaky alights to her fingers.

"Thank you, son," she says, and kisses his head. Beaky lowers his head and flies down to Kit.

"I say, child, are you well?" The woods-woman steps closer, and her movements sound like the wind sighing along the spindly paths. "You look as though you've seen the Devil."

I stare at this impossible person, a dumbstruck smile on my face. "What else could you be? After all this time, the Devil is real, and she's found me."

"Dear one, I thought you were past that." Her smile reveals shards of starlight as seen through thickened treetops. "Now, to your friend. You said you'd give anything." She slinks closer still. "How about thy pretty face? Thy youth?"

"Yes," I say on a breath.

"Thy future? Her life for thine?"

"Yes, dammit." I scrape tears away on the back of my unbroken hand. "Anything."

She smiles, and her lips are roots to trip unwary travelers. "Make me an offer. It's better when the bargain is thy own idea."

I think through the things she asked for—all trite to me now, with my family almost entirely gone, my home burned, and my dearest friend dying. My looks and youth and life are pennies dropped in a street: Not worth going back for.

There's only one thing I can think to offer. Nothing I would miss, but something this creature might relish. Something the forest has longed to take back, ever since we staked our place here.

I meet her river-rushed eyes above the flickers of fire. "The village," I say.

She feigns a gasp. "And all therein along with it?"

"Spare the children," I ask. "Let them...live here, with you. Wild and untamed. Let them be creatures other than what they'll grow into aught. But the rest of it? Do what you will."

"How cruel," she says, grinning her starlight. "It's a bargain."

She holds out her hand and places her bark-skin against Kit's side. Kit breathes in once, a slow shudder which I think means death. But a moment later, her chest rises again, and again. She slips against my side, exhausted, eyes fluttering.

"I'll to my prize now," the woman says, backing into the shadows.

"Wait. Who are you?" I cradle Kit's head against my lap.

The woman blinks. "I had a name, once. It's harder to remember every day." She stares up between the trees. "Gods, it was so long ago. I think...it doesn't matter. No." She turns, and a moment later, there is only the forest, only trees and dark and stars.

No, that's not right. She's still here. She always has been.

I once thought the forest gave nothing up, that it only took from us. But she's willing to make bargains to those who can hear her.

"Thank you," I whisper.

"Liv," Mem says, her voice trembling. "Was that...the Devil?"

"No, Mem. It was the woods." I stroke Kit's hair. Her eyelids flutter.

"I...don't feel dead," she says.

"You aren't dead," I tell her.

She snorts into my lap. "Why do I sense you've done something mad to save me?"

"The forest brings out our madness. I've just decided to embrace it." I draw her close against me. Mem eyes me, still wary, but takes my hand.

"Can we go home?" she asks.

"It's been burned," I say.

She brightens. "Will we go back to Boston?"

Kit snorts. "Just as fond of witch-making in Boston."

She's got a point. Besides, rumors fly. We may be far from Boston, but this story will reach them soon enough. Their ministers will preach on us—a small settlement beset by the Devil, sunk into chaos by witchcraft.

It's the story they'll tell. No one will speak of Thomas's atrocities. They'll only whisper of the witches that flew off.

"We have to go," I say. "Far."

"London-far?" Kit asks.

"Aye."

Beaky caws from the trees above. "God save the king."

I shudder. "Is *he* coming?"

"Yes, he bloody well is," Kit says.

"King William the Third," Beaky says.

I sigh and sink back. Beast nestles into my side. Mem ducks under my arm. "Will I like England?" she asks.

"You'll adore it," Kit says. "You won't have to wear a coif anymore, if you don't want."

She beams. "Really? And no more chores?"

"Let's not get ahead of ourselves," I say.

"We'll have to find jobs." Kit pushes herself up onto her elbows. "There might be danger, as well as adventure. It's not a perfect place. But we could do worse." She glances my way. "Liv, who were you talking to? While I was..."

I smile. "The trees. And the sky. The river, stars, and wind."

She lets out a small breath. "'There are more things in Heaven and Earth, Horatio...'"

"What's that?"

"*Hamlet*. We'll read it." She takes my hand and kisses it. "We'll stay here tonight? Think of a plan in the morning?"

"Aye," I say. Beast snuggles down at my feet and rests his chin over my boot. He lets out a contended huff.

"We'll all see the world," I say. "Together."

There's hope, finally. After everything, there's that.

More than my house burned.

The wind pushed embers like a sour breath to the trees along the road, and from there, toward the village. Smoke crawls among the trees and small fires still burn with the early dawn of the sky.

"Well," Kit says. "No one left to hang us."

I know she's trying to be light, to jest, but she speaks truth. The fire grew through the night, leaping between wood buildings and trees, catching at hay and thatch and timber. The snow's all but melted. There was nothing to stop the ravage.

Everything in this village has been eaten by fire.

The woods got the land back.

If you let this deed happen, if you condemn me as a witch and claim to walk in righteousness, God will answer thee in kind.

I shudder. Goody Nash got her wish after all. But it was not her hand which cast this plague. It was mine. I traded these lives and homes and hopes for Kit.

I'd cheerfully do it again.

Children wander the burned streets, wide-eyed and blinking. Goats butt heads by the meeting house. A cow, udders swollen and red, walks into our path with a sorry moo.

Footsteps sound in the direction of the parsonage. Tace and Temperance, Thomas's eldest sisters, stumble down the path in their haste to reach us.

"Liv!" Tace drags me into a hug. "I'm so sorry, so sorry! He made me do it, he—he did awful things, I know, but I *had* to!"

"Tace." I disengage from the girl and hold her shoulders. "It's all right. Thomas...can't hurt you anymore."

"He's dead," Temperance says. "The...well, the...she..."

"The woods," Tace says. "She told us." She nods. "Yes, and now we're part of her, too." She smiles, some of the madness still clinging to her blue eyes. "But not you. You go now. Father's horse is at the meeting house. And the constable, he left that big cart by the jail. Come by." She pats my cheek in a motherly way. "Get supplies. We'll see you off."

"Is your father there?" I ask cautiously.

"Oh." Her grin goes sloppy. "He *burned*. Talking about *God* on that *pulpit*. And some people sat and listened. They were all eaten up, and the fire was still hungry. It only stopped when she whispered its name."

"Tace." Temperance takes her elder sister by the arm. "Let's go pack for the ladies, hm?"

"She says thank you," Tace sings as she's led away. "Thank you for the tasty meal. Thank you for the room to breathe. Cruel girl. Strong girl."

"Right," Kit says. "Puritans are all mad. I told you so."

I shake the eeriness away. "Let's find that horse and cart and get the hell out of here."

We fetch the horse, then lead him to the jail where the constable's cart still sits. We load into what little we have. Kit brought her things from her camp—the lantern, some blankets, and—most importantly—a map. Maine is new to us, so the map may not be accurate, and certainly isn't complete. But there's the sea, and ports along the coast. There are ways out of here.

"We'll try for Falmouth," Kit says, unfolding the map. *Falmouth* is written in a fresher pen, and the old name, Casco Bay, is scribbled over. The map may be terribly out of date, then. We may run into other villages that have since cropped up, or a wall of wilderness.

But there is no life left for us here. We could become like Tace, a part of the forest, slowly drinking in the wildness. But I promised Kit the world. I let the village burn for it.

"East," Kit says, and climbs up onto the horse. Beaky flutters down to perch on her shoulder. I settle Mem and Beast onto the cart, then climb up behind.

We meet Temperance on the street. She offers two stuffed sacks of goods for our journey.

"Tempe, I'm so sorry," I say. "This—"

She shushes me. "She's listening. Tace told right: She's pleased with you. And she'll watch over us." She looks off toward the tree line. "The forest can give things, too. If you know how to ask."

She turns back toward the parsonage without another word. Small figures await her there: Her sisters, circled around Tace. Waiting.

I don't know what will happen to them. But I hope their lives are lovely and green and fresh every day.

I wave goodbye, then turn away and join Mem on the cart. Kit gets the horse moving, away from the village, into a corner of forest I've yet to explore.

"Is it very far?" Mem says.

"I don't know," I tell her. "This is all...new."

Mem smiles. "That sounds nice."

"Aye," I say. I look up at Kit and find her gazing back at me. She winks. I blush. But I smile, too. Because this will be my life now.

The forest opens like a grin. We enter.

The End

Author's Note

This book came to me in trickles over several years, and then in an absolutely flood in the span of a few months. I had no idea in those antediluvian years that *The Witch of the Wilderness* would ever see daylight. I envisioned it as a YA thriller, and it became trade horror within two revisions. I always knew how it ended—well, except for *that* part. I just came up with that. But I hope you liked it regardless!

I did my best in this book to stay true to the customs and beliefs of Puritans and Quakers as I understand them from my research. Stacy Shiff's *The Witches* was instrumental in helping me understand not only Puritan culture, but the witch trials going on across New England. *The Ruin of All Witches: Life and Death in the New World* by Malcolm Gaskill, was also invaluable. Thanks, too, to the many scholars whose papers are generously available online for plebians like me. You are very cool and smart.

Puritans are often seen as absolute bores at best, witch-killing lunatics at worst. But it's important to remember them as people. They fell prey to ludicrous ideas from time to time, and yes, they persecuted many to escape their own persecution. But let's not leave this story thinking they were a black-and-white History Channel horror. They were normal folks for the most part. Many of my ancestors are Puritan (hello, possible great-x8-Granddad Constable Herrick, jailer of the Salem witches!), and if they could produce me, well, they can't have been all that holy.

I can see this book being rather offensive to some. While I am critical of rigid religions systems in this book, I want to leave space for everybody's spirituality, curiosity, and questions. The world is a big, mysterious place, and we discover more about it by having thoughtful discussions. Those discussions may get heated, but let us never fall into fanaticism. That's what got so many witches hanged (and burned, European-style).

Lastly, any errors in the sparsely, but I hope enjoyably, used ye olde grammar and syntax are entirely my stubborn fault. Being your own editor is like being your own defense attorney, and mistakes are usually left in because I've read the manuscript a dozen times, my eyes and brain have gone fuzzy, and the idea of googling grammatical rules from four hundred years ago makes me want to throw my laptop into a fire. Apologizes to those out there who know exactly how, when, where, and why *thine* might have been employed for purposes other than dramatic syntax. I tried.

Acknowledgements

Thanks, fist and always, to my beta-reader, Mom. This story first came into my head after you told me about Beast leading you to that girl in the woods. Your childhood was very much an unpublished Stephen King novel, and I thank you for the stories you've shared. I plan to steal a few more, if you don't mind.

Thanks to Dad, who has always given me encouragement and love. I will never forget the day you came home with a bunch of Tim Burton DVDs for me to watch. I'm still waiting to write something as clever as *The Corpse Bride*.

To Eric, the Best Brother. I would genuinely not be where I am without you. Thank you for feeding my Taylor Swift addiction across many birthdays and Christmases.

To my dog, Hermione, who lets me write without disturbance; and my cats, Winnifred and Zelda, who will not f*#%ing leave me alone while I'm trying to type, but you're cute, so it's okay. I don't mind editing out the pawstrikes you leave behind.

To my coworkers in vetmed: You're all goddamn heroes. I did not let the dog die. You're welcome.

To my friends who love books like I do: I feel less mental around you.

To my huge, sprawling extended family, especially Aunt April, who brags about me on Facebook. I love you all.

Lastly, I want to talk about Grandma Lolo. She was born in 1922 and lived in Nebraska. She wrote children's stories and did little drawings to go with them. She wrote articles for her college's newspaper. She was talented, witty, and smart. Every time I managed to get a poem published in my college magazine, she wanted a copy. She demanded copies of my books as I slowly produced them. Sadly, I only managed one half-baked manuscript and a pretty decent short story before she passed in August 2020. I think she'd have been stoked to hold one of my finished books in her hands.

She's someone I think of often while writing. I cry when I realize she'll never read these books I'm writing now, especially since I can read *her*. I have her diaries, her articles, her stories, her photos. She wanted to read this. She never got to. That makes me sad. But I know I inherited my love of words from her. She's still here, every time I write. She made this story possible just by being her.

Moreover: She still exists as long as her many children, grandchildren, and great-grandchildren talk about her. So, I'm letting you, dear reader, know: There was a very cool lady, born Lois Edna Herrick. She was possibly descended from a jailer of witches, but I bet she would have been the chilliest Puritan. I can see her there in Salem, teaching kids to read, feeding the crows, and being decent to everybody, no matter their belief or heritage.

I began this book before she died. I wish I'd had the stuff to finish it sooner. But stories come as they will, and hers ended before I had the guts to tell mine. Either way, Grandma Gum, this one is for you.

Memento Mori

New England gravestones are known for their *Memento Mori*, reminders to the living of death. It wasn't considered uncouth or even grim to carve a crude skull or a reposing skeleton above the headstone of the recently deceased. "Here lies the body of…" was common on grave markers, none of the "Rest in Peace" and "In Eternal Slumber" frippery of the next few centuries. Nope! The Puritans wanted you to know that death was real, it was coming for you, and it was fucking *happy about it*. Skulls never grinned so widely as they did in New England graveyards of the 17th century. Popular epitaphs express this quite well. I'll share one with you here:

> As you are now, So once was I
> Rejoicing in my bloom;
> As I am now, you too will lie;
> Dissolving in your tomb.

Cheerful! And correct.

Now, I'll leave you with this: *Memento vivere*. Remember to live. Life is not all grim tasks. It's not about shrinking yourself so others feel comfortable. It's not about dimming your shine, widening your smile, or being anything other than *you*. I spent my youth trying to twist myself into shapes that would please grumpy and/or disturbingly cheery Evangelical ministers into thinking I was the best version of a perfect person.

Ha-ha-ha. Lol. Burn on you. No stars. Not the vibe, as the kids, I assume, are saying these days. (Are they? I don't know. I'm very out of touch.)

Memento mori should always lead to *memento vivere*. Yes, you will die. So, live, dammit.

Ask him out.

Go to the concert.

Drink the wine (or dump the wine!).

Move to that place you want to go.

Book the plane tickets. (I recommend Iceland.)

Kiss the girl.

Tell your pastor you're actually very gay, and bye!

Break up with him.

Drive there.

Walk around town.

Stay home and read.

Watch your favorite planet rise and set.

Kiss your cat on the nose (boop!).

Hug your dog. Do it. Now.

Paint, write, sing, break, shout, love, dance, *exist*.

Be yourself, you beautiful human. You've got one guaranteed life. Live the shit out of it.

Someday, you'll be a corpse. Today, be you.

XOXO, E.R.

About the Author

E. R. Griffin is most certainly not a witch. She never did any witching, ever! What? Of course she can swim! She grew up in *Florida*! What sort of question is...oh, no.

...Sorry. My copy person is being given the water test. So, I'll tell you about myself, till the constable notices I'm here, too. I live in West Virginia, work in a veterinary ER as a nurse, and have the best dog. One of my cats in very nice, the other is evil. I love them both to little pieces. I've written two other books, *The Queen of Ruin* (sequel coming soon, pinkie-swear), and *Bad at Magic*. My short story, "What She Left Behind," can be enjoyed in *Betty Bites Back: Stories to Scare the Patriarchy*.

Shit. The constable just noticed me. Um, I'll be back, just...

runs